The "Volunteer"

A Novel by

D.H. Jonathan

Naturale Publishing
Fort Worth, TX

Copyright © 2016 by D.H. Jonathan

All Rights Reserved. No part of this book may be reproduced or transmitted in any form or by any electronic or mechanical means, including photocopying, recording or by any information storage and retrieval system, without the written permission of the publisher, except where permitted by law.

This book is a work of fiction. While Andrew Martinez, John Stossel, and Miley Cyrus are (or were) real people, they are used fictitiously in this book. All other names, characters, and events depicted herein are either the products of the author's imagination or are used fictitiously, and any resemblance to any actual events or persons is entirely coincidental.

Naturale Publishing
Fort Worth, TX

Cover art and design by SliceReality (http://slicereality.deviantart.com).

First Edition

ISBN: 1534635246
ISBN-13: 978-1534635241

"What spirit is so empty and blind, that it cannot recognize the fact that the foot is more noble than the shoe, and skin more beautiful than the garment with which it is clothed?" - Michelangelo

Chapter One: The Proposal

"Forgive me for disturbing your weekend," Dr. Hallum, the president of Coachella Valley University, said to me after introducing himself. I was still trying to fathom why a university president would be calling a lowly undergraduate student's personal cell phone and not just any undergraduate student but one facing a suspension for academic dishonesty.

"That's OK," I said after swallowing my mouthful of meatloaf.

I was in a mostly deserted dining hall, eating lunch on a Sunday, the last day before spring break ended. I had flown back here via the Palm Springs airport the day before after spending an anxious week with my parents at home in Texas. I had only ever seen Dr. Hallum once, at my disciplinary hearing two days before the beginning of this spring break.

"This is highly unusual, which is why I'm calling you personally, but there may be a way for you to have your suspension rescinded."

My heart jumped in my chest. "Really?"

"Yes. Dr. Lorraine Slater is hoping to launch a landmark study, and she needs a... Well, she needs some assistance. She's the chair of the Sociology Department, you know."

I didn't know, but I said "Uh huh" anyway. "What about my scholarships?"

"If you cooperate fully with Dr. Slater, your whole record would be expunged. It'll be like the incident never happened. So your scholarships would continue, provided you maintain the GPA requirement."

This sounded too good to be true. Daddy had told me

throughout my life, over and over again, that if something sounded too good to be true then it probably was.

"What would I have to do?" I asked, trying to keep the skepticism out of my voice.

Dr. Hallum cleared his throat. "Well, it's not something I can really talk about. Dr. Slater wants to go over it with you herself. In person. Can you be in her office at 8:00 tomorrow morning?"

"Yes, I can."

"Good. Oh, she did want me to have you Google something. 'Andrew Martinez, Berkeley, 1992.'"

I scrambled to find a pen in my purse and jotted the terms down on a paper napkin as I repeated them back to him, the napkin ripping twice as I tried to write.

"Yes, that's it. And one other thing; what's your shoe size?"

"Six and a half," I replied, wondering why he would possibly need to know that.

"All right. That's it then. Remember, Dr. Slater's office at eight AM tomorrow. It's in the sociology department office in Carlisle Hall."

"OK," I said. "Thank you so much for this opportunity."

"Well, you may not want to take it. But whatever you decide, I wish you the best of luck."

I may not want to take it? How bad could it be? I had visions of having to write some kind of full thesis as I scarfed down the rest of my lunch and rushed back to the dorm. I bounded up the stairs to my room, and I resolved that no matter how ridiculous the offer sounded, I had to take it, even if the work required killed any semblance of a social life. Getting my degree was the long term goal, and I was going to do what I had to do to achieve that.

When I got into my room, I sat down at my computer and typed in the search terms. Google came up with a long list of results starting, of course, with a Wikipedia article. I read with curiosity and wonder how, in the early 1990's, Andrew Martinez had attended his classes at the University of California at Berkeley wearing nothing but a pair of sandals and a backpack. I had to laugh at the photos of him walking across campus naked. Apparently, he got away with this for quite a while and had become a minor celebrity, appearing on a few nationally televised talk shows.

Martinez was once quoted as saying, "When I walk around

nude, I am acting how I think it is reasonable to act, not how middle-class values tell me I should act. I am refusing to hide my dissent in normalcy even though it is very easy to do so."

I learned from that Wikipedia article that his naked student act ended in December 1992 when UC Berkeley explicitly banned public nudity on campus. The city of Berkeley passed a new ordinance against public nudity the following year, and Martinez was, of course, the first person arrested for violating it. He started wearing clothes after that but struggled with various things for the rest of his life, including problems with mental illness, and committed suicide in a jail cell in 2006.

The whole story was both funny and sad, and I wondered what it had to do with Dr. Slater's offer. I figured I would have to be her research assistant as she wrote a dissertation or book on the guy. I sincerely hoped I wouldn't have to write the book myself.

I spent the rest of that afternoon unpacking from the trip home and working on a paper for one of my lit classes. Sleep was difficult to come by that night, especially when Diane, my roommate, returned from her San Diego vacation at one AM.

"Sorry," she kept saying every time she bumped into something in the dark.

I thought about telling her to just turn the light on, but I thought that if I kept pretending I was asleep maybe sleep would finally come. If it ever did, it was not the restful sleep that made getting out of bed difficult. When my phone's alarm went off, I got up only because lying in bed hadn't been doing me any good. The shower didn't revive me much, and after brushing my teeth and hair, I shuffled back to my room in my robe and slippers in a haze. With the effort to keep my eyelids up, my eyes didn't want to focus. This was no way to go to a meeting that would determine my entire future, so I took one of Diane's energy drinks from her mini-fridge, resolving to pay her back for it when I saw her awake later. I drank it as I got dressed, deciding against my normal campus attire of jeans and a tank top. Instead, I put on my sleeveless yellow dress with the full pleated skirt, which I have always liked because it hides how thick my thighs and butt are.

I am only 5'4", and I have always thought that my body was too wide for my height (or lack thereof). My ex used to tell me that my legs looked like those of a bodybuilder due to my years of softball and Tae Kwon Do, but I could still never get over my self-consciousness about them. I rarely wore shorts even in the hot climate of the Coachella Valley. At least my breasts were a somewhat normal size and shape.

The energy drink seemed to be helping as I noticed that eight o'clock was nearing. I checked my purse to make sure my room key, cell phone, and wallet were inside, slung the strap over my shoulder, and headed toward Carlisle Hall. During the walk over, I reiterated to myself that it didn't really matter what Dr. Slater asked me to do; I was going to take her offer, avoid suspension, and finish my degree program.

The Sociology Department office was on the second floor of Carlisle Hall, right at the top of the main stairwell. I went inside, and a receptionist in a white blouse looked up and smiled at me.

"Good morning," she beamed with far too much enthusiasm for the Monday after spring break, looking at me from head to toe, almost as if she were evaluating me.

"Hi, I'm Danielle Keaton," I said, and I couldn't help but hear the nervousness in my own voice. "I have an eight o'clock appointment with Dr. Slater."

"Oh yes. Just have a seat, and I'll tell her you're here."

I turned to where she gestured and sat in one of the three chairs against the wall across from her desk. I clasped my hands together to keep them from shaking and said a silent prayer that I could handle whatever it was I would have to do. The receptionist continued to glance from her computer screen toward me every few seconds, smirking whenever she did. I looked at the two paintings on the wall behind her and tried to pretend that she wasn't there.

After a couple of minutes a tall woman with graying red hair emerged from one of the inner offices. I recognized her as one of the three members on the disciplinary board at my hearing. She beamed at me, holding her hand out.

"Danielle!" she said. "I'm Lorraine Slater."

I stood and shook her hand. "Hi."

Dr. Slater looked at the receptionist and made some kind of facial gesture, but I couldn't see what it was.

"How was your spring break?" Dr. Slater asked me as she led me into her office.

"To be honest, it could have been better."

I walked in, and Dr. Slater closed the door behind me. Her office was small with several photos and degree certificates on the wall behind her desk. There was one window, and it looked down upon the commons, a large open space in front of the library. Her desk was clear except for a small gym bag.

"I can understand that. Did you go home to Texas?"

"Yes," I said as she went around and sat behind her desk. She motioned for me to sit in the chair facing her.

"How were your parents?"

"They were OK," I said as I sat down.

"Now, it was your uncle who passed away, right?"

"Yes."

It had been my Uncle Robert's sudden and fatal stroke that had started my downfall. I had gotten a late start on a history paper, and I had intended to pound it out over the weekend before its February 26th due date. But Uncle Robert died the Thursday before. He and I had never been close, but he had been my mom's only brother. I felt compelled to fly home to Dallas that weekend to be with her. So I canceled my Saturday date with Kevin (I hadn't been that excited about going out with him anyway) and booked a flight home.

The day before I flew out, Amanda Johnson, valedictorian of her Oregon high school class and with a perfect 4.0 grade point average throughout her college career, had come into the print shop where I worked wanting to print out an assignment on the color laser printer. I helped her open the file from her USB drive and get it formatted and printed. The name Dr. Finfrock on the cover sheet had caught my eye, and I realized that she was in the same course I was in, although in a different section. I distracted her long enough to make a copy of the file on the PC's hard drive, which I then copied over to my own USB drive.

I flew home that Saturday morning and spent a difficult weekend with Mom before flying back late Sunday night. I had just a few hours to get that paper ready, so I changed the font and what I hoped would be enough of the text on Amanda's paper, removed her illustrations, which hadn't been required for the paper anyway, put my name on it, printed it, and turned it in. What I had failed to change was the citation page, which listed sources for those illustrations (with the phrase "Used by Permission" notated as well).

A week later, Dr. Finfrock asked me to stay after class and confronted me about it. I confessed, telling him about my uncle and the difficult time my mother was having. He told me that that was no excuse, which was something I really couldn't argue with, and that he would have to refer the matter to the dean. The resulting hearing had been, for me, an ordeal of humiliation. I did the only thing I could do, falling on my own sword and absolving Amanda Johnson of any guilt. But I had received a one semester suspension, which wouldn't have been so bad if it also hadn't resulted in the loss of my scholarships. Without those scholarships, I could never hope to afford to continue at Coachella Valley University. My plans of finishing my undergraduate degree with no debt and then starting law school had been shattered.

"I'm sorry for your loss," Dr. Slater said.

"Thank you." I nodded and forced a smile.

"Did you tell your parents about the trouble you've had?"

I shook my head.

"Why not?"

"I just couldn't bring myself to do it," I said with a shrug. "My mom was still dealing with Uncle Robert's death, and Dad had a big project going on at work."

"Well, maybe you can get out of this without ever having to tell them a thing."

"That would be so incredibly wonderful!"

She leaned back in her chair, and her face turned serious. "Did you read anything about Andrew Martinez?"

"Yes, I did. It was… interesting."

"Yes, he was an interesting guy. I was a graduate student at Berkeley the semester that he was running around naked."

"Really!" I said. "Did you know him?"

"No, we never talked. But he did fascinate me. I used to follow him around campus, at a distance of course, and study people's reactions to him. I was sad to see the university enact that prohibition on nudity just to get him to stop. It was a blow against true freedom of expression."

She stopped for a moment and looked out the window and down at the students walking across the Commons. With a sigh, she leaned forward and put her arms on her desk.

"I think attitudes are changing though," she said. "Brown

University hosts an annual nudity week, designed to promote body acceptance. They have naked yoga sessions, nude body painting sessions, and other clothing optional events on campus."

"That sounds interesting," I said when she paused, trying and failing to imagine such a thing at any school I had ever attended.

"Yes. Outside of academia, ESPN Magazine publishes an annual Body Issue with photos of top ranked athletes posing nude."

She pulled a copy of one out of her desk drawer and slid it toward me. The cover featured a photo of a nude Venus Williams. She was in profile, arms over her breasts and her hip thrust out toward the camera, the curve of both buttocks very visible. I didn't even know ESPN had a magazine; I had thought they were just a television network. Dr. Slater continued speaking as I thumbed through the magazine.

"Discovery Channel has a very successful reality show called *Naked and Afraid* where two survivalists, a man and a woman, have to live for three weeks in the wilderness without clothes, food, or water. Have you ever seen it?"

I shook my head no.

"VH-1 has a show called *Dating Naked*, one of those silly reality shows like *The Bachelor* except that everyone is naked. There's also a show about a realtor who specializes in property in an upscale nudist community in Florida. The genitals on all of these are pixelated of course, but I have a feeling that in ten or twenty years, these kinds of shows will be airing unaltered. And in the last few years, World Naked Bike Rides have been held in many cities. Nudity in public has also been prevalent at several different events in the San Francisco Bay area despite a city-wide ban on nudity that was imposed within the last few years. In fact, a small group of committed 'urban nudists' is vigorously fighting the new ordinance."

Dr. Slater seemed to be in full lecture mode. I was trying to make sure I remembered the names of these TV shows she had recited, and I shifted nervously as I closed the magazine on her desk and pushed it toward her. "Should I be taking notes?" I asked when she paused.

"Oh no, no, not at all. This is just background information for the project I'm launching, an in-depth study of people's reactions to nudity and how those reactions change after continued exposure. If you volunteer and participate for the full project, your suspension will be cancelled, and your scholarships continued, pending your grades of course. I couldn't get you your job in the print shop back, but you might feel comfortable with a new campus job in the art department that pays a lot more."

"OK," I said tentatively. A higher paying job didn't sound like much of a punishment, so I was worried about a catch. "What, exactly, would I have to do?"

"Well, you would be confined to campus. But you live in the dorm and eat in the cafeteria, so that shouldn't be a problem. As for a social life, I know there are dances in the Student Union as well as other events. You could go to those if you wanted."

"I'm OK with that," I said, eager to get my scholarship restored.

"As for what you will be doing, you'll be attending classes like you normally do. I'll have a team of six research assistants who will take shifts monitoring your interactions."

Dr. Slater stopped talking and looked at me, as if trying to gauge my response. I was still perplexed.

"Is that it? Going to class. Is that really all I have to do?"

"Yes, that's all you have to do. The research assistants will monitor people's reactions to your nudity and keep all the records. They'll take video, and you'll be wearing a tiny microphone that will transmit to a receiver that the RA on duty will have. That will record all the audio that we can then go back through in detail."

She kept talking, but I didn't hear any more of what she said. My head was spinning.

"Wait," I said, holding up my hand. "Did you say my nudity?"

"Yes. If you accept this assignment, you would be required to spend the rest of the semester without any clothing."

Dr. Slater had an intense expression as she looked at me, and I realized that, as outrageous as her proposal sounded, she was serious.

"You mean go to classes naked?" I said, thinking aloud more than anything. "I could never do that. No. Not in a million years. That's crazy."

"Are you sure? Andrew Martinez did it."

"And he was crazy. The articles that I read said he was diagnosed with mental illness."

"Several years after he left Berkeley," Dr. Slater said. "And after policymakers had squashed his freedom to be who he really was, to make a bold statement about our society. It's sad really that he was never accepted. We as a society can be cruel to those who are truly different, who don't fit into what is considered the norm."

Silence descended on the room as Dr. Slater sat and watched me as I thought. I had been going to Coachella Valley University for a year and a half. I had friends. I had two guys that I had dated briefly during my freshman year. And there was Kevin who had been trying to get me to go out on a date with him for over a month. How could I ever just let them all see me naked? And not only once, but on an ongoing basis for the rest of the semester? Today was March 16, and the semester ended in the middle of May. That was two months. I couldn't think of a time that I had ever been naked for longer than two hours; now this woman was asking me to run around naked for two months, and in public?

"That's nuts," I said. I thought of my two options: leaving CVU forever after this semester, my reputation in tatters, or staying and doing this and ruining my reputation in other ways. I felt trapped, like I was being blackmailed or extorted. They couldn't do this to me! "How can this be legal?" I said, breaking the silence in the room. "This, as an alternative punishment?"

"It's not an alternative punishment," Dr. Slater said. "It's an alternative TO punishment. If you do this, you would be performing this department, the university, and the entire field of sociology a huge service."

I was still shaking my head. The idea of someone freely walking around the university bare ass naked was ridiculous. That I would be that naked someone was so far beyond the realm of possibility that I couldn't believe it. Was this meeting even happening? Perhaps I was in a dream, one of those dreams I used to have in high school where I went to school in my underwear without realizing it.

"I can tell you're having a problem with this," Dr. Slater said, "but that's because of the years of social conditioning you've undergone, conditioning that has ingrained in you this notion that our bodies always have to be covered when interacting with others of our own species."

"But what if I get arrested?" I said. "Aren't there indecent exposure laws or something?"

"No, not really. Thanks to court rulings, nudity in public without any lewd conduct is legal in the state of California. That's how Andrew Martinez was able to get away with attending classes nude in 1992. There are quite a few cities who have implemented nudity bans, like Berkeley unfortunately, but Coachella Valley University doesn't fall under any of those."

"Palm Desert doesn't have a nudity law?" I asked.

Dr. Slater shrugged. "It wouldn't matter if they did or not. The university's mailing address may say Palm Desert, but the actual campus is on land that has never been annexed by any municipality. We are in unincorporated Riverside County."

I didn't know what was more unbelievable, that it was perfectly legal to walk around naked or that my university was asking me-—no, requiring me--to do that very thing. Of course, this was California, and I had just read the stories about Andrew Martinez.

"There may be people who will call the police on you," Dr. Slater continued, "but any calls to 911 on campus are routed to the University Police Department. Everyone there is aware of this project and are even helping us compile statistics on the calls they receive, whether it's people calling to complain because they're offended or calling because they're concerned for your safety and well-being. But you will have nothing to worry about, legally."

I thought back to the summer between ninth and tenth grade. I was spending a Friday night with my friend Samantha. She lived in an apartment complex and as we were talking, she said that she had always had thoughts of sneaking out late at night and skinny-dipping in the apartment complex pool. That sounded so exciting to me at the time, and I told Samantha that we should do it. We stayed up until almost two in the morning working up enough nerve just to leave the apartment. Once we did, we made our way to the pool, which officially closed every night at ten o'clock, and climbed over the gate. We huddled in the darkest corner, quickly stripped, and darted into the pool, careful not to splash or make any noise. Being in the water naked had felt strange and wonderful. Samantha and I held onto the side and whispered to each other. I had forgotten what we talked about so long ago, but I remember being startled by the sound of footsteps and seeing the figure of a man walking outside the pool enclosure. I felt real terror right then, and I think Samantha felt it too. We both held our breath and froze. I remember how vulnerable I felt, naked and in the water so far away from any clothing. I couldn't even move for fear of making waves in the water that the guy, whoever he was, would hear. My biggest fear had been of getting in trouble. I had visions of being arrested and taken to jail and of having to call my parents to bail me out. Luckily, the guy kept walking. We thought at the time that he was just some drunk who had walked home from a bar up the street. But we jumped out of the pool as soon as he was out of hearing distance and put our pajamas on over our wet bodies because, like idiots, we had forgotten to bring towels.

I never skinny-dipped again after that. In fact, I always made doubly sure that everything I ever wore was properly buttoned up whenever I was with other people and that I wouldn't have a "wardrobe malfunction" anywhere embarrassing. Now, Dr. Slater was proposing that I just go everywhere without a wardrobe and that the university would be just fine with it.

"If it's legal to just walk around campus naked," I asked, "why doesn't anybody do it?"

"Because it isn't 'socially acceptable,'" she replied, using her fingers to accentuate the quotation marks. "And that's the point of this entire project. Can it become socially acceptable? Which groups of people will accept you; which will applaud you; which will shun you? Will there even be anybody who joins you?"

"Joins me?"

Dr. Slater shrugged. "You never know."

I turned my head and looked out the window at the Commons. Students were walking to and from different parts of the campus. A guy and girl were sitting on the bench beneath the three tall palm trees, talking and drinking coffee. Another girl in shorts and a halter top was lying on her belly on a blanket on the grass, text book opened in front of her as she studied. I tried to picture myself walking through the area with nothing on. What would it feel like to be so naked and vulnerable and free? Something caught in my throat when I thought of the word free. Would being naked really feel free, I wondered. Was I actually considering doing this?

I turned back to Dr. Slater and asked, "Would there be any alerts going out, telling people about the project."

"Oh no. If people knew about the project, they would alter

their responses and interactions with you."

"So if I did this, what would I say to people about suddenly going everywhere naked?"

"I'd prefer that you never said anything," she replied. "Just act like you normally do when you're dressed whenever someone talks about what you're wearing. But I know that's not realistic. People will be persistent about something so… unusual. So, you could just say that you wanted to try becoming a full time nudist and that you just discovered that nudity on campus was legal. And if that doesn't work, use some of Andrew Martinez's quotes. That's one of the reasons I had you look him up on the Web."

I turned and looked back out the window. I thought of the people in my dorm, in the food hall where I ate, in my classes, and I wondered what they all would say to me, what they would think. How did I feel about that? Afraid, mostly. I had spent a year and a half building up a network of friends and acquaintances here, both male and female. All of that had the potential for falling apart. But the alternative was leaving the school forever at the end of the semester. That social network wouldn't matter one tiny bit after that. And I didn't come to Coachella Valley University to socialize; I came to get a solid degree that would get me into law school. I had promised myself on the walk over here that I was at least going to try to do whatever it was that Dr. Slater proposed, no matter how outlandish it sounded.

"OK," I said, still looking out the window at the people outside and imagining myself naked among them, my voice sounding far away as if someone else were speaking. "I'll do it."

Chapter Two: Preparations

"Wonderful!" Dr. Slater exclaimed, and I could see a sense of relief in her expression. She had been almost as tense as I was, with her lecture-like spiels, but I was just noticing it now that she was relaxing. She pulled a manila file folder from her desk drawer, set it on her desk, and pushed it toward me. "Here's a contract for you to read over. It spells out our expectations of you and what you will get in return for finishing the study."

I opened it and started reading. The contract was pretty straightforward. I was to remain nude and on campus from now until the end of final exams, the last day of which was May 16th. I could only wear a hat, cap or visor, protective footwear, and minimal jewelry (rings on my fingers and ears only). I also had to wear a special necklace with a tiny embedded microphone that I was to charge every night while I slept. I was expressly prohibited from wearing pants, skirts, socks, shirts, bras, underwear, backpacks, and any shoulder bag with a strap wider than two centimeters. I looked at my current purse, which I was only carrying today because my dress didn't have pockets, and wondered how wide the shoulder strap was on it. There was a release for photos and videos of me should any be used for any academic publications related to the project, and my stomach turned as I thought of how many pictures would be taken of me over the course of the next two months. Everyone I knew carried a smart phone at all times, and every one of those smart phones was equipped with a better than decent digital camera.

"While we'd like to prohibit people from taking photos of

you," Dr. Slater said when she saw where I was reading in the contract, "that just isn't feasible in today's world."

"I know," I said and went back to reading.

Upon successful completion of the study, my suspension was to be rescinded and my disciplinary record expunged, just as Dr. Slater had said. My scholarships would be continued, pending only my grade point average. I would also be awarded six credit hours of Sociology 4950, a special topics course, with a grade of A, something that would greatly help my grade point average after the anticipated lower grade in Dr. Finfrock's history class. It would also save me from having to take two elective courses later on. But there was a clause at the end of all this stating that if any representative of the University of Coachella Valley Sociology Department caught me wearing clothing of any kind before the end of the semester, the entire contract was null and void.

"I can't wear anything ever?" I asked Dr. Slater.

"Correct. We are studying long term social patterns relating to the acceptance or rejection of a nude person. That person needs to be nude at all times for this. In fact, I would recommend packing up all your clothes and having them stored here in the Department. It's not required of course. And you can always withdraw from the project at any time. But having your clothes removed from your room and stored here would help ensure that any decision you make would be done with some premeditation and calculation and not in the heat of the moment."

My immediate inclination was to reject this suggestion out of hand, and I started to say something to that effect. But I thought of my morning routine and how I never felt fully awake until I had gotten downstairs for coffee and breakfast. I could see myself getting dressed automatically, without thinking, and then violating the contract before I even realized it. And it might also be good to have temptation removed. I had no idea how difficult it was going to be to go nude anywhere, but I could imagine that the urge to cover up might, at times, become overwhelming.

"OK," I said and thought I sounded too meek. Then I realized that I was going to be naked in a world of clothed people, where clothing denoted status and power. How could I not feel meek?

"Excellent. I'll have one of the RA's meet you at your dorm

to take them."

"RA's?" I asked, thinking of the Resident Assistants in charge of each floor of the dorm. My RA was a theology major named Stacy. She seemed very religious and was very vigilant in making sure any males on my floor were properly escorted at all times and were off the floor by the ten PM curfew. I wondered what she would say the first time she caught me naked outside of my room.

"Research assistants," Dr. Slater said. "I have a team of six. They will take shifts shadowing you, taking video and making sure that the audio from your microphone is being received and recorded. All covertly, of course. Their video cameras are very small and will be mounted on some part of their clothing. They will follow you at a distance, and the people you encounter will never know that they are being recorded. They will also serve as your bodyguards and will intervene if your safety is threatened."

"That's good to know," I mumbled as I continued reading the contract.

"Any questions?" Dr. Slater asked as I looked up from the last page.

"Backpacks," I said. "What am I going to use to carry my stuff?"

Dr. Slater smiled and unzipped the gym bag on her desk. "I think you'll like this," she said as she pulled out a gray binder. She set it on her desk facing me, unzipping and opening it. She pulled a Kindle from the pocket on the left side. "This has all of your college text books, including the entire reading lists from your literature classes." She set the Kindle aside. "That will be yours to keep, by the way, once you complete the project. Here's a spot for your phone, room key, and pens or pencils. You have paper here for note taking, and a copy of that contract." She flipped the pocket page over. "And here you have several towels to use as seat covers." She pulled a black cloth from the back pocket. When she unfolded it, I saw that it was larger than a washcloth but smaller than a hand towel. "For sanitary reasons, you know. It's common nudist etiquette to sit on a towel. You just put one of these down wherever you sit, either in class or the library or wherever."

Dr. Slater put the Kindle back in its spot and zipped the binder closed again. "And there's a pocket on the outside here where you can keep your current seat cover," she said as she folded the black towel and stuffed it inside the front pocket of the binder.

She left the binder on her desk, and I looked back down at the contract. Seeing the black towels and hearing what I would be using them for just made me even more conscious of the fact that I would be completely naked for the next two months. Surely, this had to be some kind of joke. Maybe the experiment was seeing what Dr. Slater could get a student to agree to do. Once I signed the contract and started taking my clothes off, she would stop me and tell me April Fools or something. I could only hope.

"Any other questions?" she asked.

I shook my head, picked up the pen, and signed on my space at the end of the contract. Dr. Slater smiled as she turned the contract around and signed on her designated line. She put the contract back in the manila file and put it back in her desk drawer.

"Now that the paperwork is out of the way," she said, "let's get started."

She reached into the gym bag and pulled out a brown cord with a large sand-colored carved bead. I could see that there were clasps on either end of the cord. "This is the necklace you'll wear. It's the same kind that the people wear on that *Naked and Afraid* TV show I told you about. The little ball here is actually a microphone."

She turned it over and showed me the bottom side of it. "It has a micro-USB port here. You can charge it every night with this." She pulled a charging cord and plug from the gym bag, showed it to me, and put it in the outside binder pocket with the black towel. "Go ahead. Try it on."

I took the necklace from her and put it on. The little ball naturally hung down just past the notch of my collarbone.

"Perfect!" Dr. Slater exclaimed as she stood up and moved to my side of her desk. "We also have some sandals for you," she said, pulling them out of the gym bag. "You can go barefooted whenever you'd like, but the concrete walkways get too hot for bare feet most of the year."

"Yes," I said. It was only mid-March, but high temperatures in the Coachella Valley were already topping 90 degrees most days.

Dr. Slater dropped the sandals back into the gym bag and pushed it toward me. She was standing right over me, so I pushed my chair back and stood up beside her.

"Dr. Cleveland, the assistant chair, is on sabbatical this

semester, and his office is right next door," Dr. Slater said, pointing toward her door and to the left. "You can use it to change in if you'd like some privacy."

"Change?" I said.

"Well, undress might be a better word," Dr. Slater laughed. She took my elbow and guided me toward the door to her office, grabbing the gym bag off her desk. "Isn't this exciting?"

The word I would have used was terrifying, but I didn't say anything. I looked out into the reception area and saw a group of students standing around the receptionist's desk. She was talking to one of them, a tall guy with sandy brown hair, her cheeks blushing slightly as she batted her eyelashes at him. Under other circumstances, I might have thought he was good looking, but at that moment, I felt like I was walking to my funeral. What had I gotten myself into?

Dr. Slater handed me the gym bag as she showed me into Dr. Cleveland's office. She looked at me and must have seen the look of fear in my eyes.

"Take your time," she said. "Today will be the hardest day, but it will get better after this. You'll probably even have fun with it. I kind of wish I could get away with doing this myself. Just put your clothes in the bag and bring it back to my office when you're ready."

I forced a smile at her as she closed the door. As soon as she did, I collapsed into one of Dr. Cleveland's guest chairs and tried to fight back the tears. I remembered my first trip to Coachella Valley University and how the tour guide had said that there were fifteen thousand students enrolled. I wondered how many faculty and staff could be added to that number. And all of them, all fifteen thousand plus, would soon have free visual access to my naked body. I knew I had just signed the contract, but how could I do this? I should just get up and walk out, withdraw from the university, and never look back. That was my only other option. But then I would have to explain to my parents how I had cheated on that history paper, stupidly thinking that the professor wouldn't notice the similarities to Amanda's. Surely, I remembered thinking, with all the students he had, he didn't actually read all of our papers.

It's only two months, I told myself. Once I got through those two months, I could accelerate my plans, take summer classes, and graduate early. The extra six credit hours I would get from this project would help. I figured that no one would want to hang out with the girl who had inexplicably run around naked for two months. But that didn't matter. I didn't need a social life after this. I was just going to get my degree and get out of here to go to law school. I could do it. It was just two months.

I took off my shoes. The sandals were still in the gym bag. I took them out and placed them on the floor in front of me before putting my flats into the bag. Taking a deep breath, I stood, unzipped my dress and let it fall to the floor. Just in bra and panties, I stepped out of the dress, picked it up, and folded it as well as I could. I put it into the gym bag on top of my shoes. Taking another deep breath, I pushed the straps of my bra down until my breasts were exposed. I turned the bra around so that the clasps were in front, unhooked them, and dropped the bra into the bag. The air blowing from the A/C vent above me felt strangely stimulating on my nipples. I looked down and saw how hard they had become. I told my body to stop it. This was not supposed to be exciting or sexual. I pushed my panties down and stepped out of them. I crouched down to pick them up, put them in the bag, and zipped the bag closed. When I stood up, I realized that I was completely naked in the office of a professor I had never met. It felt strange and somewhat naughty. Other than that late night skinny dipping episode, the only places where I had been naked had been bathrooms and locker rooms. I looked around at the office, which was about half the size of Dr. Slater's. There were family photos on the credenza behind Dr. Cleveland's desk, and I wondered what he would think if he could see into his office right then.

I felt a chill in the core of my spine, and I wondered if it was from the cool air conditioning or from nervous excitement. I looked down at myself, glad that I had trimmed my pubic hair and glad that I hadn't shaved it completely off. I was in a swimming for fitness class, and the way my one piece swimsuit was cut practically forced me to keep the hair trimmed. Running my fingers through my pubic hair helped to straighten it out and fluff it up after it had been pressed flat by my underwear. I almost had to laugh at the thought that I was combing my pubic hair so it would look good when I went out.

My legs looked as tan as my arms, but I could see the shape of my one piece on my white skin. At least I would be getting rid of the tan lines soon. I took a walk around the office, and my hands brushed against my bare thighs and hips. When I got back to the sandals, I slipped my feet into them. I had to bend over to tighten the Velcro straps. The soles were thick, but I could run in them if I had to. I don't know why I thought of that. But I knew I was going to be very vulnerable when I left that office, and I guess being ready and able to run just sounded like a good idea.

Being naked and wearing footwear was another new sensation for me, and it felt unnatural. I took another walk around the office, feeling the weight of the sandals on my feet. My nerves were still frayed, and I kept telling myself that being naked in this office was all right, that I wasn't going to get in any trouble for it. But I still felt wrong, somehow. It must be that "social conditioning" that Dr. Slater had mentioned, I told myself.

I took another look down at my thick thighs, my curly strip of dark brown pubic hair, the pasty white skin of my belly and breasts, and the shriveled and puckered brownish pink nipples and areolas. I pulled on my nipples, trying to stretch them out and make them less erect, but my touch only kept them stimulated.

"Shit," I said out loud. Maybe, I hoped, getting out from under the air conditioning vent in this tiny office would help.

After grabbing the gym bag in my right hand, I turned the door knob with my left and inched it open. When I got it open wide enough to peek into the reception area, I was happy to see that the group of students had gone. The receptionist in the white blouse was at her desk talking on the phone. She was facing the glass outer doors of the Sociology Department offices. I cracked Dr. Cleveland's door open a bit wider so that I could see those glass doors. Two people passed by in the hallway but didn't look in at the receptionist.

Dr. Slater's office was just out this door and a few paces to the right. I could quickly get over there without being seen. Why that concerned me, I don't know. I guess part of me hoped that this was just a test to see how badly I wanted to stay in college and that once I had shown Dr. Slater that I was willing to strip naked, she would tell me I could get dressed and keep my scholarship. I knew that was crazy. She had obviously put a lot of work and money into this project. But then, this project was crazy.

Stop overanalyzing everything, I told myself. I took a deep

breath, gathering my resolve, and dashed on tip toes over to Dr. Slater's office. As I slipped inside, I kept my gaze on the receptionist and on those glass doors, making sure that no one saw me before I could get Dr. Slater's door closed. I turned around to see if Dr. Slater was at her desk and gasped. The students who had been out in the reception lobby were now gathered in Dr. Slater's office! I instinctively covered my breasts with my free arm and moved the gym bag over my crotch. I must have had that deer-in-the-headlights wide eyed look, because Dr. Slater rushed to me.

"It's all right, Danielle," she said in a soothing voice. She stood in front of me, blocking the others' view of my body. "It's OK, really. I know this is difficult, but it will get easier. I thought meeting the team would help put you at ease."

"The team?" I said.

"Yes, the research assistants. They're all graduate students in the department."

"Oh," I said, remembering our conversation. Taking a deep breath, I said, "OK."

"Wonderful!" Dr. Slater stepped aside, showing me to the group. "All right team. This is Danielle Keaton." She turned to me and asked, "Do you go by Danielle?"

"Most people call me Dani," I said, my voice soft and almost cracking.

Dr. Slater turned back to the team. "You can call her Dani. She has bravely volunteered to be our test subject, and we all owe her our gratitude. Dani, this is Ginger, Linda, Emma, Greg, Cindy, and Jeremy," she said, pointing at each person.

The only name that really registered was Greg, the handsome sandy-haired guy I had seen talking to the receptionist. He smiled and gave me a little wave when Dr. Slater said his name, his dimples becoming pronounced with that smile. I would have blushed if I hadn't already been blushing from the embarrassment of being naked in a room full of people. As Dr. Slater continued with the introductions, I forced myself to lower my arm, revealing my breasts to everyone. I was happy to see that my nipples were not as erect as they had been. Greg's expression didn't appear to change when my breasts were revealed, and I felt a twinge of disappointment, although I don't know what I was hoping for from him.

"Now," Dr. Slater said when she had finished the

introductions, "let's have a look at you."

She held her hand out, and I automatically passed the gym bag to her. I stood with my feet close together, my thighs touching. But everyone could still see my pubic hair, and I fought the urge to cover myself with my hands.

"Dani, you are beautiful," Dr. Slater said. She turned to the team. "Don't you all think so?"

I heard a bunch of yes's, and I saw some of them nod. But Greg just looked, his mouth slowly turning up into a smile when he saw that I was looking at him and no one else. I must have turned fifty shades of red.

"Greg, how is the microphone working?" Dr. Slater asked.

Greg put his hand to his ear, looked at me, and said, "Say something."

"Uh," I stammered. "Something?"

Greg gave Dr. Slater a thumbs up.

"Wonderful! All right. Dani, your first class is at 11:00, correct?"

"Yes," I said, trying to think. "British lit."

"OK. It's 9:30 now. What we'll do is have you go back to your dorm room so you can start packing your clothes. Greg here has first shift, so he will trail behind you. He'll stay in the dorm lobby, but he'll be able to hear everything. This first day is very important to the study. We need to register the shock that most people will feel and see how they respond to it. Ginger will meet you at your room around 10:15 or so to pick up your suitcase or trunk or whatever you brought your clothes in."

"It's just a suitcase," I said. I hadn't brought many clothes to college, especially since I didn't need any winter wear in the Valley.

"Good," one of the girls, Ginger I assume, said.

"That should give you plenty of time to get to class," Dr. Slater continued. "Sound good?"

I shrugged and said, "I guess."

Dr. Slater put her hand on my shoulder. "Don't worry. You'll do fine."

"Should I respond to anyone if they…," I started to ask, but I paused to try to find the right words, "well, if I hear any rude comments?"

"That's entirely up to you," Dr. Slater said. "Just be yourself and do whatever comes naturally. People will respond how they respond. It's all part of the study."

"OK," I said.

We all stood there looking at each other for what seemed like a long and uncomfortable time. Dr. Slater finally grabbed my purse from the chair where I had left it and handed it to me. She was almost bubbling with excitement.

"All right," she said as I took my purse.

Dr. Slater leaned past me and opened her office door. I turned and faced the outer office. The receptionist in the white blouse looked up at us and smiled. Remembering her smirks just after my arrival, I wondered if she was suppressing a laugh at me. I felt ridiculous in my sandals and nothing else.

"Now, you have a wonderful day Dani," Dr. Slater said.

"Thank you," I muttered.

I was really doing this. I was really going to walk out of this office and all the way back to my dorm completely naked. I couldn't believe it, but I stepped forward anyway. The receptionist gazed at me for just a second before looking back at her computer screen.

"Have a wonderful day, Miss Keaton," she said as I passed by her desk.

"Thanks. You too," I replied automatically.

I stopped at the glass doors and looked back at Dr. Slater's office. She was still standing there watching me, with Greg at her side. The rest of the team was behind them, trying to see around. Feeling like a circus attraction, I pushed the glass door open, poked my head out, and looked up and down the corridor.

Chapter Three: Coming Out

I don't know why I checked the hall first before leaving the Department of Sociology office. I knew I was going to be seen going back to the dorm, but I was still dreading that first time someone saw me. It had been strange standing naked in front of Dr. Slater, the team of RA's, and the receptionist, but I knew that they were all in on this project. What I dreaded was that first look from someone outside of the sociology department.

The corridor was empty, so I scurried across to the top of the stairwell and then down to the landing where the stairs turned and went the rest of the way down to the first floor. The stairs emptied right in front of the main entrance of Carlisle Hall. I looked back up the stairs and saw Greg standing at the top. He was now wearing a green backpack. He nodded and winked at me, mouthing the words, "It'll be all right."

I looked back down the stairs and saw the feet of two people walking past and then turning toward the front doors of the building. I felt the flutters in my belly when I realized that they just as well could have turned and come up the stairs. Oh, what the hell was I doing? I felt like I was hyperventilating and wondered if I should run back up to Dr. Slater's office and ask for a paper bag. Greg was still at the top of the stairs, waiting patiently. His gaze made me feel like covering up, but I also found it stimulating at the same time. He was so handsome and well built, and he was looking at everything I had. I'm sure he had watched my big ass as I scurried down the stairs. That Sir Mix-a-Lot song came to mind, and I wondered if he was one of the guys who liked big butts and cannot lie. I hoped he was and then thought myself silly for even wondering about it. He was a grad student, working on a masters or a doctorate, and I was some college sophomore who had been caught cheating and now had to run around naked like a lab rat in some experiment.

The lobby at the bottom of the stairs looked empty now, although I could only see a small part of it from the landing on the stairs. I knew I had to stop distracting myself with thoughts of Greg and get on with walking to my dorm. I took a slow, deep breath, trying to get my nerves and my body under control. My nipples were still hard, and I couldn't help but feel aroused, feeling the air circulation hitting every part of my body. I took one step down, then two, then three and four. The lobby still looked empty, but it was a big lobby, sitting directly under the sociology department offices. My next step down allowed me to see all the way to the building's main doors. No one was in sight. I breathed a sigh of relief, although I realized I was being silly because there was no way I was going to be able to get across campus without being seen by someone.

I bounded down the rest of the stairs, my breasts bouncing almost obscenely, and I realized that I couldn't run or even walk fast without making a spectacle of myself. I laughed, realizing that, naked, I was already a spectacle. The double doors of the large lecture hall to my right, which seated at least a hundred students, burst open just as I was stepping away from the stairwell. My stomach seemed to jump up into my throat. I stopped like a deer in the headlights and thought I should rush back to the stairs. But I knew that many of the students leaving that hall would be heading upstairs. And where would I go then? I couldn't run back to Dr. Slater's office.

"Holy shit!" I heard a male voice say.

People coming out of the lecture hall stopped in their tracks and almost got run over by students behind them. My knees felt weak as I continued to make my way across the lobby.

"What the hell?" someone else asked.

I could almost feel their gaze on my naked buttocks as I walked to the exit doors. My head was down, my eyes on the floor in front of me. I tried not to look at the people looking at me as they continued to file out of the huge lecture hall. The flesh of my butt jiggled with each step. How could I let all of those people see me like this? How could I be naked and so out in the open? I wanted to run, but I remembered how my breasts had bounced on the stairs. I had to walk at a normal pace. This was going to be my life for the next two months, I realized, and I wondered how I would be able to stand it. I was naked! No one, especially anyone male, was supposed to see me naked like this.

"Hey!" someone called to me, but I kept going, pushing the door open and walking out into the warm desert sunshine.

As unnatural as I felt being naked and in sandals, I felt even more unnatural outside. I paused for just a moment, wondering how long it would be before I started hearing the reactions of people on the Commons. When I heard the doors behind me open, I started walking. My purse was in my right hand, clutched against my belly. I was afraid to put the shoulder strap on since I didn't know if it was under the maximum width in the contract, whatever that had been; I couldn't remember right then. I lowered the purse and put both hands on it so that I was holding it over my crotch, trying to hide my pubic region from view. I knew I couldn't hide everything, breasts and butt especially, but I had to at least hide the most intimate part of myself. It was awkward to walk with both hands on the purse so I let my left arm drop and swing naturally.

"Hey," a voice next to me said as a girl I had never met rushed to walk beside me. "Are you OK?"

"I'm fine," I said.

"You know you're naked, right?"

I wasn't in the mood for a conversation. I just wanted to get to the safety of my dorm room. "Is it that obvious?" I snipped.

"Yeah, kind of."

I walked another few steps, fighting the urge to break out into a run. The girl stayed with me.

"Why?" she asked.

I looked at her, slowing as I did, and then turned my head even further to see a group of guys, and even a few girls, following us. I could see three of them with phones out taking photos or videos. Shit, I thought, already?

"It's an experiment," I said. "I just read that it's perfectly legal to walk across campus naked, so I thought I would put that to the test."

People walking on the Commons were noticing me now. Several of them had stopped walking and just stood looking at me with their mouths hanging open. I've never liked being the center of attention, and I usually dressed and acted in such a way that I was never noticed by a crowd. Now, everyone was looking at me simply because I was naked. It made me feel lower than everyone else somehow, and the only word I could think of to describe it was humiliation. And yet, seeing those shocked expressions, especially on the guys, made me feel quivers that started in my nipples and travelled through the core of my being down into my belly and beyond. What the hell was wrong with me? This should be the most embarrassing thing anyone could ever experience, but I was feeling some kind of electric charge from it.

"You're either very brave or very crazy," the girl next to me said.

"Thanks, I think," I said.

"You don't need any help, right?"

"No, I'm fine. I'm just going back to my dorm room."

I walked on, and the girl slowed and merged back into the crowd following me. I heard snippets of conversation and laughter, but I tried to ignore it.

"Wow, titties!" a guy ahead of and walking toward me exclaimed. I wanted to lift my purse and cover my breasts, but I knew that would uncover something else. And I sure didn't want to hear what he would say about my vulva. He would probably call it a pussy, a word that I hated when referring to any part of the female anatomy. I had hated hearing guys in high school talking about "getting pussy" as if we were some big achievement or conquest, so I swore that I would never use the word myself.

I kept walking, passing just a couple of feet away from the guy as he slowed and gazed. I don't think he ever looked at my face. He did tilt his head as I passed by, like he was trying to look at what was behind my purse.

"Nice!" he said, nodding, with a smug look on his face, and I was afraid that he might reach his arm out to stop me. Thankfully, he didn't. I wondered how long it would have taken Greg to come to my aid if he had. I looked behind me to see the guy checking out my butt. I ignored him and tried to see where Greg was. There were so many people following me, looking at my naked buttocks flex and jiggle with every step I took. I wanted to crawl into a hole and die. If only I hadn't dawdled for so long on the stairs, I would have been out of Carlisle Hall before that huge class had let out, and I wouldn't have this group following me. Greg did not appear to be in that group. As I turned my head back around to face where I was going, I saw him off to the side, facing the people following me.

I put my head down and quickened my pace. Holding the purse over my crotch was awkward as fast as I was walking, so I let my arm swing normally, showing my vulva to the world. Two guys jogged up beside me, and one of them said, "Hey, can we get a picture with you?"

"No," I replied instantly.

"Oh please? No one will believe us without some proof."

"I'm trying to get somewhere," I said.

"Well, are you going to be like this later?"

"Like what?"

"Naked!"

"Yes," I admitted, thinking of those two months. How could I possibly do this for that long?

"Maybe later then? A photo, that is."

"Maybe," I said, and I quickened my pace even more. But that just made the bounce in my breasts even more prominent. I was glad that the two guys slowed down and merged back into the group so that I could slow back down myself.

"She says she'll still be naked later," I heard one of them say.

"Awesome," someone said, and I heard another voice say, "Why?"

"Hey gorgeous!" another guy yelled. "Why are you doing this?"

I couldn't stand having them follow me like this, so I stopped and turned around, facing the entire group. There was a collective gasp when they got a full frontal view of me. My knees weakened, and I prayed that I wouldn't collapse. The people with phones in their hands held them up to get better shots of me. I couldn't believe I was doing this.

"My God, you're beautiful!" a guy said, and I must have blushed scarlet.

"Thank you," I said. I heard the clicking of cameras as I continued to stand there and let everyone look. "After thinking about things, I decided that I didn't want to hide behind any more masks or costumes," I said, not sure what I was trying to say or that it was coming out correctly. "I want to live a natural life without worrying what anyone else thinks of me. So here I am. I'm going to be like this for a while, so get used to it. I'd appreciate it if you didn't follow me around whenever you see me. Like you're doing now."

"You mean, you're going to be naked all the time," a girl asked.

"Yes. As long as I can get away with it," I stuttered, my momentary burst of confidence gone.

With that, I turned and started walking again.

"How do you not get arrested?" someone asked, but I ignored them and kept on walking. "I think I'm in love," I heard someone else say. He sounded like the same guy who had said that I was beautiful, and the thought of that sent another shiver through my belly that I felt all the way down between my legs. I kept walking, taking a quick glance back to see the group dispersing. No one was following me, thank God.

I reached the other side of the Commons. My dorm was only two buildings away.

"Holy shit!" someone said, and I turned and saw three guys coming out of their dorm building and stopping when they saw me. "What the hell?" one of the other ones said.

The shame I had felt since taking my clothes off in Dr. Cleveland's office was now overpowering. I put my head down, watching my sandaled feet take each step, and clutched my purse to my belly, my arms covering most of my breasts. I made it all the way to the back entrance of my dorm, Holcombe Hall, ignoring anyone I saw and everything I heard. Slamming the door open, I burst inside and took the stairs two at a time up to the third floor. My room was right next to the back stairwell. I pulled my room key from my purse while still bounding up the stairs. I burst through the stairwell door and quickly unlocked my room. No one was in the hall to see me, and I felt a surge of relief. Letting people I had lived with all year see me naked like this was going to be worse than letting strangers on the Common see me, and I wasn't ready for that yet. Of course, I wasn't ready for any of this. I had gone into a morning meeting hoping to keep my college hopes alive, and I had left that meeting stripped of both my clothes and my dignity.

I closed my door, threw my purse on the desk, and collapsed onto my bed, glad that Diane was gone. My hands trembled as I covered my face with them. I sobbed and cried for a bit before I sat up and took off my sandals. I caught a glimpse of my reflection in the full length mirror on my closet door. I stood and walked over to it, trying to wipe the tears and redness from my face. My hips have always been wide, but they didn't look so bad now, I thought. I turned to the side, put my arms over my breasts, and moved one leg forward, emulating the pose I had seen Venus Williams doing on the cover of that *ESPN Magazine* that Dr. Slater had shown me. My butt looked smaller than Venus's had looked in that photograph. I turned this way and that, looking at myself. My butt did round out behind me, but it seemed in proportion with my thickly muscled thighs and my pubic mound. Everything looked in balance as I looked at my full body profile. I turned and faced the mirror, seeing myself the way the guy on the Commons had, the one who had said I was beautiful. And I did look beautiful. The only criticism I could find was my two toned white skin, with the areas normally covered by my swimsuit far too pale. I figured that wouldn't be a problem much longer, exposed to the desert sun as often as I anticipated.

Lying back on the bed, I stared at the ceiling and tried to process everything I was feeling. How could I have gotten so desperate to stay in college that I had agreed to go everywhere naked for two months? The walk to the dorm had been humiliating and embarrassing and exhilarating. I shuddered as the word "exhilarating" imposed itself on my thoughts. But how could I have felt exhilarated when I had also felt so ashamed? I thought of that moment when I had stopped and stood in front of that group of people, mostly guys, and just let them look at me, and I felt a surge of nervous energy. Before I realized it, my hands were between my legs, and I was surprised to find how wet I was. What was wrong with me?

Instead of stopping, I kept touching myself, massaging my labia as I thought of the guy who looked at me naked and proclaimed me beautiful. I thought of the glint in his eyes as he looked at my breasts, my nipples, my pubic mound. I had discovered the joys of masturbation in middle school, and I remembered how dirty I had felt after every time. And then I went to high school and heard other girls talking about sex, and I didn't feel so dirty anymore. Since an unplanned pregnancy would have destroyed all of my future plans (kind of like getting caught cheating on a paper could have), I had remained a virgin. Outside of a couple of oral sex encounters with boys in high school, masturbation was my only sexual release. And I needed a release right then.

I plunged one finger into my vagina, then two, using my other hand to stimulate my clitoris, lying on my back with my feet flat on the bed and my pelvis raised high up in the air. As worked up as that walk across campus had made me, I brought myself to a quick orgasm, with a cry escaping my lips as it rushed over me.

Spent, I lay back down flat on my bed and tried to catch my breath. I felt the weight of the necklace on my chest, and I cringed when I remembered that it was a microphone. Greg was supposedly in the dorm lobby and could hear everything. Shit! Now he was going to think I was just some horny girl who ran around naked and got herself off every time she was alone.

I sat up, remembering that one of the other research assistants was going to come and take the clothes I was supposed to pack. All of my clothes-- every single garment. I must be crazy for agreeing to that part of the deal, letting them take every single thing I had to wear, but I got up and retrieved the suitcase from the closet. Before I could unzip it open, I was overcome with the urge to go pee, one of the normal after-effects of my orgasms.

The floor had two full bathrooms, each with eight stalls and six shower units. The closest to my room was down the hall, past three other rooms. I opened my door and peeked out into the corridor, looking both ways and wondering if that was going to be my standard procedure for leaving a room for the next two months. I didn't see anybody, so I grabbed my room key, just in case Diane popped in and out and locked the door when she left, and scurried to the restroom.

"That feels better," I said out loud to myself as I peed, sitting on the commode. As I wiped, I thought about Greg again, knowing that he was probably listening. Would there ever be an end to my embarrassment? "Sorry Greg," I said to try to make myself feel better, "when you gotta go, you gotta go." I washed my hands and walked back to my room.

"So, I guess you're still listening," I said as I started packing my clothes. "That walk back here was…weird. I'm wondering if you envisioned having to follow a naked girl around campus as part of your graduate degree requirements. It's pretty crazy when you think about it. I hope this gets easier."

I got my closet cleared out, the clothes off their hangers and lying flat in the suitcase. I started on the drawers, but all I had in those were socks, underwear, a few t-shirts, and four pairs of jeans. The knock on the door startled me. I instinctively looked for something to put on so I could answer it before realizing that I would have to answer it naked. I opened it slightly and saw one of the girls from Dr. Slater's office standing in the corridor.

"Dani?" she said.

I opened the door the rest of the way and said "Hi."

She was a large girl with light brown hair and striking blue eyes.

"Hi," she said as she walked in. "You forgot your binder." She pulled it out of the bag she was carrying and handed it to me. I looked at it and at the corner of the black towel sticking out of the external pocket. In just a few minutes, I would be spreading that towel out on a seat in my Nineteenth Century British Literature class so that my bare bottom wouldn't touch that seat.

"Thanks," I said and set it down on my bed.

We stood looking at each other for an awkward moment, me naked and her in her frilly blouse and Capri pants.

"I also brought you a couple of other things," she said, reaching into a plastic grocery bag that she was carrying. She pulled out a strapless hand purse and gave it to me. "For when you go out and don't need to carry the binder," she explained.

The purse was only large enough to hold my phone, my room key, and a little bit of money. I could carry it easily in the palm of one hand.

"Thanks…?"

"Ginger," she said. "I know. It was kind of crazy this morning. I couldn't believe it when you came in all naked and everything. She has been pushing for this for a long time, and I never thought she would find someone to do it."

"Dr. Slater?" I said.

"Yeah. She's been trying to get this project going for I don't know how many years."

"Wow."

"I know. She had two volunteers last semester. The first one never did get her clothes off before backing out. The second one never made it out of the office. So you walked all the way over here like that?"

I looked down at my bare feet and said, "Not exactly. I had

sandals on."

She looked down and giggled. "Cool."

She was silent as she slowly looked up from my feet, taking in the rest of my naked body. I really wanted to cover up right then, but all my clothes were in the suitcase on my bed. I don't think I could ever be attracted to a woman, but the way Ginger looked at me excited me somehow.

"What else did you bring me?" I asked, nodding toward her bag.

"Oh, yeah." She pulled several cans of spray-on sunscreen and set them on my bed.

"Awesome!" I exclaimed. I took one, saw the SPF90 label, went to one of the corners of the room, and started spraying myself.

"You should probably spray that on at least three times a day if you're outside a lot," Ginger said.

I got the front with no problem, but Ginger came and helped me when she saw I was having trouble getting it sprayed evenly on my back.

"Thanks," I said when she was done. I took the can from her and threw it on the bed with the rest of them.

Ginger looked at my open suitcase and said, "Did you get everything in there?"

"Yeah," I replied. "Everything that's clean, that is." I had my clothes from Saturday and Sunday in my dirty clothes hamper.

"Here," Ginger said, holding out the bag that she'd used to carry the sunscreen in. "Put your dirty clothes in here, if they'll fit, and we'll have them laundered and put with the rest of your clothes."

I grudgingly grabbed the hamper from the closet and dumped my dirty clothes into the grocery bag. Ginger tied the bag shut and zipped up the suitcase. She pulled it down onto the floor and lifted the handle so that she could wheel it out with her.

"OK," she said. "I guess that's it."

"Yeah," I said, looking at my suitcase.

"I'll be seeing you around. Although Dr. Slater doesn't want us interacting with you very much."

"I know."

"I did see Greg downstairs, and he wanted me to tell you that he was very impressed with how you handled that crowd following you."

I couldn't help but smile. "Thanks."

Ginger shrugged. "Well, I had better get this stuff to Dr. Slater. Good luck. And have fun with this."

"I'll try," I said.

I watched Ginger wheel all of my clothes out of my room and out of my life for the next two months. I wondered if Dr. Slater's two previous volunteers had been in the same position I was in, where saying no would have come at great cost. But I couldn't think about it for long; I had to get to my British lit class. After making sure I could navigate through the Kindle in my binder, I got my sandals on and the binder zipped back up. I paused at my closed door, looking at the last remaining guardian of my privacy. And once Diane saw me naked later, even the door wouldn't provide me much refuge. I wished Dr. Slater had been able to get me a room without a roommate for this experiment. Diane was such a party girl that I was sure she would make a big deal out of my nudity. She'd probably even invite a few guys up to the room, just to be a bitch.

I pushed thoughts of her aside and tried to mentally prepare myself for class, giving a brief thought to skipping today. But my grade point average was more important now than ever before, and skipping classes was just not an option for me. As strange as that walk to my room had been, I knew I had to try to act as normal as possible and even try to ignore the fact that I was naked, as impossible as that sounded. So I opened the door and walked out of my dorm room without even so much as a peek into the corridor first.

Chapter Four: First Class

Heading toward the back stairwell, I was just starting to think that I was going to make it out of my dorm without being seen when I heard someone open one of the room doors behind me. Maybe whoever it was wouldn't look this direction, I hoped as I started to push open the door to the stairwell.

"Dani!" I cringed when I heard the voice of my floor's RA, Stacy. "What in the world!?"

I had thoughts of just ignoring her and rushing down the stairs, but I knew that, like everyone else, she was going to see me soon enough anyway. I turned and faced her, holding my binder in front of my crotch. The embarrassment of being caught and seen naked would just not go away. My heart was beating so hard that it felt like it was trying to bang right out of my chest. I took a deep breath and tried to remain cool and collected.

"Hi Stacy," I said.

She had stopped in the hall, her mouth hanging open. "What is going on?"

I shrugged. "Just going to class."

"You can't go like that!"

"Like what?" I said, wondering how long I should continue to play dumb.

"You're naked," she said after stuttering a few times.

"I prefer the word nude," I said.

Stacy stood without moving, her eyes wide. She looked like

she was trying to figure out what to say, and I didn't have time to wait on her.

"See you later," I said, pushing the door open and stepping into the stairwell.

Afraid that Stacy might follow me, I bounded down the stairs, almost tripping at one point. The thick soled sandals felt heavy on my feet. It seemed ironic that the only things I was allowed to wear, the sandals, were not very comfortable. I slowed down on the bottom floor. The walk from Carlisle Hall to the dorm had been short. I was about to go out for a much longer time. My regular routine had me walking across campus to my Nineteenth Century British Novels class and then back across campus to eat lunch in the dining hall. After lunch, I had to cross the campus again to go to my world history and Spanish classes. I usually didn't return to my room either before or after lunch, although today I thought I might need another coat of sunscreen.

I stopped at the bottom of the stairwell and tried to gather myself before going outside. I thought back to that skinny dipping adventure and remembered that the thing I had been most afraid of was getting arrested or in trouble. Dr. Slater had guaranteed that I would face no such consequences, so I should be able to go naked without any fear. And yet my knees felt weak at the thought of walking out in public naked again. I knew I needed to change my attitude, to think of going nude as a privilege instead of a punishment.

"I get to be naked," I whispered to myself. "I don't *have* to be naked; I *get* to be naked."

Taking a look out the window on the door, I was dismayed to see that foot traffic around the dorms had greatly increased.

"Shit," I whispered, remembering the crowd that had followed me half way across the Commons. I wondered how many people would follow me this time.

I didn't want to be late for class, so I put my hand on the bar of the door.

"I'm going out the side exit," I said, hoping that Greg was paying attention.

After taking a deep breath, I pushed the door open and stepped out into the sunlight. I didn't pause to wait for anyone to notice me but just started walking. My nipples stiffened in the gentle breeze. I saw a guy glance at me, then back toward where he was walking for just an instant before his head jerked back around again. I almost laughed at the classic double take, but I kept walking. Others were looking in shock or surprise as I merged onto the concrete walkway. I tried to ignore the looks of the oncoming people, but I couldn't help but see the widened eyes and dropped jaws. One guy smiled at me and said, "How you doin'?" like Joey from the TV show *Friends* used to do. I smiled and said, "Fine," but I didn't slow down when the guy stopped almost in front of me. I wanted to look and make sure Greg was back there somewhere, but I also didn't want to encourage the Joey guy to follow me. So I kept my eyes forward.

The warmth of the sun felt good on my bare shoulders. It was another beautiful day in the valley. I carried my binder at my side in my hand, my fingers curled around the bottom. The tips of those fingers would brush against my hip every few steps, reminding me that I was naked. People still continued to stop and stare when they saw me, but I did my best to ignore them. I GET to be naked, I told myself again, but I still couldn't help but feel the shame of having to do this to keep my college career intact.

"Are you OK?" I heard a girl ask.

I nodded and kept walking. That bravery I had felt when I had stopped and confronted the following crowd on my way to the dorm had left me. I just wanted to get inside, away from the eyes of EVERYONE. My British lit class only had about fifteen students, so at least my exposure there wouldn't be so public.

I was halfway across the Commons when I saw Diane, my roommate, walking toward me with her boyfriend James trailing behind her.

"Dani?" she said in a loud voice.

I wanted to turn and run, but I stopped walking and held my ground. Diane seeing me naked like this had to happen sooner or later. I had just imagined, and hoped, that it would have been in our dorm room.

"What the hell?" James exclaimed, and I moved my binder so that I was holding it with both hands in front of my pelvis, hiding my pubic region.

"Hi," I said meekly when Diane and James neared.

"Where are your clothes?" Diane said, shaking her head and

laughing.

My mouth felt dry, but I couldn't let Diane see my humiliation. I forced a smile and said in as cheerful a voice as I could muster, "I gave them up for Lent."

The two of them burst into laughter, and I couldn't help but laugh with them.

"Got off to a late start then," Diane said.

James pointed his phone at me and hit a few buttons. I blushed, wondering where those photos were going to wind up.

"Seriously Dani," Diane said, "what the fuck?"

"I'll tell you later. Right now, I have to get to class."

My standing still was starting to attract a crowd, so I walked past Diane and James toward Preston Hall and my literature class. Diane hurried along beside me with James trailing behind again. I was never more aware or self-conscious of the jiggle of my buttocks as I took each step.

"So did you lose a bet?" Diane asked me.

"No."

"And you're just going to go into class like that?"

"Yep," I replied.

"I don't believe this."

I didn't believe it either, but I couldn't tell Diane that.

"You think your professor is just going to let you into class like that?" Diane continued.

I shrugged, but based on what Dr. Slater told me about this study, I didn't think I would have any problems with professors. "I guess I'll find out," I said.

I increased my walking pace, hoping Diane would drop off and go away.

"But why!?" she wailed.

"It's complicated," I replied. "I'll tell you later."

"You'd better."

She slowed down, and I could hear her say to James, "What are you looking at?" I didn't hear his reply.

Once Diane was left behind, I looked around and felt the butterflies in my stomach when I realized just how many people were looking at my naked body as I walked. My breasts were bouncing painfully and obscenely with each step, and I had been so intent on getting away from Diane that I had ignored them. Slowing down, I probably blushed, and I once again had to resist the urge to cover up and run away. As I neared Preston Hall, those butterflies in my stomach turned into a tingling sensation in my groin, the kind of thing I felt just before getting on the Titan roller coaster at Six Flags, that nervous excitement of doing something that I couldn't believe I was doing. I looked around and spotted Greg following me off to the side, making sure that the front straps of his backpack were pointed toward me and the people around me. He nodded to me, and I smiled back.

Preston Hall was one of the older, smaller buildings on campus and hosted mainly upper level English classes. The building was dark and quiet compared to the brightness and hustle and bustle of outside. The air conditioning hit me as soon as I walked in, turning my nipples hard in an instant, reminding me that I was naked in a place where I would normally be clothed. My nineteenth century British novel class met three times a week, so in this eighth week of the semester, I had walked into it over twenty times. I had been fully clothed for all of those previous times, so walking in naked was the most unnatural feeling thing I had done to that point.

As I neared the room, I took my black seat towel out of the exterior pocket of my binder. I wanted to get in and seated under the cover of a desk as quickly as I could. The door was in the back of the room, so everyone was facing away from me as I slipped in and sat in a desk in the middle of the back row rather than my regular seat near the front, hoping the desks around me would help hide my body somewhat. Keeping my head down but my eyes raised so that I could see my fellow students, I unzipped my binder and turned on the Kindle. The ten or so students already in the room were talking amongst themselves. The tingling in my groin and belly hadn't gone away as I waited for someone in the class to notice that I wasn't wearing clothes.

Quentin, a short black guy with dreadlocks, noticed me as he walked in the room. He did a double take as he passed me, then sat down in what had become his regular seat. Leaning over, he whispered something to the girl next to him. She looked back at me, and I saw her eyes widen. The chatter that had been present ceased as the whispered news made its way around the room. People kept taking glances back at me, but I couldn't bring myself to acknowledge them. I pulled up a copy of the book we were supposed to have read for class, *North and South* by Elizabeth Gaskell, on the Kindle and read through the introduction. I had managed to read the entire novel over spring break, although I really didn't get much out of it. The murmurs of the other students increased, and I wondered who would be the first one to speak to me. Greg was nowhere to be seen, and I wondered how he could miss getting this video if the purpose of all this was to study people's reactions to me. Then I noticed the black bubble on the ceiling at the front of the room, and I remembered reading about how high definition security cameras had been installed in almost every classroom on campus within the last two years. I lifted the Kindle so that it was between the camera and my breasts.

Three more students came into the room and sat down. I started hearing giggles which ceased when Dr. Trostle breezed into the room and set her briefcase down on the instructor's desk.

"Good morning, everyone," she said. There was a smattering of replies. "Oh, I think we can do better than that. Is everyone still hung over from spring break? Good morning!"

"Good morning!" the class responded in much more robust voices.

"That's better. I hope everyone had a—" Dr. Trostle stopped when her gaze seemed to find me. Her eyes narrowed, and she took a deep breath. "Spring break. I hope you all had a restful and fulfilling spring break. And I hope you had an opportunity to read at least the first half of *North and South*."

From there, Dr. Trostle launched into her lecture about the novel. She talked about feminism (like she always did), tradition versus modernity, and the differences in the social classes in 1854 England. I took a few notes on the pad in my binder, but I couldn't really get into the lecture. People in the class kept taking looks back at me. I tried to ignore them, to really listen to the lecture, but my mind wandered. Dr. Trostle herself seemed distracted as, several times, she trailed off in the middle of a sentence and didn't finish the thought.

I wondered if I could really go into the dining hall naked. Of course, Dr. Slater would have arranged it so that the workers would allow it, but could I really go in, stand in line, get my food, and sit down at a table to eat, with everyone I knew from both dorms watching me? And I had no doubt that they would be watching me.

I was the only naked person in the whole university. That's what made this so difficult, being singled out so that everyone couldn't help but notice me. Even more difficult was having no privacy, my private parts on public display all the time, for two months. Would I be able to stand this for that long?

"Miss Keaton!"

The sound of my name being called out by Dr. Trostle snapped me out of my own reverie. I snapped to attention and looked at her.

"Would you come up here please?"

Everyone in the room was looking at me now, and I wanted to shrink down into my desk. But Dr. Trostle wanted me to come up to the front of the class! The tingling sensation in my gut was back in full force as I slid out of the desk, stood up on wobbly legs, and staggered to the front of the class. My nipples tightened as I reached the instructor's desk and turned around to face my fellow students.

"Now, Miss Keaton has decided to come to class without any clothes," Dr. Trostle said. "Can you tell the class what kind of statement you're trying to make?"

Shit, I thought. I really had nothing to say, especially since I couldn't tell them the real reason I was doing this. "Ummm, well. It's my objection to current fashion trends," I said, making up something. "I mean, why do we always have to cover ourselves?"

Everyone was looking at me, and I was standing with my hands at my sides, resisting the almost overwhelming urge to cover my breasts and pubic area. The students whose names I could remember, Quentin, Suzanne, Roberto, and Marco, were, like everyone else, taking in all of me. In that moment, I sincerely hoped that I could go away and never have to see any of them again.

"Well," Dr. Trostle said after an uncomfortably long silence, "your verbal presentation may need some work, but I do support your empowerment. Now, I want everyone to take a good look at her now so that, when she goes to sit back down, you are all looking at and paying attention to me. No more trying to sneak peeks at her. Is that clear?"

"Yes ma'am," several voices said.

"All right." She nodded to me, and I made my way back to my desk.

As I sat down, I looked down and was dismayed to see how

erect my nipples had become. I also felt wetness down below, and I was glad that my seat cover was black so that the wetness wouldn't be easy to spot. Had Dr. Slater anticipated something like this? And how could something so embarrassing be so arousing?

I don't know if our little demonstration helped the other students pay attention to the rest of the lecture, but I know it didn't help me. I kept thinking of myself naked and on display, unable to move or cover up, and how sexually aroused that had made me. Part of me kept wishing Dr. Trostle would call me up to the front of the room again, and another part dreaded it at the same time. If I had been alone, I would have masturbated myself to orgasm like I had done earlier that morning. Then I developed the fantasy of Dr. Trostle calling me up to the front and telling me that I had to masturbate in front of everyone. I shifted in my seat as I couldn't get the image out of my head.

Class finally ended, and I hadn't taken a single note since I had sat back down. What was wrong with me, and how did I ever expect to get my much needed A in this course if I didn't pay attention to lectures?

I stood, grabbed my damp seat cover from the desk, stuffed it and the Kindle into my binder, zipped it up, and rushed out of the class before anyone had the chance to stop and talk to me. The sun was overwhelmingly bright when I walked out of the building, and I had to slow and let my eyes adjust. I kept walking though, wanting to get away from everyone. I knew that, for Dr. Slater's experiment to work, I needed to act like I normally did, but that wasn't going to happen. I didn't know if I could ever act normal while I was naked and everyone else was clothed.

Greg was nowhere to be seen, but I did spot one of the other RA's, a tall redheaded girl whose name I couldn't remember. She had on the same green backpack that Greg had worn when leaving the Sociology Department office. The redhead nodded to me, but I ignored her and quickened my pace.

"There she is!" someone exclaimed.

"Holy shit, it's true!" someone else said.

I glanced up and saw a line of what seemed like several hundred people on the Commons next to the concrete walkway. Most of them had their cell phones out and were taking pictures and videos. I wondered if there was another way for me to get to my dining hall and then realized it was too late for that. The crowd would just follow me wherever I went. I took a glance behind me and saw the tall redhead closing in. Hoping she had a panic button somewhere, I put my head down and walked as quickly as I could without my breasts bouncing around.

"Nice necklace," someone said, and I almost had to laugh. If only you knew that the necklace was recording everything you say, I thought to myself.

I heard all manner of things from the crowd, but the words beautiful, awesome, brave, and sexy stood out. Of course, I also picked up the words slutty, shameless, exhibitionist, and skank, but I ignored them and kept walking. I was relieved that no one tried to touch me or stop me in any way. By the time I reached the dining hall, I wanted to cry, laugh, and scream, all at the same time. And this was only the first half of the first day. I still had 59 and a half days left.

Walking naked into the dining hall where people were sitting around eating was the most unnatural and embarrassing thing I had ever done to that point. All the chatter and lunchtime conversations came to a sudden and complete stop when I walked into the room. Being twelve o'clock, about twenty people were waiting in the serving line. I was not about to wait in that line standing still and naked with everyone in the hall looking at me. I would just have to skip lunch. Turning around, I marched out of the dining hall and toward my dorm building. Laughter erupted from the dining hall before I could get far enough away to not hear it.

That was it! I couldn't face people any more. I was just going to go tell Dr. Slater that I was giving up and that she should give me my clothes. I would pack up and go back to Texas and make ends meet somehow. I would tell my parents that I had cheated on a paper and gotten kicked out. I would never, ever tell them about going around campus naked for half a day.

The crowd that had watched my walk to the dining hall had, for the most part, dispersed, but there were still a few stragglers around when I walked back outside. Two young guys ran up to me as I strode across the grassy area between the dining hall and the dorm.

"Oh my God!" one of them exclaimed. "You are so awesome!"

"Why do you think that?" I asked, tired of everyone talking about my nakedness.

"Because you are so brave, to go out without any of the disguises that we all wear." I stopped and looked at him. "I mean," he continued, "we all dress for other people. Look at me, the little alligator on my shirt here. What does my Izod shirt say about me? And is that really accurate? I don't feel like anyone knows the real me. If I were as brave as you, I would go around in my pure state too."

"Pure state?" I asked.

"Yeah." He looked down at my body and back up, but he did so in a simple, non-leering way. "You look pure and beautiful. Like a statue. Venus de Milo. Except you have arms."

I couldn't help but laugh. He laughed with me. The guy with him just stood with his mouth hanging open.

"I'm Michael, and my tongue-tied friend here is Dave."

"Nice to meet you," I said, and I actually shook his hand.

We stood looking at each other for just a moment, but I could see, in my peripheral vision, people stopping and snapping pictures with their phones.

"Well," Michael said, "I just wanted to tell you that you are awesome."

"Thanks. See you around."

"Yeah, definitely."

I turned and headed toward the side entrance of Holcombe Hall and thought about the laughter I had heard in the dining hall. To hell with those people, I said to myself. To hell with all of them if they can't handle me in my "pure state" as Michael called it. My path to law school would not be derailed, I decided.

With my newfound confidence, I climbed the stairs to my room, thinking about my less than stellar response to Dr. Trostle's question about why I was doing this. When I got to my room, I was going to get on Google and look up something on the benefits of nudism. If I couldn't reveal the real reason I was doing this, I could at least come up with a consistent story and not keep making things up on the fly (although I had to laugh when I thought about how I had told Diane that I had given up clothes for Lent).

Feeling more confident than I'd felt since I had admitted cheating to Dr. Finfrock, I burst through the stairwell door on the third floor. Before I had a chance to look for my room key in my binder, I noticed that the door to my room was open.

"Holy shit, you weren't kidding," someone said when I stepped into the room.

Diane and James were in the room with four guys I didn't know!

Chapter Five: First Afternoon

"There she is!" Diane exclaimed. "I told you."

"Holy shit!" one of the guys said. The others just stared at me with dumbfounded expressions on their faces. I resisted the almost overwhelming urge to cover my breasts and pubic mound with my hands, and I was glad I had let Ginger take all of my clothes. I probably would have put them on right then. Rather than stand there and make a spectacle of myself, I walked into the room toward my desk. One of the guys was sitting in my chair. He gazed at me, and I felt that strange tingling in my gut again. Did I actually like being looked at naked?

"I need to get on my computer," I said.

The guy turned and looked at my monitor then back at me. "Uh, sure." He stood up and stepped over to Diane's side of the room.

I didn't use one of Dr. Slater's black butt towels since this was my seat, and no one else should be sitting in it. I plopped down and unlocked my workstation as I slipped my sandals off.

"So, are you going to tell us why you're nature girl all of a sudden, and why your closet is empty?" Diane asked.

"Why were you looking in my closet?" I said as I pulled up Google in my web browser.

"Oh come on Dani! What is going on?"

I turned around and looked at her. "Why do you have all these guys in our room? You know you're only allowed to escort one guy at a time in the dorm."

"We just wanted to have a look for ourselves," one of the guys said. "It's kind of unbelievable, a naked girl running around campus."

"Well, I haven't been *running* anywhere," I said.

"How long are you going to stay like this?" another guy asked.

"The rest of the semester, at least," I said, and I immediately wondered why I added the "at least" at the end. I would never consider extending this past the end date. In fact, I already couldn't wait for it to be over so that I could feel clothes on my body again.

Pushing those thoughts aside, I typed "benefits of nudism" into Google and tried to ignore the guys' gazes on my naked body. A long list of articles filled the screen, and I clicked on one about women in nudism and started reading.

"Well, if she's not going to talk to us, let's go get some lunch," Diane said.

I only vaguely heard them all leave the room as I read article after article having to do with health benefits of nudism, how pools stay cleaner when people don't wear bathing suits, and the compatibilities between Christianity and nudism (which had some good references I could use with Stacy, my overly religious Resident Assistant). The only issue I had with all of these articles was that they dealt with groups of nudists. I started to search for instances and information on lone nudists among clothed people, but all I found were fantasies and fiction. One interesting thing I found was a whole series of stories about a girl named Tami who, when trying to avoid expulsion for streaking on her college campus, claimed that nudism had become her religion. In the stories, she was then forced to continue the charade of going nude everywhere when the college dean took her at her word. I had read enough to get the gist of the series when I noticed the time. I would have to hurry to make it to Dr. Finfrock's class without being late.

I locked my workstation, grabbed my binder, and got up. It was only then that I noticed that Diane had left the door to our room open. She had done it on purpose, I knew. Was she getting some kind of perverse pleasure out of showing me off? A girl and a guy were standing in the hall wide-eyed as I stood up. I looked at them, and they jumped as if startled and wandered off. Shaking my head, I made sure my room key was in its spot in the binder, and headed out, closing and locking the door behind me.

I took my first step down in the stair well when I realized that I had left my sandals in the room. Since the day wasn't that hot outside and since I was in such a hurry to get to class on time, I decided to just go barefooted. The straps of those sandals had been rubbing a raw spot on the tops of both of my feet anyway. The plopping sounds of my feet hitting each step echoed throughout the stairwell as I descended. Once I reached the ground floor, I pushed through the exit door, only realizing that I hadn't paused until I was out in the sunshine. Maybe I was getting more used to this.

The afternoon was warmer than the morning had been, but the concrete wasn't too hot for my feet. I walked as normally as I could, trying to step lightly so my feet wouldn't make those plopping sounds. The sun felt hot on my shoulders, and I wished that I had put on another coat of sunscreen before leaving my room. Rounding the dorm, I merged into the main walkway and, for the fourth time that day, started walking naked across campus. I had just entered the commons when a girl and a guy jogged up beside me.

"Hey," the girl said. "I'm Clarissa, from *The Coachella Clarion*, our school newspaper, and I'd like to do an interview with you."

"I can't right now," I said without slowing down. "I'm late for class."

"Oh, it can be later," Clarissa explained. "What time are you free?"

"Um, I get out of class at four."

"OK, how about five o'clock?"

"That's fine, I guess," I said, wondering if I should clear the interview with Dr. Slater.

"Awesome! Where would you like to meet?"

I knew I didn't want to do the interview in my room, but I couldn't think of any other place where we could have some privacy. "How about the lobby of the dorm," I finally said, even though I had yet to appear there in my new "naked girl" persona.

"Sounds good to me. It's Holcombe Hall, right?"

"Yes."

"Cool. Blake here will take some photos of us talking."

"Hi," Blake said, waving to me.

"Maybe you could pose for some too," Clarissa continued.

"Something we could actually put in the paper, you know. With nothing showing."

"OK," I said, thinking how ironic it was that everyone on campus was seeing my nipples and vulva on a regular basis, but they still wouldn't publish photos of such in the newspaper.

"And what is your name again?" Clarissa asked.

"Danielle. Danielle Keaton."

She typed my name into her smartphone.

"You wanted to interview me before you even knew my name?" I said.

"Well, yes. Word of your..., well, being naked, has gotten around, and I wanted to be the first one to get the story on it."

"OK," I said, glad that I had just spent the last hour doing research for the kind of questions that I thought she might ask, especially since I had been forbidden from telling the truth.

We had almost arrived at Preston Hall. I looked at my phone and saw that I had three minutes before class started. I would need all of those since I had to pee.

"Great. We'll see you at five o'clock," Clarissa said.

"See you then," I said without stopping.

I bounded up the four steps and entered through the front door. Several people walking by stopped and stared at me as I walked in and turned toward the ladies room. Once inside, the dirty floor made me wish I had worn those sandals after all. I ignored the dirt, did my business, washed my hands, and rushed to class.

Dr. Finfrock was checking the roll when I entered. He was the only professor I'd ever had at Coachella who took attendance before each and every class.

"Kim Halsey," he called as I slipped in and carefully closed the door behind me. When I turned to take my seat, he was staring at me with his mouth hanging open. His face softened with something like recognition, and he nodded at me as I took my seat.

"Kim Halsey," he repeated.

"I said here," Kim said.

"Right. Sorry."

I pulled one of my black butt towels out of my binder, spread it on the chair of what had become my regular desk, and sat down. As Dr. Finfrock continued with the roll, everyone in class had turned to look at me.

"Danielle Keaton."

"Here," I called.

Dr. Finfrock paused only for a moment before continuing. I looked down at my Kindle as the stares of my fellow students started to get to me. They finally all turned around once Dr. Finfrock started his lecture. I took notes on the pad of paper in my binder, but I kept getting distracted whenever I'd notice one of the guys in class looking at me. It still felt strange sitting in a classroom naked, listening to a lecture, like I had been doing in clothes all semester. What made this class even stranger than my literature class that morning was that I was also barefoot. The floor felt cold and hard on the bottoms of my feet. I shivered as I noticed Dr. Finfrock looking at my breasts as he talked. That tingling sensation in my gut just wouldn't go away. This was only the first day, I told myself. I would get used to this. I *had* to get used to it.

My mind wandered away from Dr. Finfrock's lecture, and as I contemplated my situation and my walk to my current history class, I realized that, unlike my trip to British lit that morning, I had not once looked behind me to see if one of Dr. Slater's research assistants was following me. When starting out this morning, I had talked into the microphone to make sure the RA knew where I was, but such a thing hadn't even occurred to me this afternoon. I could only figure that I had forgotten because I had left in such a hurry after staying at my computer longer than I had intended. It couldn't have been because I was growing more comfortable with the idea of going out naked and alone, I thought. This was still only the first day, and I couldn't imagine going out naked would ever get that easy even at the end of these two months.

In the middle of Dr. Finfrock's lecture, during one of his pauses for effect, my stomach growled rather loudly, and I wished I had gone ahead and eaten lunch. Of course, all eyes turned to me again, and I wished I could sink into the floor. I had never been so embarrassed in my life. If I had had clothes on, I could have handled it better, but once everyone turned to look, many of them kept gazing at my naked body. Dr. Finfrock himself had a smirk on his face. I slid my butt forward in my chair, lowering myself, and lifted my binder, holding it upright and hiding myself from most of my classmates. Thankfully, Dr. Finfrock continued as if nothing had happened. After a few minutes, I had to lay my binder back on my desk to take a few notes, but by then, everyone else had gotten back to their own note taking.

Dr. Finfrock ended his lecture by announcing a quiz during the next class on Wednesday. As soon as he dismissed the class, five of my fellow students surrounded my desk.

"What the hell, Dani?" a guy named Martin said.

"Did you not have anything clean to wear?" another girl asked. I couldn't even remember her name even though we had spoken at almost every class meeting before this one.

"It's a long story," I said, "and I have another class to get to."

"I'd heard that there was a naked girl running around and going to classes," Martin said, "but I had no idea that it was someone I know. Why are you doing it?"

"Like I said, it's a long story."

I put my Kindle in the binder, zipped it up, and stood, discreetly grabbing my butt towel and stuffing it in the binder pocket.

"This is just crazy," another guy said, shaking his head as he gazed at my nude body. The way he looked at me, not leering but with mere admiration, caused the butterflies in my belly to start stirring again.

"Whatever the reason, you are awfully brave," Martin said as he turned and left the room.

The rest of the group followed, and I was right behind them when I heard, "Miss Keaton."

I stopped and turned toward Dr. Finfrock. "Yes?"

I clutched my binder to my chest, hiding my breasts from him. As vulnerable as I felt being naked out on campus among the students, standing naked in front of my instructor, especially this one, made me feel more vulnerable than ever, like a child even.

"When I got an email from the president of the university saying that I would have a student attending class in the nude and that I should accept it and continue on with class as usual, I didn't believe it. And now that I see you here in this state, I feel somehow responsible. Something tells me that this has to do with that plagiarized paper."

I shrugged, not knowing what I could or couldn't say.

"You know, I only referred that to the dean because it was my obligation to do so. I had hoped that you would be granted leniency, but that decision wasn't up to me. The rules stated what I was supposed to do, and I did it. But this goes beyond anything I've ever heard of."

"It's all right," I said.

"Are you telling me that your current state of dress, or undress, has nothing whatsoever to do with that paper?"

I shook my head. "No, I'm not saying that."

"Is there anything I can do to help? I can't really withdraw my report, but I can go talk to the dean. To the president even."

"No. This is something I signed up for, voluntarily."

"And what is it that you did sign up for?" Dr. Finfrock asked.

"I can't really say right now. I'm sorry."

"That's OK," Dr. Finfrock said after a short silent pause. "Is there anything I can to do help?"

"No," I said. "I'm good."

"All right. If you'd like, you could re-write that paper, your own work, and I could give you partial credit. A C on it would be better than a zero when I average your semester grade."

"You don't have to do that," I said.

"It's all right. I know there were extenuating circumstances, and now that I see what you're having to do, I think a little understanding is in order."

"Thank you. That's... That's wonderful." I wanted to hug him, but I refrained. A C on that paper might even help me get at least a B for the course. And with the extra hours for doing this nudity experiment, my grade point average would be just fine.

"Can you get it to me by next Monday?"

I couldn't think of anything else I was doing over the weekend, especially since I knew that I wasn't able to leave campus.

"Sure."

"All right. If you ever need anything, please let me know. And don't forget about that quiz on Wednesday."

"Thank you, Dr. Finfrock."

He nodded to me, and I took off for my next class, Spanish III, which was two buildings over.

"You go, girl," someone said to me as soon as I walked out of Preston Hall, smiling as she said it.

"Awesome!" another guy said.

"Holy shit, there she is," I heard someone else say.

Being naked makes even a normally mundane walk between

buildings an event, I thought with amusement. I felt like a rock star, although I was still uncomfortable with all the attention. I got to my Spanish class just in time. I saw one of my classmates just ahead of me, and I heard Ms. Castillo say "Buenos tardes," to him.

"Buenos—" Ms. Castillo began to me as I walked in the room. All eyes turned to me when the students heard our instructor stop suddenly short of finishing her normal greeting. I was holding my binder at my hip, but I swung it around and held it in front of my pelvis as everyone looked at me. I felt my nipples tighten as those now familiar feelings of shame and vulnerability washed over me again.

"Hola," I said, trying to lighten the tension.

"Hola!" everyone answered back, as if I were teaching the class.

I smiled and probably blushed a deep shade of crimson as I shrugged and headed toward my seat. I slapped my butt towel down as quickly as possible before sitting. Other than my nudity, the class proceeded normally, with Ms. Castillo going over our vocabulary words and the conjugation of past tense verbs. At the end of class, she passed out our homework, to be turned in on Friday. I was relieved that it was only a two page worksheet. It would probably only take me an hour to do.

As usual, I was the first person out of the room when Ms. Castillo dismissed us. On Mondays and Fridays, I had a swimming class, which fulfilled part of the four semester recreation and fitness university requirement, in the Phys Ed Building over a quarter of a mile away. I had less than ten minutes to get to the building, changed, and into the pool. Of course, changing wouldn't take me very long now, I thought and almost laughed when I thought that I had finally found a real advantage to going everywhere naked. I heard several compliments and comments as I hurried to my swimming class. I walked fast, ignoring my bouncing breasts, although I saw several guys staring as I passed by. The embarrassment and the fear were starting to go away as I slowly realized that this was my new normal, what I had to do, as taboo as it had always seemed, and that I wasn't going to get arrested or otherwise in trouble.

There were several double takes when I walked into the Physical Education building, but I walked past everyone, ignoring the people who called to me, wanting to know why I was naked. I hurried to my space in the women's locker room, quickly dialed in my combination, and opened the metal door. My swimsuit was hanging on the hook inside. I had used the mechanical ringer to squeeze all of the water out of it after class that last Friday before swim break, but after more than a week, it didn't smell that great. The good thing was that I didn't have to wear it. In fact, I was prohibited from wearing it. I put my binder in the locker and grabbed my cap and goggles. As I went to put them on my head, my hands brushed by the necklace, and I remembered that there was a microphone inside.

"Hey," I said, ignoring the looks I got from some of the other girls in the locker room. I talked in a quieter voice and said, "whoever the RA is, I have swimming. Can I get this necklace wet, or should I take it off?"

I looked around and realized that there was no speaker included with the microphone, and that if the RA happened to be male, he wouldn't be walking into the women's locker room.

"Meet me just outside the locker room," I said.

I closed my locker, leaving it unlocked for the moment, and walked out through the double doors and into the main corridor. I saw one of the girls from Dr. Slater's office that morning running up.

"Sorry," she said, out of breath. "I was over by the pool. Dr. Slater says to take it off, just to be safe."

"OK," I said.

I didn't have time to chat, so I turned around and went back into the locker room, stopping to drop the necklace with my other stuff and to lock up everything. I made it to the outdoor pool at 2:58.

"Holy shit, Dani," Rick, who was usually in the lane next to mine, said as I walked over. The other six swimmers just stared. The pool only had eight lanes, so each section of swimming for fitness had been limited to that number.

"What?" I replied to Rick, feigning ignorance, as I dropped into the pool.

"So you're the campus naked girl that I keep hearing about," Rick said after I came back up.

"Yep. Makes getting ready for swim class a lot easier."

"I'll bet."

Just then, Ms. Martin, our blonde, six-foot-tall swimming

coach, strode into the pool area, blew her whistle, and shouted, “Warm up, 200 yard freestyle.”

“You look great, by the way,” Rick said before we all kicked off across the pool.

Swimming naked felt wonderful. I had full range of movement without the swimsuit binding me. And in the water, I felt somewhat covered. Ms. Martin didn't even notice that I was swimming naked. Unfortunately, skipping lunch on a swim day had been a very bad idea, especially after taking the week off for spring break and not sleeping much the night before. Just the 200 yard warm-up drained me. I did somehow manage to avoid being the last swimmer to finish the warm-up, although just barely.

"Get your kick boards," Ms. Martin said.

We all pushed ourselves up and out of the pool. Everyone's eyes immediately turned to me. I took a glance down and was amazed at how my body looked when wet and glistening in the sun. When I looked back up, Ms. Martin was staring at me in amazement. The kickboards were in a bin right next to where she stood.

"Keaton, is there something wrong with your suit?" she asked as I grabbed a board.

"No ma'am," I said. "I just decided that there wasn't anything wrong with my body and that I didn't need to keep covering it up."

“Well, all right,” Rick said.

Ms. Martin looked like she wanted to say something else, but she stopped. I suspect that she had received the same email that Dr. Finfrock got. I took my board back to the pool and dropped back in. The next thirty minutes were spent exhaustively kicking from one end of the pool to another. I didn’t count how many laps I did, but I know Rick passed me at least three times. Ms. Martin usually had us swim laps doing different strokes: butterfly, breaststroke, backstroke, etc., but today, she kept us on the kick boards working legs the entire time. I was so relieved when she finally called an end to class.

My first attempt at getting out of the pool failed as my foot slipped off the edge, and I fell backward into the water. Laughter erupted from the other side of the fence surrounding the pool. I looked and saw a group of about fifteen guys and a couple of girls watching my comedic show. The research assistant was right there among them, recording them, I’m sure. I wondered if she was able to get audio since I didn’t have my necklace on. I tried getting out of the pool again, this time using my knee to push myself out, something that was uncomfortable on the rough concrete around the pool.

"We'll get back to our regular routine on Friday," Ms. Martin said to the class.

I staggered on wobbly legs over to the bin, put my board up, and made my way back to the locker room, trying to listen to the people watching from the other side of the fence. The guys in the swim class stood by the pool until I got through the door; I'm sure enjoying the view of my wet naked body. As I got to my locker and exchanged my swim cap and goggles for my binder and my microphone necklace, I could sense several girls from another class whispering among themselves. I stood by my locker for a moment, trying to ignore the whispers, thinking that there had to be something else for me to do there. I usually showered after swim class, but my legs felt too weak to stand that long. With nothing to change into, I closed my locker and went to the mirror to do something with my hair, wishing I had put a brush in my binder. There were two girls at the mirror when I arrived, and both of them gave me a quick look and scattered.

The RA should have been there, recording the reactions of the girls in the locker room. I almost had to laugh as I thought that, in the one place where it is somewhat customary to be naked, I was being shunned by just about everyone. Once I got my hair looking somewhat reasonable, I grabbed my binder and walked out. The guys who had been watching me from beyond the fence were standing in a group near the main door of the Phys Ed building.

"You just made my day," one of them said as I walked past.

I smiled but kept walking. My legs felt barely able to support my weight, so I moved slowly. I expected the guys to follow me like that bunch this morning had, but they all stayed where they were. The concrete felt hotter than before, so I walked on the grass beside the walkway, enjoying the feeling of dampness on my feet. I felt light-headed, almost dizzy, and I thought about dinner. The dining hall opened at 4:30, and I planned on being first in line. And then I remembered that I had that interview at 5:00. If I had been thinking clearly, I would have scheduled that for tomorrow, not right after my swim class. Still, I thought I would have enough time to eat before the interview. If the pictures were for the school paper, they would be seen in a grainy black and white. I shouldn't need make up or anything for that, I thought.

I got the usual stares and heard the occasional comment on my walk back to the dorm, "Naked girl!" being the most common. Feeling too drained to walk around the dorm and take the side stairs, I decided to walk in the main entrance and go through to the dining hall. I was going to be in the lobby doing an interview soon anyway, so I couldn't avoid the common areas forever.

As soon as I walked in the door, I saw him: Brandon, the man of my dreams, my crush for the past month. Why was he here? And why was he sitting near the TV room talking with Kevin, the guy I didn't care much about but who had been pursuing me relentlessly for the past few weeks? My first thought was to turn and run, go around the side of the building and drag my tired ass up that side stairwell. Then Brandon saw me, and I wanted to shrink into the floor. I clutched my binder to my chest, hiding my breasts, and covered my pubic area with my hand, feeling humiliated and ridiculous, as Brandon stood up and started walking toward me!

Chapter Six: The Interview

"Danielle?" Brandon said, and my knees almost buckled. He always used my full name, never "Dani," and I always loved hearing it in his baritone voice.

"Hey," I said, feeling myself continue to shrink.

Stay confident, I thought, and I forced myself to stand up straight, my arms to my sides. Brandon stopped when he saw my breasts and my pubic mound fully exposed, his mouth falling open in astonishment. I felt that electric charge through my body, starting in what felt like the core of my vagina.

"Wow," he said, and my knees almost collapsed.

I thought then that I would forever remember the look of pure desire in Brandon's eyes. Knowing that I was the cause of that desire was the single most erotic moment of my life to that point. That electric charge I felt might have been a mini-orgasm.

"Wow, are you cold?" Kevin said with a laugh, approaching from behind Brandon and looking straight at my almost painfully erect nipples. My sudden burst of arousal dissolved to shame as Kevin leered at me. Still, I resisted the urge to cover myself, but I did look down at the floor.

"What are you doing Danielle?" Brandon asked. "Why aren't you wearing clothes?"

I couldn't tell him the truth, of course, but the story I had come up with for everybody and for my impending interview with the school paper seemed inadequate for Brandon. "It's a long story," I wound up saying.

He looked over at Kevin, and they both smiled. "Whatever it is," Brandon said as he walked in a circle around me, "I like it."

Brandon slapped my butt, the sound reverberating throughout the room. "Ow," I said, stepping forward, shocked at the sudden burst of pain from the spank. "Stop," I said, rubbing the spot where his hand had landed.

Kevin was laughing as Brandon said, "Sorry. I couldn't resist."

"That wasn't funny," I said, trying to get Kevin to stop laughing.

"So when we finally do go out on that date, are you going to dress like that?" Kevin said, still laughing. "Or undress, I guess. It's OK with me, but I might just want to stay in the room. Rather than go out."

Kevin and Brandon exchanged a look. "Not if I ask her out myself," Brandon said with a mischievous smile.

Only a few moments before, I would have been thrilled to hear Brandon say he wanted to ask me out, but now I just felt disgusted and degraded. They were thinking of me as their plaything. How could Brandon have suddenly turned into such an asshole? Or had he been an asshole all along, and I was just blinded by my schoolgirl crush?

"Screw you," I said to both of them and walked past them toward the dining hall.

People were already sitting at tables, people I knew and had talked to regularly for the past year and a half. I stopped at the glass doors, feeling humiliated and embarrassed. I couldn't just walk in there and let them, non-strangers that they were, see me naked, but I also couldn't starve myself. Without an income, this was the only place I could get food. If I hadn't taken Dr. Slater's deal that morning, I told myself, I would never be seeing any of these people again anyway. I took a deep breath and pushed through the glass door.

All conversation stopped as I walked in. I found a seat at an empty table near the exit, and set my binder down. I looked at my phone and saw that I still had fifteen minutes until the serving line opened. In one fluid movement, I slid the black butt towel from the outer pocket of the binder and dropped it onto the seat as I slipped in and sat down. I pulled my Kindle out of the binder, thinking I would get a jump on tomorrow's Chemistry class, but I glanced up and saw everyone's eyes still on me. How could I concentrate on chemistry with everyone watching me? My nipples hardened as the tingle of excitement coursed through my nerves. My buttock burned where Brandon had spanked me, and I shifted in my seat to take pressure off that side and felt the dampness on my butt towel against my inner thighs. What was wrong with me? How could something so humiliating be so stimulating?

"Danielle," a soft voice said.

Two freshmen girls, both of them tall and athletic, approached from behind me. One was named Liz; I couldn't remember who the other one was.

"Hey," I replied.

"Can we sit with you?" Liz asked in a timid voice.

"Sure," I replied, fearful that they would do something to try to further embarrass me, as if I could be any more embarrassed.

"I like your solution to the heat," the other girl said as they both sat across the table from me. "I wish I had the courage to do that."

I shrugged, not feeling particularly courageous. For the next fifteen minutes, we talked about what we did on spring break, classes they were taking that I had had the previous year, and even the NCAA women's basketball tournament. They both played on the Coachella Valley University team, which had been eliminated early in our conference tournament. It was nice to be included in a conversation that didn't involve how naked I was. Even though Brandon and I had never been on a date, the end of my crush felt like the end of a relationship. The sadness and anger kept me from really engaging in the conversation with Liz and her friend. I caught them both taking cursory glances at my bare breasts a couple of times, but for the most part, they looked me in the eyes.

When the serving line opened, I jumped up, my meal card in my hand, and got my tray first. The ladies running the line frowned at me as they gazed and served a plate of beef stroganoff, mashed potatoes, and green beans to me, but none of them said anything. I wondered if they had gotten the same email that my professors received. Liz and her friend, whose name I still hadn't managed to catch, went through the line beside me, whispering and giggling between themselves when they thought I couldn't hear. When we all reclaimed our seats, I ate fast, knowing that I was supposed to meet Clarissa from the paper at 5:00.

They both talked while I scarfed down my food, and I managed to figure out that the other girl was named Audrey. I tried not to notice the procession of students entering the dining hall. Soon, the line was long enough that three guys at the back were standing right by our table. I felt their eyes on me, looking straight down my breasts to my naked lap. I sat with my legs tightly together as I shoveled one bite after another into my mouth. Swimming had built up a huge appetite, and I could have eaten an entire second dinner. But I had someplace to be.

"You got a hot date or something?" Liz asked when I had finished and was gathering all my trash onto my tray.

"I'm meeting someone at five."

"A guy?"

"No."

"Oh. Well. Audrey?"

"There's a dance this Friday at Mary Ellen's," Audrey said. "Do you want to go with us?"

"What's Mary Ellen's?" I asked.

"A bar," Audrey replied. "We go there every weekend."

"Is it on campus?"

They both laughed. "No, silly," Liz said.

"I can't go. I have to stay here."

"They would let you in like that, I think," Liz said. "In fact, you would be a big hit."

"Sorry," I said. They looked disappointed as I stood up, slipped my butt towel into my binder, tucked the binder under my arm, and grabbed my tray. "Thanks for the company."

"Any time," Liz said.

I set my tray on the conveyer belt back to the dishwashers and hurried out. I tried not to look at everyone in the dining hall, but I could feel their gazes on my naked body. That exciting tingling sensation in my gut and down between my legs just would not go away. I glanced at my phone and saw that it was eight minutes until 5:00. I ran up the stairs to my room. It was empty, thankfully. Diane usually spent her afternoons and evenings away with her boyfriend or wherever she went. I really didn't care. I threw my binder on the bed and grabbed my cell phone, a fresh butt towel, my room key, and the small hand purse the Sociology Department had given me. In the shared bathroom, I brushed my hair in front of the mirror and put on a tiny bit of makeup from the compact in my purse. At least I didn't have to worry about what to wear to the interview, I thought and almost laughed out loud.

I made it down to the Holcombe Hall foyer at 5:02. Clarissa was sitting on a love seat waiting for me, with a small microphone attached to her phone. Blake was standing across from her, checking the camera that hung from the strap around his neck.

"Hey Dani," she said as soon as she saw me.

"Hi," I replied.

Now that I was here, I didn't think I could do the interview. Sure, doing this project, spending an entire two months naked in front of everyone, was going to save my college degree, but what was going to happen after that? People had already been taking photos of me. There were fancy new video cameras all over campus. And now Blake was about to take some shots of me. How many of those photos and videos were going to wind up on the Internet? And when they did, would my name be attached to them? Would simple Google searches of my name return those photos? How could I possibly hope to pass a pre-employment background investigation with my naked body all over cyberspace? I felt a sudden urge to turn and run. But I knew that once the study was over, I could divulge the real reason for my nudity. Perhaps the study would become an important landmark in the sociology field.

"Come on and sit down," Clarissa said.

I stepped forward, pulling my black towel from my handbag and setting it down on the open end of the love seat, and took my place.

"Before we start," I said, "could you not use my last name in the article?"

Clarissa's eyebrows furrowed in a look of surprise. "Oh. OK. I guess so."

"I mean, I can't stop my photos from appearing everywhere, but I'd rather not have my name attached to them."

"OK. I don't know how long you can prevent that from happening, especially if you keep up the public nudity. This could be national news, which is why I wanted to break the story first."

I shuddered at the thought of seeing national news trucks on campus as I walked everywhere completely naked, news anchors saying my name and calling me the naked girl. What if my friends back home saw it? Even worse, what would my parents think?

"I'll worry about that if it happens," I said.

"OK," Clarissa said and started the recorder app on her phone. Blake was already walking around the room snapping photos from different angles. "Do you go by Danielle or Dani?"

"You can call me Dani."

"OK, Dani. I think it's safe to say that quite a few people on campus were shocked today, the first day of classes after spring break, at seeing a naked girl on campus, just going about her regular business. What prompted this sudden change in your attire, or lack thereof?"

"Well, I had a bit of a revelation while I was at home on the break," I began, starting my made up story as Clarissa held the microphone close to my face. "My cousin had gone down to South Padre Island, but she came home early. She's a big girl, but she said she had worn a two piece. A bikini basically. She told me that people, other girls mostly but some guys too, had criticized her and told her that she should only wear one piece bathing suits. She felt humiliated, of course, and didn't feel like staying after that. So, she and I spent some time together. We watched last year's season of *Game of Thrones*, and in that last episode is a sequence where Cersei Lannister, one of the least likeable characters on the show, is forced to do this long walk of shame, naked, through the city with some annoying nun, or whatever she was, behind her the whole time, shouting 'Shame!' every few seconds."

I did have an overweight cousin who went to South Padre Island, but I didn't see her during the break. The last time I had seen her had been the month before, at my uncle's funeral. And it had been a few months since I had watched season 5 of *Game of Thrones*, but that Walk of Shame sequence was very memorable.

"I read an article about that scene right after that. They had hired a body double and used CGI to put the actress's face on the model's body for the full frontal shots."

"Lena Headey," Clarissa said.

"What?"

"The actress was Lena Heady."

"Oh yeah. And of course, the body double they used was

just perfect, you know. Or what Hollywood says is perfect. And I got to thinking about what had happened to my cousin and how Hollywood has set our unrealistic expectations of what a naked woman should look like. I thought that if more people saw what a real woman looks like, outside of Hollywood, people's expectations would change. We would be much more accepting of all kinds of body types. I mean, look at me. I've got a bubble butt and really thick thighs. I would never have been asked to be what's-her-name's body double. But I still think I'm attractive, even if I don't fit that Hollywood mold. So, we got to talking about it, my cousin and I, and she said I should just go back to school naked."

"So it was your cousin's idea?"

I frowned. I hadn't wanted to make that claim; it had just come out in the telling of the story. "She was joking, of course. I didn't take it seriously until I saw something about the nudity laws in California on some website. I realized then that simple nudity, without any intent to sexually gratify anyone, is perfectly legal here."

I glanced away from Clarissa and saw that the edge of the foyer had filled with people pressed against the walls, watching the interview but staying back to give Blake room to move around as he continued snapping photographs. I recognized most of them as being from the dorm, and I felt especially self-conscious, sitting there naked on the love seat and talking about my nudity.

"What website?"

"The article was somewhere on the AANR website. I probably couldn't even find it now without some searching."

"And what is the AANR?" Clarissa asked.

"The American Association of Nude Recreation," I replied, hoping that I had gotten it right.

"So you're doing this for your cousin?"

"No, not for her. For all women. Or, at least, any woman who has ever been made to feel ashamed of her body."

Many of the people in the foyer burst into applause at this statement. I looked around and saw that most of those clapping were women of varying sizes.

"That's awesome and admirable," Clarissa said. "But there's a big difference between the idea and actually carrying it out. How did it feel, that first time you stepped outside without your clothes?"

I smiled, glad that the fictional portion of the interview was over. "It was terrifying. But at the same time, it was exciting and empowering. I mean, I felt extremely vulnerable, being naked, but I also felt amazingly free. And pure. When we wear clothes, when we cover ourselves, it's like pretending to be something. We dress up for a job interview because we hope to make the interviewer want to hire us. But that's not us, what we are inside. Being naked is truth. It's purity."

I felt like I was laying the bullshit on too thick, so I stopped. But bullshit or not, I did kind of believe what I was saying. I did feel true, even though so much of this interview was a lie.

"So, how long do you plan on doing this?"

"Until the end of the semester."

"Two months?" Clarissa asked in an incredulous tone.

"Yes. Unless they change the laws on me."

I heard several boos at this prospect, mostly from guys.

"Let's hope that doesn't happen," Clarissa said.

I had a feeling that Dr. Slater would be very active in preventing any such thing.

"Now that we know why you're doing this, I think we can all agree on what a noble cause it is," Clarissa continued.

"Thank you," I said, not sure what else I could add.

"I think that's it," Clarissa said. "You're a sophomore, right?"

"Yes."

"And what is your major?"

"English. Pre-law."

"Awesome. Thank you so much for taking the time to talk to me. Do you have any questions of me?"

"When will this appear in the paper?"

"I am going to get it written up tonight, so it will be on the stand the next issue, Wednesday morning."

"Ok."

I actually thought having the story out on campus would ease the shocked looks I kept getting and make people more accepting of me. That would make getting around less of an adventure than it had been today.

Clarissa switched off her recording app, disconnected the speaker, and dropped everything into her purse.

"Could you stand up and take a few poses?" Blake asked me.

He had been respectful, and the interview, short as it was, had turned out well, I thought. So I stood up and took a few poses. Just about everyone in the foyer behind him started snapping photos with their phones. Almost everyone here knew my last name or could easily look it up on the dorm roster, so my hopes of keeping my name off my online photos seemed hopelessly futile. Still, I was loving the attention, and that tingling sensation returned with a force. I turned and gave everyone both profile views; I spun around and gave everyone a back view, looking over my shoulder at everyone.

"Thank you," Blake said when he had taken several shots. "This is awesome."

"Thanks again," Clarissa said as Blake packed his camera into the bag.

Very few people had left the foyer of Holcombe Hall, and those remaining all stood watching. With a bit of embarrassment, I picked my black butt towel up from the love seat, folded it up, and stuffed it into my tiny hand purse.

"You're welcome," I said to Clarissa.

"Are you sure about not wanting your last name in the article?"

I shrugged. "I don't think it matters much anymore."

"So I can go ahead?"

"Sure."

"Awesome! I think what you are doing is admirable, unusual as it is."

Blake got his gear packed up, and he and Clarissa started walking out the front door of the dormitory. Wanting to get away from the crowd, I walked outside with them, wearing nothing and carrying only my little hand bag, as the people in the dorm murmured among themselves.

I walked with Clarissa and Blake until they turned to walk back to the journalism department. I decided to keep walking and let the group in the dorm disperse. The campus was not busy at this time of day, so I could walk with very few people watching. Still, every time I caught someone, especially a guy, looking my way, that tingling feeling reasserted itself. I knew I needed relief, and I thought that I would probably have the dorm room to myself if I went back. But with Diane and her boyfriend already having seen me a couple of times, I wouldn't be surprised if she altered her normal routine. She and James were probably in the room now, waiting for me to show up.

I went into one of the science buildings and found a ladies room on the first floor. Thankfully, it was empty, and I went to the toilet farthest from the restroom entrance. It was the ADA-compliant handicapped stall, so it was very roomy. I straddled the commode without sitting down, and quickly went to work on my swollen clitoris. The first orgasm wasn't satisfying enough, so I got myself off two more times, hoping I wasn't making much noise. I managed to not cry out or scream, but the squishy sounds my hand made as I worked on my sopping wet vagina seemed to echo throughout the room.

I froze when the door to the ladies room creaked open, and I slowly lowered myself down onto the commode, two fingers still inside me. I heard the first stall door swing open, then close with a thud. Whoever-she-was peed, wiped, and walked out. I caught a glimpse of her through the space between the partition and stall door. She was a goth chick with hair dyed black and earbuds in her ears, her head bopping to the music. I was thankful that she had probably never heard me. I shuddered, and almost came again since my fingers were still inside my vagina. As soon as she left, I went back to work and orgasmed one more time. I waited until I caught my breath, then peed. I cleaned myself up with wet paper towels while standing at the sink counter, wondering how I would explain myself to anyone else who walked in. Thankfully, no one did. Once I was somewhat clean and dry, I looked at myself in the large mirror. My labia were more noticeable than usual, poking out from between the outer folds. Trying to tuck them back in would just further stimulate them, so I had to just go like I was.

During the entire walk back to my dorm, I couldn't help but think that everyone who looked at me knew what I had just done in the ladies room. It was silly paranoia, and I know that being naked just made those feelings of shame and vulnerability even more intense. I took the side entrance and went up the stairs to my room, seeing no one once I was in the building. Diane and James were not waiting for me as I had feared, which was a wonderful thing. If either of them had noticed the state of my labia, no hole would have been deep enough to crawl into.

I spent the rest of the evening trying to work on that

replacement paper for Dr. Finfrock’s class. I was always conscious of being naked, and that kept distracting me. Still, I made a lot of progress, and when Diane came in at 9:30, alone, I was almost finished with my first draft.

“Oh my God, you’re still naked,” she said.

“Yep,” was all I said in response.

She left again, and I saved my work and went to take a shower. I went to bed feeling tired but refreshed. The sheet felt strange against my bare skin. I had never even slept nude before, but it was comforting, letting the sheet caress my entire body, thankful just to be covered. The contract that I had signed for Dr. Slater had had a clause allowing me to sleep under a sheet and/or blanket during nighttime hours. I reflected briefly on just what a strange day it had been: the nervousness at meeting with Dr. Slater, the disbelief at her proposal, the feelings of both fear and arousal at being seen naked by everyone. Just before sleep overtook me, I wondered if anyone had ever had a day as strange as this one had been for me.

Chapter Seven: Day Two

I awoke at 6:15 on Tuesday morning feeling confused and disoriented, wondering why I had taken off my pajamas in the night, before everything came back to me. I rolled over and fumbled around for my phone to stop the alarm. The volume was set to get slowly louder until I woke up enough to turn it off so that it wouldn't disturb Diane. I remembered waking up at one in the morning, realizing that I hadn't plugged in my phone or my necklace microphone. Diane was sleeping in her bed by then. I hadn't heard her come in. After running to the restroom to pee, I stumbled around the room in the dark getting both my phone and the microphone charging before going back to bed.

Just thinking about the microphone reminded me that at least one research assistant had been listening to me masturbate in the restroom of that science building last night. I wondered if it had been the incredibly handsome Greg, even though he had drawn the first shift yesterday morning. Imagining him listening to me caused those tingling sensations to return, and when they did, I pictured him not only listening but standing in the stall with me, watching. My hands were on my belly under the covers, and I slid one down, feeling the curve of my pubic mound, my first two fingers hovering past my labia close enough to give myself shivers. I don't know how long I would have continued if Diane hadn't snorted and turned over in her bed.

With a sigh, I rolled out of bed, grabbed my shower pack and towel, and headed down the hall. Stacy, my floor's Resident Assistant, also had early classes on Tuesday and Thursday and was standing at the sink brushing her teeth when I walked in. She abruptly stopped brushing when she saw me in the mirror and spit a big mix of bubbly toothpaste and saliva into the sink.

"Couldn't you at least wrap up in the towel?" she said.

I figured that would violate the rules of the study that Dr. Slater had spelled out, although there were no cameras in the bathroom (at least, I assumed there weren't). No research assistants were around, and I wasn't wearing the microphone because I was about to shower. But I still wasn't going to take any chances.

"I could," I replied, "if I felt ashamed of my body. But I don't." I shrugged, hung my towel up, and stepped into the shower stall.

I would like to say that I just showered and got out, but thoughts of Greg and the rest of the RAs looking at my naked body the previous morning in Dr. Slater's office were too stimulating. As I touched myself, I relived the nude photo shoot with Blake in the dorm foyer, with at least two dozen people looking on at my bare breasts, my exposed buttocks, and my pubic region. When the orgasm came, I gasped and tried to hold back my scream but wasn't entirely successful. I just hoped Stacy had finished brushing her teeth and had left the bathroom.

As I washed, I felt the regular post-orgasm shame that I usually felt. I couldn't believe that I had done this three times in less than 24 hours. What was wrong with me? Dr. Slater had said that the focus of the study was how others reacted to me, but how could she not care what this study was doing to me? I had to push those thoughts and questions aside as I prepared for my day.

I had two early classes on Tuesdays and Thursdays which left most of the rest of the day free for work. Since I had been fired from the print shop, I didn't know what I would do now. After brushing my teeth, blow drying my hair, and putting on just a dab of makeup, I slung my towel over my shoulder and returned to my room. Since I didn't have to dress – couldn't dress – I had some extra time. I logged onto my computer and checked my Facebook. Kevin had posted on my Timeline, "I love the new naked look." There were no comments or likes, and he had just posted it last night about ten o'clock, which would have been midnight Central time.

But all my friends back home, including my parents, could see the post. I clicked the delete button, wishing I had never approved Kevin's friend request. I thought about all the other people from CVU I had added, any of whom could post something about my new nude adventures, either in text or, worse, a photo. How many were there? I couldn't remember them all. Facebook had been wonderful for keeping up with my friends back in Texas, but that had been when I didn't have something to hide from them. I clicked on my account settings, and with some sadness, I deactivated my Facebook account.

I went over to my email and saw a message from Dr. Slater. "Dear Dani," it said, "Thank you so much for volunteering for this project. I looked at some of the footage and listened to some audio from your first day, and you were wonderful. I thought your answers in your interview were genius. Please keep up the good work, and if you have any questions, please don't hesitate to ask." I was tempted to just delete the message. The more I thought about the project and how Dr. Slater had presented it to me, either strip now and go naked for two months or get kicked out of school, the angrier I got. She can call me a volunteer all she wants, but the fact is that I was forced into doing this.

I closed my email page without either deleting or replying to the message and put my microphone necklace on. All I could see was a tiny green light to indicate that it was fully charged. Diane started to move around in her bed, so I grabbed my binder, making sure my phone, room key, and Kindle were inside. I started to put some sunscreen on but thought that I wouldn't need it this early. I had a break between classes just before 9:30, but that walk between buildings was short. My last class ended at 10:50, and I could duck into the bathroom to put some sunscreen on then. So I added the bottle to my binder, zipped it up, and left the room.

I went barefoot again since I didn't like how the straps of those sandals rubbed the tops of my feet. And it had felt strange being naked with shoes on. If the only things I was allowed to wear made me uncomfortable, I didn't see a reason to wear them. Forgoing the back staircase, I instead went to the elevator and pressed the down button. The butterflies in my stomach started up as I waited. Yesterday hadn't been a dream, and I was really heading out naked into the world again. I shook my head, marveling that I was even allowed to do this, much less forced to.

When the elevator door opened, four girls' jaws dropped at the sight of me. I smiled and stepped inside, turning to face the doors as they slid closed.

"Umm, did you forget something?" one girl asked.

"Shh," someone else said. "She's the naked girl. Didn't you see her getting interviewed downstairs yesterday?"

"It's all right," I said, turning to look at them. "I know this is strange, but I think everyone will get used to it soon."

"But how do you get used to it?"

I shrugged. "Once you get past the fear of it being so taboo, it's not that bad."

The elevator doors opened, and I burst out into the lobby, eager to get some distance between myself and the girls behind me. I sauntered through the foyer, not slowing as I glanced over at the love seat where I'd had my interview and my stimulating photo session the evening before, grinning slightly at the memory. I hadn't thought Blake was that attractive, but imagining him copying the pictures of me onto his hard drive and looking at each one turned me on. I had to stop thinking such things. Looking down at myself, I was dismayed and embarrassed by the pink color of my vulva and that my labia were still poking out like they had been last night. But I couldn't stop now. I had been naked all day yesterday, and my photos and video had been taken more times than I could count. Quitting now would be a waste of my only opportunity for a college degree. And the fact was, I was enjoying this, as embarrassing as it would be if certain people back home found out about it.

The morning temperature was still in the sixties, and goose pimples popped up on my arms and everywhere else as I walked away from the dorm. The concrete felt cold against the bottoms of my feet. I skipped down the steps and started walking toward the Commons, thinking to myself that the area outside the dorm building was unusually crowded. It was then that I realized that all these people had gathered just to wait for my appearance. Flash bulbs blinked everywhere as I turned to walk on the concrete path, and the chatter of the crowd increased. There was even a smattering of applause. I wondered what they thought of my glowing pink vulva. Could they tell I had been playing with myself in the shower? That thought made me feel a deep sense of shame as well as excitement.

Confusion reigned. Was I losing my mind?

I was acutely aware of the jiggle of my buttocks with every step I took away from the crowd. When I took a quick glance behind me, I saw that about half of the group was following me from a distance, most of them with their phones raised, taking video of those jiggling buttocks. I wondered where my assigned research assistant was. Greg had had the early shift yesterday, and I hoped he was back there somewhere now. How could I go anywhere and carry on with a normal day with a crowd like this following me all the time? I wondered if this was how movie stars felt, with people panting after them everywhere. At least they got to wear clothes when they went out in public.

This was only the second day, I reminded myself. They couldn't keep this up. After all, they were all college students too with their own classes to keep up with. At least, I hoped they were all college students. The campus was generally open to the public, so conceivably, anyone could show up. I looked back again, trying to see if any of the people following me looked to be over college age, but I couldn't pick anyone out.

I walked fast, not caring that my breasts were bouncing almost obscenely. The people I was walking away from couldn't see them anyway, although I did see some eyes widen on the faces of the few oncoming pedestrians as I passed by. My nipples were pointy and erect both from the cool temperature and the arousal at being so exposed to so many people. I was beginning to think I should email Dr. Slater to get the name of a psychologist, maybe a professor in the psychology department, who could help me through this. And if she did set me up with one, would the consultations be confidential or would they be included in the sociological study. The life of a naked guinea pig, I thought and sighed.

I passed the science building that I had used for my little escape last night, and I put my head down in shame, watching my feet slap on the concrete. The chemistry building was just past that, and I turned and bounded up the steps to get inside and to my class. So far, the level of scrutiny and the number of people seeing my naked body had been worse than yesterday. Would tomorrow's newspaper article help or hurt that?

I walked up the stairs, glad that only two people, both guys, had followed me into the building. They took the stairs behind me, and I wondered what they could see when they looked up and ahead at me. Maybe later on I could get someone to follow me up some stairs taking video just so I could know how much of myself I was exposing with each step, but I couldn't think of anyone to ask.

"Holy shit!" someone said as I scurried into my chemistry class and took my seat at my regular desk, pausing for only a fraction of a second to drop my butt towel into the chair.

I took the Kindle out of my binder, turned to the current chapter in my chemistry text book, and then looked up. Everyone was staring at me. I decided to play dumb, and just said, "What?"

"Did the campus dress code change or something?" the guy next to me said.

Before anyone could answer, Dr. Biden, our middle-aged but still nerdy professor, swept into the room. He set his stack of books on the instructor's desk with a sigh, looked up at us, and stopped when his eyes fixed on me.

"Um, good morning," he said.

"Good morning," the class said in response.

"I trust everyone had a nice relaxing spring break. Or a fun filled very active break. Whichever you were shooting for."

There was a smattering of laughter before Dr. Biden went into his lecture. Normally, he was a very good speaker and kept his eye contact floating from student to student, but today, his eyes never left my breasts. A couple of times, he realized that I had caught him, and he smiled sheepishly and looked down at his lecture notes. I thought his reaction was both sweet and funny, but his eyes kept returning to my breasts.

I don't know what came over me toward the end of class. I do know that that ever present tingling sensation was stronger than usual because of Dr. Biden's stares. To his credit, he never wavered from his lecture or even stumbled over any words. As the class continued, I slid my towel forward on my chair. I'm sure Dr. Biden thought I was trying to hide my breasts under the desk, and he did try to look at other students for a few minutes. But when I spread my legs and gave him what I thought was a clear view straight at my vagina, he froze and dropped the pen he had been holding.

"I'm sorry," he said, bending down to pick the pen up and getting an even better view of my spread vulva.

I should have felt like such a slut and been ashamed of

myself, but Dr. Biden's stuttering for the last ten minutes of class was both funny and endearing. By that time, I was impatient for class to end. The way I was sitting wasn't very comfortable, and part of my butt started going to sleep. I was having too much fun to change positions though. My right knee started bouncing, hoping to keep the blood flow going. I could feel the wind from the air conditioner vent hitting me right between my legs, making me want to escape again like I had last night. I had never thought of myself as being horny before. I was still a virgin after all, so I didn't even know what it was like to have a man inside me. But I did have to admit that right then, I was horny. Being naked was making me constantly horny, I think.

'We'll have a lab Thursday afternoon," Dr. Biden said, "so be ready to experiment with crystals. I'll see you next time."

The class gave a collective sigh as everyone started packing up and heading out. I had a survey of American literature class next. Unlike my MWF British lit class, which was an advanced class for English majors, this one was a sophomore level class required on almost every degree plan in the university. No one said anything to me as everyone filed out of the class, but I could feel their eyes on me.

"Miss Keaton," Dr. Biden said just as I was about to leave.

"Yes sir?" I said, cringing. How could I have taunted him like I had done? I still had to sit in his class for another two months. He probably thought I was such an incredibly shameless slut.

"Lab," he said. "I've been asked to excuse you from any lab work for the rest of the course. Could you explain why?"

"Um. I don't know."

"Specifically, I was asked to exclude you from any activity that required the wearing of a lab apron or coat. Which is pretty much all of them."

I hadn't even thought of lab coats. I wondered what would have happened if I had shown up to lab and put one on, although I probably would have stopped to ask Dr. Slater if I was permitted to wear anything required by the safety regulations of the university. It looked like she was trying to eliminate those issues before they even came up.

"Um, I don't know who would have asked that," I lied.

"I think you do. But, be that as it may, I have agreed to the request as long as I could assign you make up activities. Is that all right with you?"

"Sure. I think so."

"All right. I'll email you your lab make up assignment tomorrow."

"OK," I said, hoping that the make-up work wasn't going to be more difficult than the actual lab. "Thank you."

"See you Thursday," he said as I hurried out of the room.

I bounded down the stairs and out the front door. At just a few minutes before 9:30, the temperatures had risen into the upper seventies, with a nice breeze that tickled every inch of my skin. If everyone knew how good it felt to be naked outside, more people would do it, I thought. My literature class was in the building diagonal to the Chemistry building, so I cut across the lawn, enjoying the feeling of the still damp grass on my feet and between my toes.

"Naked!" a guy yelled from somewhere.

"Wow!" I heard someone else say.

"Will you marry me?" another voice asked. I just shook my head and kept walking.

Pausing at the entrance to the building, I took a quick look behind me to see if I could spot one of Dr. Slater's research assistants. Were they really following me like she said they would? Or have I been left out to dry, naked and alone? Out of the people walking or standing within sight, ninety percent of them were looking at me. I probably blushed, but that tingling sensation intensified. I felt like covering up, but I also felt like turning and giving everyone a full frontal view. I did neither. Just before I was about to turn and enter the building, I spotted Ginger, the large girl who had helped me pack my clothes yesterday morning. She nodded to me when I smiled at her.

My American lit class was taught by a young TA still working on her PhD by the name of Karen Armstrong. She hated being called Ms. Armstrong and insisted that we all call her Karen. She was already at the lectern when I walked into class, and her eyes widened. I smiled at her and took my regular seat. Karen preferred classroom discussions to regular lectures, so she started her intro to our last reading, "Bartleby, the Scrivener" by Herman Melville. I had read the story on the plane back from spring break, and at the time, I didn't think my reading of it would matter as I had expected to lose my scholarship. I pulled the story up on my Kindle and skimmed it as Karen talked.

"So Danielle," Karen said. "Could you tell us your thoughts on the story?"

Wondering if my nudity was making me a target for the discussion and being in the middle of skimming the story, I thought I would be a bit of a smart ass and give the quote most often given by Bartleby. "I would prefer not to."

There was a smattering of laughter, and even Karen smiled herself. But still, she waited, so I felt compelled to continue. "I mean, it's a reflection on freedom. How free are we to do or not do what we want? Bartleby just prefers to not do anything, and how people react to that says more about them than it does about Bartleby."

"Hmm. That's interesting. Do you apply this to yourself in any way? Like, why didn't you wear clothes today?"

I shrugged and smiled and said, "I would prefer not to." I thought I was lying, but the more time I spent naked, the more part of me enjoyed it. Still, I longed to wear clothes like everyone else, hated that I was being singled out in the prohibition of clothes, while still enjoying the attention I was getting. Insanity must be setting in, I thought.

The discussion on Bartleby continued, from topics of clinical depression to the use of force against an individual. I tuned it out as I noticed my male classmates continually looking at me. I still felt ashamed of the way I had exposed myself to Dr. Biden, so this time, I folded my arms over my chest as I tried to listen to the discussion.

Karen usually ended the class early, so we got to leave at 10:30 with our assignment to write a report on the Bartleby story. I stayed in the room while everyone left, checking my phone. I'd had four missed calls and two voice mails. The first voice mail was from my mother, wondering how I was and why she couldn't find my Facebook profile any more. The second voice mail was more interesting.

"This is Matt Moore calling for Danielle Keaton. I got your name from Dr. Slater. I teach figure drawing in the art department, and the model for my eleven o'clock class cancelled today. I was hoping you would be available to model. The class is three hours and pays twenty-five an hour. You'd have to fill out some paperwork in the art department office, but we could take care of that after class if we need to, and if you are available.”

Matt recited his number. It was the same as two of the missed calls I had received, so I called him back immediately. Twenty-five dollars an hour was more than double the rate I had been making at the print shop. I figured it was nude modeling (and given my participation in Dr. Slater’s study, it would have to be nude), but at least I would be naked where a person would normally be expected to be.

“This is Matt,” he answered.

“Um, hi. This is Danielle Keaton. I just got a voice mail from you.”

“Yes!”

“I’m sorry; I just now got out of class. Do you still need a model?”

“Yes, I do, very much so.”

“OK. I’d love to do it, although I’ve never done anything like this.”

“It won’t be too bad. We start with a bunch of short gesture poses, about one minute each, then three twenty minute poses, and finish with a one hour long pose. But you can have a break or two during the long pose, and the whole class has a break after the first hour to hour and a half.”

“OK.”

“I can give you some pointers on the poses too. And it’s nude, or course. Are you OK with that?”

I laughed out loud. “Yes,” I replied.

“Well, all right. I’ll see you soon. We’re in room 210 in the Fine Arts Building. Bring a robe if you’ve got one.”

“I don’t think I have one.”

“Don’t worry about it. We have one in the studio. Talk to you later.”

He disconnected, and I laughed again. Twenty-five dollars and hour for three hours? That was going to help a lot. Dr. Slater had mentioned something about the possibility of a higher paying campus job, but I hadn’t expected the pay to be that much. I put my phone back into the binder. The room had cleared out, so I sprayed myself with sunscreen right there by my desk. A guy with red hair and glasses walked in, apparently for the next class, and just stopped and stared.

"Did I just die and go to heaven?" he said.

My body was glistening with the sunscreen, the smell of coconut wafting through the room.

"Nope, not yet," I said. I popped the cap back onto the bottle of sunscreen and replaced it in my binder.

"Who are you? And why are you in here naked?"

"I'm Dani, and it's a long story. But, if you read tomorrow's school newspaper, you'll learn more."

The guy's hands shook as he pulled his phone out of his pocket. "Could I get a picture of you?" he asked in a shaky voice. "Nobody will believe me when I tell them this."

"Ok," I said. His nervousness was kind of endearing.

I stood by the desk as he pulled up his camera app and snapped a photo. I smiled and said, "They still may not believe you," and stepped next to him, putting my arm around his waist. "Now, take a selfie with both of us."

He held the phone high and snapped a couple of pics. I didn't let go of him until he had checked to make sure they had turned out well. I looked at them too and saw our smiling faces along with my bare breasts.

"Thanks," he said, as I turned away to grab my binder. "I'm Rusty, by the way."

"Rusty? I'm Danielle. Nice to meet you."

"So, you just decided to be a nudist one day?"

"Yeah, kind of. Check out tomorrow's paper."

I walked past him and started back to the dorm. I still had half an hour before the art class, and I wanted to leave my binder in my room. I didn't know how much my Kindle was worth, and I didn't want to leave it lying around while I was stuck up on the platform in art class.

The sun was shining brightly, and the temperature had shot up into the lower 80s. My bare feet made plopping noise on the walkways, the concrete not yet too hot for bare skin. Like yesterday and this morning, I was aware of the looks and stares I was getting, but I didn't mind anymore. Was I even growing to like them? The way everyone looked and snapped photos of me with their phones made me feel like some kind of movie star. All I was doing was walking across campus. I didn't have any special talent. I was just in my natural state, not wearing clothes. Why, in a warm weather environment like this, were we as a species so compelled to wear clothes all the time? God, my thoughts were starting to sound like Dr. Slater's speech to me the previous morning when she introduced this crazy project to me. My feelings toward her went from anger to amusement, just as my feelings about being naked in public went from fear, embarrassment, and humiliation to liberation, exhilaration, and maybe even euphoria. I was one confused naked girl.

Holcombe Hall had apparently acquired a dedicated group of squatters. Several people, mostly men, were sitting cross-legged on the lawn beside the street in front of the dorm building. They rose in unison as I approached. I turned away from them as quickly as I could, cutting across part of the lawn to get into the building.

Some of them were calling to me, but I ignored them. They weren't seeing me as a person; I was just a naked girl to them, an object. The suppressed humiliation returned, and I again felt anger at Dr. Slater for making me do this.

Determined to not allow my nudity to alter my regular activity, I took the elevator and ignored the stares I got from the people in the lobby. Diane and James were in the room when I got there.

"Holy shit," Diane said, shaking her head. "We need to have a party or something to celebrate your coming out."

"My coming out?"

"Yeah, little Miss Nudist."

"I wish I had a naked girl living with me," James said, and Diane punched him in the shoulder.

I put my binder away and pretended that Diane and James were not there making comments. I got my phone, towel, and room key stuffed into my tiny hand purse and started to head toward the art building.

"You should shave your pussy," Diane said.

"What?"

"I mean, if you're going to show it off, you should shave it. People don't want to see hair."

"How do you know?"

She and James both smiled. I had never seen Diane completely naked even though we were roommates. I shook my head and walked out of the room. It was just like Diane to suggest, and therefore criticize, my grooming choices.

I took the side stairwell and went out the back entrance to avoid my fans outside the front doors. The walk to the art department had been like all my other naked walks, with lots of wide-eyed staring and gasps. I ignored it and just went about my business. I arrived at the Fine Arts Building early, so I stopped in the art department office. Matt had mentioned something about paperwork, so I thought I would be proactive and get it taken care of. If anything, it would make a good impression on him.

The receptionist gave me the usual reaction when I walked in, open mouthed expression of incredulity.

"Hi, I'm Danielle, and Matt just booked me to model for his figure drawing class."

"Oh. Well, I guess you would be a good fit for that job. But why are you naked now?"

"It's a long story. But it will be in the school paper in the morning."

"OK."

I gave the receptionist my full name, and she looked me up in her computer. My termination from the print shop hadn't been completed in the system, so all she had to do was change my job title and pay, making sure that I wasn't still employed at the print shop. After signing the simple change form, I was all done. The receptionist did say that the department chair would have to sign off on it, but that that wouldn't be a problem. She gave me a blank timesheet, and I took it with me up to the drawing studio.

Five students were setting up their easels when I walked in. I took my place on the model stand, setting my timesheet and purse down on the back corner of the platform and removing my towel from the purse.

"You're the campus naked girl I've heard about?" one of the artists, a slightly overweight blonde girl with thick-rimmed glasses, asked me.

"The one and only," I replied.

She gave a snorty, nerdy laugh and said, "Cool!"

A young guy in jeans and tie-dyed t-shirt walked into the room and came straight toward me.

"Danielle? I'm Matt."

I smiled and shook his hand. He barely looked older than the students. "Hi."

"You weren't kidding when you said you didn't need a robe. I guess you're the one everyone's talking about."

"Yes," I replied, blushing at my sudden fame.

Matt went over the kinds of poses he wanted for the gestures, demonstrating a few of them for me. When class started, I did my best, imagining myself as a ballerina, a gymnast, or a volleyball player. The gestures were almost a kind of dance, and I felt like I was performing. The longer poses were simpler. Of the three twenty minute poses, one was standing with one hand on a hip, another was sitting cross-legged on the platform with one knee up, and the third was reclining. For the one hour pose, he had me seated in a chair. I surprised myself by being able to keep still. Matt marked the position of my feet and hands with masking tape halfway through the long pose and then told me to take a break. I walked naked around the room looking at the drawings of myself, which were all amazing. Everyone seemed to see me differently, but each drawing was beautiful in some unique way. When I got back into the pose, only a little instruction was needed to get me back into the same position. At the end of the class, all the students applauded, and Matt was very complimentary. He was also impressed that I had taken care of the paperwork. Matt helped me fill out and sign my timesheet, signed it himself, and told me that he would turn it in for me.

"Are you available next Tuesday, same time, 11 to 2?" he asked before I left.

"Absolutely," I said.

He smiled, the dimples in his cheeks stirring those familiar tingling sensations again. "Good. Consider yourself booked."

I smiled back at him. I was going to like my new job and my new boss.

Chapter Eight - Violation

Even though my first class wasn't until 11:00 Wednesday morning, I still got up before 7:00, showered, dressed in only my special microphone necklace, and went downstairs to check the campus newspaper rack just inside the front door of the dorm. The new edition was there, with the banner headline "Full Exposure" in large block letters. The subtitle directly underneath it was, "Naked Girl on Campus Speaks". A black and white photo of me on the love seat was next to the article, my arm positioned in such a way as to block my nipples from view. My hip was clearly visible and very clearly naked, but no pubic hair or buttocks were showing. I took two copies, reading the article as I walked over to the dining hall, trying to ignore the stares of my fellow students. Clarissa had done a good job detailing the surprise most people on campus had received at my earliest naked appearances. She also made me out to be some kind of crusading hero, quoting the story I had given her about my cousin. If the story had been true, I would have felt really proud. As it was, I felt like I had dodged a bullet by coming up with a plausible story without divulging the secret of Dr. Slater's study. And even though we had talked about the use of my last name at the end of our interview, she had left it off, referring to me once as "Danielle, a sophomore from Texas majoring in English and pre-law" and then as Dani throughout the rest of the article. At the end was a statement that more photos were posted on the newspaper's website along with a warning that most of them were NSFW. It took my brain a second to translate that acronym as "not safe for work".

I went through the serving line and got a heavy breakfast of scrambled eggs, bacon, sausage, and biscuits covered in gravy. I wasn't normally a breakfast eater, but yesterday's art class had caused me to miss lunch for a second consecutive day. Luckily, there hadn't been a swim class yesterday to drain almost every ounce of energy from my body like Monday. Still, I knew I couldn't get by on just one meal a day, so I dove into my breakfast. Liz and Audrey walked in, spotted me, and sat across from me after going through the serving line.

"Good morning," Liz said.

"Hey."

"I saw a certain naked girl on the front page of the paper this morning," Audrey said with a grin.

I smiled back at her, my mouth full of food, and pushed one of my copies to her.

"In England, they used to put those girls on page three," Liz said, and she and Audrey both laughed. I had no idea what they were talking about, so I just let the comment fly over my head.

"Hey," one of two guys said to Liz. I had seen them both before, but I'd never talked to them. One was taller than the other, but both were athletically built with finely combed hair and smooth skin.

"Hey Zack," Liz said. "Sit down. Our under-dressed friend here is Dani. Dani, this is Zack and Bruce."

I shook their hands, noting that the taller one was Bruce.

"Hi Dani," Zack said. "That's a heck of a way to get famous."

They both sat down, and we all started talking. I ate my breakfast, looking around at the rest of the dining hall. The people who used to sit with me all the time were at a table across the room. As far as I recall, none of them had ever talked to any of the people at my current table. I wondered what Dr. Slater would think of these results, the avoidance of my old friends and the draw of new ones. At least, I hoped they were friends. After what had happened with Brandon yesterday and as exposed and vulnerable as I felt, I questioned everyone's motives.

I could tell from the way they talked and their hand gestures that Zack and Bruce were gay. It made me wonder about Liz and

Audrey. Were they lesbians? They had invited me to a bar called Mary Ellen's, so I made a mental note to look that up once I had looked at my photos on the school newspaper's website. Diane's "coming out" comment from the day before came to mind, even though I wasn't gay and had never even felt attraction to another girl. Here I was sitting at the table for gays, lesbians, and nudists.

After breakfast, I went back upstairs to get on my computer and look at my photos. They were amazingly vivid high definition shots of me. I was, of course, fully naked, but I had a smile on my face and not the sultry look like I seen on the models in the few adult magazines I had looked at. The photos of me seemed to depict a girl who just liked to be free and naked. And while the full frontal photos were rather explicit, they didn't seem dirty or pornographic. I just looked like a free spirit, plain, with very little makeup. I was OK with them on the university website, given that everyone on campus sees me naked on a daily basis anyway. I just hoped that no one back home saw them.

Diane stirred, farted, and sat up in bed. She looked at me as I closed the newspaper site and switched to my report for Dr. Finfrock's class. I had just about finished it the night before, along with writing the assignment about the "Bartleby the Scrivener" story.

"Morning," I said.

"Hey."

She stumbled up, grabbed her stuff, and headed toward the bathroom. I got to work on revising and proof-reading my paper. It wasn't anywhere close to being as good as Amanda Johnson's report, the one I had plagiarized, but it would suffice, I thought. Diane walked back into the room after twenty minutes or so wrapped in a towel, her dirty pajamas in a bundle under her arm. She would normally put on panties and jeans or shorts under her towel before removing said towel with her back to me to put on her bra and shirt. For some reason, seeing her now in her towel made me think about the comment she had made to me yesterday.

"So you think I should shave, huh?" I said.

"What?" Diane looked at me in a daze, still not fully awake. She had never been a morning person.

"You said I should shave my pubic hair."

"Oh, yeah. I did say that. Yeah, I mean, if you're going to go around showing your pussy off to everyone, you ought to shave it."

"Do you shave yours?"

"Yeah. Why?"

"Let me see."

Diane frowned and said, "No," with emphasis. "I'm not going to show you my kitty."

"Why not? I show you mine."

"You show *everyone* yours since spring break. And even I never saw yours before the break. I mean, seriously, what the hell happened to you?"

I stood up and tossed one of the copies of the campus newspaper onto her bed. "Read that."

Diane dropped her dirty clothes bundle and picked up the paper. "Holy shit," she said.

As she read with an open mouth the article about me, I grabbed the side of her towel and gave it a slight but sudden tug. It fell to the floor, and Diane squealed, dropping the paper and trying to cover herself.

"What are you doing!?"

Her pubic region was indeed shaved, and I thought it made her look like a little girl. Her small A-cup breasts added to that impression, making me wonder if her boyfriend James wasn't a latent pedophile.

"Bitch!" she said, picking up her towel and wrapping it back around her.

"Hey, you suggested it. I just wanted to see what I might look like. I've never shaved down there. I kind of like having a little bit of hair so I don't look too girlish."

"Fuck off," Diane replied, pulling her panties up under the towel.

"I'm sorry," I said, trying to smooth things over.

"I'm not like you," she said. "I can't just do what you're doing. Aren't you embarrassed? It's not normal to run around naked."

Two days ago, I would have agreed with her. But constant nudity was my new normal, something I had to do to get my coveted degree, and I had to at least partially embrace it or be thoroughly miserable for the next two months.

"It's just a phase," I said. "I'll probably grow out of it by the end of the semester."

"God damn, I hope so."

I returned to work on my computer as Diane finished getting dressed and left the room. My classes that day went better than they had on Monday. I was less fearful and a little more confident than I had been on that first day. Dr. Trostle gave a little giggle when she walked into the room and saw me, but she didn't single me out. The other students seemed less distracted this time, and she didn't feel the need to interrupt her lecture to regain everyone's attention.

Trying to go through my regular pre-nudity routine, I left that first class of the day, walked across campus back to the dorm, and went straight to the dining hall. People generally eat breakfast and dinner at varying times, but lunch was different, with almost everyone in our two dorms eating all at once. This was my first lunch time visit to the dining hall since my nudity had started, after skipping lunch Monday and missing yesterday due to my new job. The noise was loud as I approached but got eerily quiet after I walked through the glass doors. With everyone watching me, I took my place at the end of the line, just behind three guys whom I had rarely seen and who appeared to be in their mid-twenties. They had a surprised expression on their faces and looked me over before I smiled at them. They smiled back and quickly turned away. I turned my attention to the rest of the room. Just about everyone I was used to seeing on a daily basis was here, and they all were now getting a view of my completely naked body, some of them for the very first time. I couldn't have handled this on Monday, but after more than 48 hours of constant nudity, I was better able to accept it. Many people would turn away when I looked at them, as if they were ashamed of being caught looking at me. I had to smile, thinking that those reactions were exactly what Dr. Slater was looking for. I looked up and saw three black half globes protruding from the ceiling at equidistant points, part of the new video system installed in all of the campus buildings over the past two years, and hoped that they were catching all of these reactions. Since I was blackmailed into volunteering for this project, I was surprised that I even cared. But then again, I didn't want to have had my clothes and my dignity stripped for nothing.

"You're Dani, right?" one of the guys in front of me said.

"Yes. How could you tell?"

He smiled and blushed. "I read the story this morning. I'm

Dan."

"Hi Dan," I said, shaking his hand.

"I'm Ted," one of the other guys said, "and this is Steve."

"Hi," I said and waved at them.

"I was surprised that it was legal for you to be naked everywhere, especially here in the dining hall," Dan said.

I just shrugged.

"Do you remember the name of the court case that set the precedent?"

I paused, not knowing what to say. I had, of course, seen no such thing on the AANR website as I had claimed in my interview with Clarissa. I had just gone by what Dr. Slater had told me.

"We're in the law school here," Ted offered.

"Ah," I said. "I don't remember."

"I'll have to look it up," Dan said. "It would make an interesting study."

We had reached the serving area, and I took a tray from the stack and watched as the women passed my tray down, filling it with my requested items, and we all moved along the line.

"You said you were pre-law," Dan continued.

"Yes."

"Well, I hope you're ready to give up all semblance of a social life when you get to law school. We spend all of our time doing research in the library."

"It's a ridiculous amount of work," Ted added.

Steve, who hadn't said anything yet, leaned over to Dan and whispered something in his ear.

"Oh yeah," Dan said and turned to me. "Would you like to sit with us?"

"Sure," I said, hoping that they could give me some insight into law school.

As we walked out of the serving area, I saw Liz waving at me. I smiled at her but nodded my head toward Dan, Steve, and Ted, then shrugged. I followed Dan to a table in the corner where several other older students sat. I soon learned that they were all law students as well. Just hearing them talk about their professors, assignments, and lack of social life was almost enough to put me off law school. But I couldn't think about that now. One thing at a time, I told myself. The guys at the table all took long looks at my breasts throughout the lunch, but I was getting used to that. At one point, I looked up and caught Liz glancing my way while she talked with Audrey.

So far, I had been invited to both the queer and law school tables while being shunned by my former friends. And actually, it wasn't fair to say that they had shunned me. I just hadn't felt comfortable being naked around the people I was used to associating with when I was still fully clothed. I looked at the table where I normally sat and where the normal conversations were going on without me, although most people there kept looking in my direction. I resolved to sit with them during tomorrow's lunch.

Diane was gone when I got back to the room after lunch, so I logged onto my computer and saw an email from Dr. Biden asking if I could stop by his office after my classes ended to talk about the assignment that would substitute for my Chemistry lab. I wrote him back and told him that my Spanish class ended at 2:50 and that I could meet him right after that. My swimming class only officially met on Mondays and Fridays, but I would sometimes swim in the pool on Wednesdays anyway. Depending on how long the meeting with Dr. Biden took, I might do that today, I thought.

I surprised Dr. Finfrock when I turned in his make-up assignment, the one that had caused my current naked predicament.

"I'll have a grade for you on Friday," he said after I handed it to him at the end of class. "And if there's anything I can do to help you in your current state."

"No, I'm good. I wasn't so sure on Monday, but things are better now."

"Are you sure?"

"Yes." I appreciated his concern, even though it had been his report that had nearly cost me my scholarships (and had cost me the dignity of wearing clothes).

After Spanish class, I walked over to the Chemistry building to find Dr. Biden's office. As usual, I had a small crowd of followers with cell phone cameras. The number of double takes I saw from people in front of me seemed to be decreasing with each walk across campus I made. Could my naked body actually become a fixture around Coachella Valley University?

Dr. Biden was alone in his small office, the door propped open, when I arrived. He looked up from the book he was reading as

I approached and jumped to his feet.

"Miss Keaton!" he said. "Please come in. Sit down." He motioned to the chair in front of his desk as he walked around and closed the door behind me.

I dropped a black butt towel in the chair and took my seat. Dr. Biden walked back around and sat across the desk from me.

"Thank you for coming," he said. His voice cracked a little. I looked at his hand on the desk; it was trembling.

"No problem," I said.

He was looking me up and down. "I was trying to think about what you could do instead of the labs, but what happened in class yesterday keeps clouding my judgement."

"What do you mean, what happened in class?"

"W-with you. The way you were sitting, spreading your, you know, legs."

"Oh. I'm sorry about that. I was just… I don't know." I'm sure I was blushing.

"It's all right. Don't be sorry. I'm not."

He stopped talking and just looked at me, his gaze intense, his breath labored. I fidgeted in my seat, wishing that the door to his office had been left open. I turned away and looked past him out the window. Dr. Biden started to stand up but then sat back down again. He fidgeted in his seat but never took his eyes off me.

"I did come up with something," he finally said. "I want you to sit here on my desk."

"I'm sorry, what?" I said, looking back at him.

He put his hands on the blotter on his desk and swept them away from each other, indicating that his desk was clean and smooth. "I want you to sit right here. With your legs spread."

"Why would I do that?"

"Because you want to pass chemistry. Because you want to show yourself off, and I want to see you."

I could feel how wrong the situation was, and my anger was rising. I tried to keep myself calm. "Look," I said, "this, my being nude, is not about sex. I'm not exposing myself to get any kind of thrill. I'm sorry about yesterday. It was a case of boredom more than anything else."

"Bullshit," Dr. Biden said. "Now, get on my desk, or you can forget about ever passing my class."

I thought about turning to leave. I could drop the class before he could fail me. There was still time to do so, but the tuition money was not refundable and would come out of my scholarship fund, meaning that I would have to pay for a replacement class myself. It would also derail my graduation schedule. He just wanted me on the desk, I told myself, not on him. As long as he just looked, I would be OK, I thought. But if he tried to touch me, I would be gone.

"You know, I am the only faculty member who teaches Chemistry 1401," Dr. Biden said, "and I know you need that class for your degree plan. So get up on this desk or forget about ever being able to graduate from this university."

Shit, I thought. I stood up and took two slow steps around to the side of his desk. He pushed his chair back, and I saw with disgust that his pants and underwear were down around his ankles, his stubby but erect penis throbbing with each beat of his heart.

"Oh my God," I said, looking away.

"Come on," he said when I faltered.

Looking at the ceiling, I stepped between him and his desk and lifted myself onto it. I pushed myself back, my legs dangling off the side.

"Put your feet up on the desk, legs spread," Dr. Biden said as he stroked his penis with his right hand.

I pulled my feet up and doing so spread my legs further apart, my vulva splayed out in front of him.

"That's it," he said, pushing his glasses up with his left forefinger. "My God, that's beautiful. Lay back."

I lay back, spreading my arms out on the desk to hold my shoulders and head up since the desk wasn't wide enough to accommodate my full height, keeping my gaze up toward the ceiling. I was still a virgin. In fact, I was proud of my virginity. This was not the way I wanted to lose it, to a professor turned rapist. And that's what this was, rape. The only question was, how far was he going to go? Even though I tried to be strong and brave, tears started to fall. I sobbed when I felt his hand over my pubic mound, the tips of his fingers stroking and tickling my pubic hair.

"Shut up," Dr. Biden said. "Just enjoy it. I'm not going to hurt you, for Christ's sake."

I cringed when I felt his breath hit my vagina, and I braced myself for some other violation. I was wondering what I should do, whether I should bite his penis off if he tried to stick it in my mouth, wondering how much pressure I would need and how long it would take to completely sever it, when I realized that I was wearing a microphone that was supposedly monitored at all times by one of Dr. Slater's research assistants. Surely, someone was listening and could tell what was going on. And if not, I needed to keep talking and to keep him talking.

"I'd rather you didn't touch me," I said.

"But you're so beautiful. Your pussy looks amazing." He was breathless, the masturbating he was doing with his right hand had quickened.

I was just about to say something else when the door knob rattled. Dr. Biden jerked his hand away from my vulva. He had locked the door, of course, but the rattling was followed by three loud and insistent knocks. Dr. Biden shot up from his seat, his erect penis hitting my foot.

"Who is it?" Dr. Biden said.

He motioned me up, so I rolled off the desk and stood against his wall, wiping the tears from my face with my forearm.

"This is Lorraine Slater! Now let me in!"

"Shit," Dr. Biden whispered under his breath, but I breathed a sigh of relief. They really were listening to the feed all the time.

Biden got his pants zipped up and straightened and unlocked the door. Dr. Slater didn't wait for him to open it; she just barged in. I saw Greg in the hallway behind her, the backpack slung over his shoulders with one of the straps pointed into the office. I smiled at him, tears still rolling down my cheeks, and tried to cover myself with my hands. I had never wanted clothes more than I wanted them right then, to hide myself from the disgusting Biden.

"Just what in the hell do you think you are doing?" Dr. Slater demanded.

"I am trying to have a conference with a student over make up work. For the labs that you yourself had asked her to be excused from."

Dr. Slater took a deep breath. "That didn't sound like any student conference I ever heard of."

Dr. Biden looked at me and then back at Dr. Slater. "What are you talking about?"

"I'm talking about you demanding sexual favors from Danielle in exchange for a passing grade; that's what I'm talking about."

Dr. Biden smiled. "I don't know what you think you heard."

"Oh, I heard everything. In fact, it's all recorded. That necklace Danielle is wearing is much more than a necklace."

Biden's face fell as he looked at me again, at the necklace.

"What the hell?" he stammered. "Was this some kind of set up?"

"Nope."

Biden looked at the floor. "What do you want?" he finally asked.

"First of all, Danielle gets an A in your course. Second, she never has to attend your class again. I can't trust you with her. Danielle is an English major; she doesn't need to learn anything else about chemistry anyway, isn't that right, Danielle?"

"Y-yes ma'am," I said.

"I can't just give her an A she hasn't earned," Biden said.

"Oh yes you can. Or I will have the campus police in here in two minutes to arrest you for attempted rape and improper relationship with a student. I think the audio recording would be very compelling evidence, don't you?"

Biden looked at me, then back to Dr. Slater. "Do you know who I am?" he said with a tone of defiance.

"Yes. And I don't give a damn that your second cousin is the Vice President of the United States. I'm sure he would be just as appalled at your behavior toward this young woman as I am."

Biden was silent for what seemed like a long time. I moved from the wall to Dr. Slater's side. Even though my feelings about her were mixed, I was never happier to see anyone in my life.

"Fine," he finally said, waving us all away. "She gets an A. Now, get the fuck out of my office."

Dr. Slater took my hand and said, "Come on, Danielle."

I let Dr. Slater lead me out of Biden's office and down the hall toward the front door of the building. Greg stroked my other elbow and whispered, "Are you all right?" I nodded to him. We stopped just before the building's main entrance. Classes were in session, so we were the only people in the hall.

"I'm sorry about that," she said to me.

I realized I was shaking all over, from fear or anger or a mix of the two. "I don't think I can do this anymore."

"Yes, you can," Dr. Slater assured me. "You have been incredible so far, much better than I could have ever hoped for. And please know that we will never let anything happen to you. I know today was scary, but I did expect that eventually someone in a position of power would try to take advantage of you."

I wanted to say something, to tell her she was crazy for having me continue in this, but I couldn't get any words out. Dr. Slater stepped close and gave me a hug. In spite of myself, I put my arms around her as well. We stayed like that for just a few seconds before she broke it off and resumed her normal distance.

"So he just gets away with it?" I asked.

"Oh no. He won't be teaching here again after the semester ends. He just doesn't know it yet. I'll have someone watch him for the rest of this term. But for now, this project needs to run to the end. You understand? And you never have to see him again. Ever."

I nodded, emotionally drained by the whole thing.

"Where do you need to go now?" Dr. Slater asked.

I didn't feel like swimming any more. "Back to the dorm," I replied.

"Greg, can you walk her back?"

"Absolutely," he said.

"Good. Keep your chin up Dani. You are doing great. You look magnificent, and we are getting some very interesting observations of the people around you. This is going to be so wonderful. OK?"

I nodded.

"Good." She leaned in and kissed me on the top of my head and made a hasty exit out of the building.

I stood there for a moment, my arms wrapped around myself but under my breasts, pushing them upward.

"You sure you're ok?" Greg asked.

I nodded. "Yeah. That was just unexpected. The asshole."

"I know. As soon as I realized what was about to happen, I called Dr. Slater just like I was supposed to. She was already on her way. She likes to listen and watch as much live data as she can. But what I really wanted to do was kick the door in and beat the shit out of him."

"Thank you," I said. The thought of Greg coming to my rescue was a comforting one.

"You ready?"

I nodded, and he took my hand as we walked outside. The sun was still shining brightly; its warmth felt good on my bare shoulders. I noticed much less staring and even fewer followers with Greg walking beside me. He had let go of my hand after we had walked outside, but he stayed right by me.

"You know, I volunteered first," Greg said as we neared my dorm.

"What?" I looked at him, and he nodded.

"I was going to do what you're doing. But Dr. Slater wanted a female. She said that she had seen what had happened to Andrew Martinez at Berkeley, and she thought a female would find greater acceptance. Especially an 'attractive yet virtuous female' as she put it. I have to say, she hit the jackpot with you."

I stopped near the dorm's side entrance and turned toward him. He obviously didn't know about my plagiarized paper or how Dr. Slater had used that to force me into volunteering.

"You are beautiful," Greg continued. "Amazing in every way."

"Thank you," was all I could think of to say as I stood there near him, looking up into his eyes. I lifted my chin, hoping, praying that he would get the hint. He did, leaning down and kissing me softly and all too briefly on the mouth.

"I'll see you around, Danielle," Greg said and turned to walk away.

As I practically floated up the stairs to my room, I couldn't help but feel thankful to Greg for helping me put the awful experience with Dr. Biden somewhat behind me so quickly. And I wondered if his sensitivity toward what had just happened to me had made his kiss such a gentle one. I really hoped I would get to experience a not-so-gentle kiss from him in the near future.

Chapter Nine – Celebrity

The first thing I thought when I looked at myself in the mirror on Thursday morning, day four of my constant nudity, was that I had made a huge mistake. My conversation with Diane had put the idea in my head, and then, last night in the shower, I had been so disgusted by the memory of Dr. Biden's fingers in my pubic hair that I shaved it all off. That feeling of fresh bareness in the shower had even prompted another masturbation session. I was now getting myself off two or three times a day. I had only been a once a week gal before the whole nudity thing started.

Now, Thursday morning, I looked at myself, at how bare I looked, with my labia majora and the little hint of the inner lips poking out, unobscured by hair. And the area of skin where a razor had never before been used was still pink from the burn. In my current situation, I couldn't cover it up. I had to let anyone and everyone see me like this. The private parts of my body were no longer private, and it was frustrating, infuriating even, which was why I tried not to think about it, to just go through my day, go to my classes, as if I had clothes on. I shrugged as I continued to look in the mirror. I could start to let my pubic hair grow back, and how the stubble looked when it appeared would help me determine whether to keep letting it grow or shave it again.

When I went to my survey of American lit class, I kept my binder in front of me as much as possible, hiding my pubic area from the view of as many people as I could. I rushed straight to my seat when I got to class. The discussion on The Adventures of Huckleberry Finn droned on around me, but I had trouble keeping my mind on anything but my constant nudity and vulnerability. I kept thinking about Dr. Biden's office, at having to spread my legs for him. How had I let myself be caught like that so unprepared?

Thoughts of last night's walk with Greg helped to push aside those memories of Dr. Biden. After Greg told me what he had, I couldn't help but imagine him naked walking across campus, his long penis swinging with each step. Had he really volunteered for Dr. Slater's nudity study? Or had he told me that at the time just to calm me down? Dr. Slater had told him to walk me back to my dorm, breaking the protocol of the research assistants staying out of my regular interactions. Had his admission of being a volunteer and his gentle kiss outside my dorm been part of the plan to keep me cooperating with this crazy project? I hated to mistrust him, especially after what I had felt during and after that kiss. But I couldn't let Greg's good looks cloud my judgement, especially after what had happened with Brandon. Dr. Slater was using me, using the vulnerability created by my plagiarism, to force me to humiliate myself in previously unimaginable ways. Biden had done basically the same thing, so was Dr. Slater any better than he was? And was Greg merely one of her pawns, just doing her bidding?

I tried to push all such thoughts aside. I had grown up to be a generally trusting person, believing that most people wanted to be good. Maybe I had been sheltered. My family had attended a Southern Baptist church my whole life, and we had lived in an upper middle class neighborhood in one of the better school districts in Texas. I'd had good friends from both church and school, but when I thought about it, I had never had a real enemy.

The thought of my church friends made me cringe. What would they think if they could see me now, naked in public, exposing myself to anyone and everyone on campus? I'd probably be thrown out of the church if my pastors ever found out. That thought alone made me grateful to Clarissa for not using my last name in her article.

When my American lit class ended, I found myself with nothing to do. Chemistry was over for me, thank God, so I left English class and wandered over to the Fine Arts Building. I don't know why. Perhaps I was hoping that one of the classes had had a model not show up and would recruit me from the hallway. I had rather enjoyed my first modeling assignment on Tuesday. Of course, Matt's class didn't start until 11:00, and he had booked me for the following Tuesday, not today.

No one asked me to model, of course, but I got lots of looks and stares from everyone who saw me. Then again, I had gotten looks and stares from every single person who had seen me since I had left Dr. Slater's office that Monday morning. The looks made me feel like a circus freak, a sideshow, like something was wrong with me. And I guess there was. How could a person just go anywhere and everywhere with no clothes on? Covering ourselves was our defense against people like Dr. Biden, and that I was being denied that defense really should have angered me.

When I walked out of the Fine Arts Building, I stomped across the Commons back toward my dorm. Two guys walked past me, looking awestruck as everyone does lately, and one of them said, "Nice! I love the bare look." I didn't know if he was referring to my bare body or my freshly shaven pubic area, and I realized that I hadn't been using my binder to block anyone's view of my most intimate body part. Either way, I felt embarrassed and moved the binder back in front of me. But the thought of both guys looking at me, at my bare vulva, was also stimulating. That constantly tingling sensation kicked into a higher gear, and I felt even more embarrassed that I was turned on by their seeing me. What was wrong with me? After a few steps away from the two guys, I shifted the binder again so that it was under my arm, making my breasts and pubic area visible to any oncoming foot traffic. I felt a slight shudder whenever I saw guys' eyes look down toward my pelvis, and I sincerely hoped that Diane was not in the room when I got there. I couldn't believe how much I liked this, especially after the experience with Dr. Biden last night. I really was turning into a shameless exhibitionist. Maybe I deserved to be kicked out of my church.

The path from the Commons to Holcombe Hall passes by the edge of the university campus at one point, and it was there that I saw the first news van. It was from Channel 3, the local Palm Springs ABC affiliate. A cameraman stood beside the van, a shoulder mounted camera pointed right at me as I walked. A lady dressed in a nice skirt suit and with a heavy layer of make up on her face stood beside the path and smiled at me as I approached. I recognized her from the little local news I had watched in my almost two years as a student at CVU.

"Dani?" she said as I walked by. I didn't slow down, but she fell in beside me. "My name is Kristen Davis, from KESQ. Could I ask you a few questions?"

"No, I'd rather not," I said, feeling panicked. The newspaper and website were bad enough. I did not want to be on TV.

"I loved your story in the school paper, and my station would like to get you on camera."

"I'm not really dressed for TV," I said. "Maybe some other time."

I turned away from her and from the news van, cutting across the lawn to the front door of the dorm. The reporter stayed on the path, not following, and I breathed a sigh of relief when I reached the front door and walked into Holcombe Hall. After the door closed, I stood by it, looking out the window as Kristen Davis turned and scampered back to the van. She and the cameraman talked for a minute or two before they both got back into the van. It still sat there at the curb though. I turned away and saw three guys and a girl sitting at the little coffee table in the foyer in the middle of a game of Settlers of Catan. Their game had stopped with all four of them just staring at me.

"Hi," I said, smiling and probably blushing.

They all smiled. "Hi," one of the guys said. "Would you like to play?"

Their game, as it was laid out on the table, appeared to be fairly well along. I shook my head. "No, I have homework to do. You all go ahead."

I walked past them, marveling that I never even got the urge to try to cover myself with my binder, and scurried to the elevator. The breezes from the air conditioner vents tickled all over, and I hoped once again that I would have the room to myself when I got there. The elevator was empty, and I had to resist the temptation to touch myself. That ride up to the third floor was far too brief to really get anywhere. I rushed to my room, not bothering with the room key. The door was locked, which was a good sign. Once I got the key out of the binder, I let myself in, saw no sign of Diane or James, locked the door, and threw myself onto the bed. My fingers went to work right away.

Three orgasms later, I was spent and out of breath. I hurried to the bathroom to pee and scampered back to my room. Now that my sexual urges had been satisfied for the moment, I could think more clearly. That TV reporter concerned me. I didn't want to be on the news, even if it was just the local Coachella Valley newscast. Had Dr. Slater planned for something like this? I knew from the reading she'd had me do before our meeting that Andrew Martinez, the Berkeley naked guy, had been interviewed several times and had even appeared naked on a few talk shows. Unlike Martinez, I wasn't looking for attention, and I didn't care about any statement about anyone's right to be nude or not. I just wanted to get through this semester and keep my college degree hopes intact.

I knew though that anything could go viral and be seen by millions all over the world. A news story about a permanently naked girl on a college campus was just unusual enough to be one of those viral stories, even if it had started as a local item. What would I say if my parents found out what I was doing?

Thinking of my parents reminded me that I had never returned my mother's voice mail from the other day. I took my phone out of my binder and called her.

"Well, it's about time you called your mother," Mom answered without even saying hello.

"I know," I said, "I'm sorry. School has been so busy lately."

"Are you OK? You sound stressed. And I wanted to tag you on something on Facebook the other day, and I couldn't find you."

"I know. I deactivated my Facebook."

"Why on earth would you do that? It's so easy to keep up with you that way."

"I know. I was spending way too much time on it though. It was distracting me from my school work." I hoped this was an acceptable excuse.

"Is that all? You don't have anybody bothering you?"

"Oh no," I said, probably too quickly. "Nothing like that."

"Oh, I wish you'd reactivate it."

"I will," I said, "once I get through this rough patch." I stopped, took a breath, and asked how she and Daddy were doing. From there, the conversation went like most of my calls with Mom. She gossiped about the women in the neighborhood and at church, complained about Daddy's working too many hours, and detailed her latest ailments, telling me that she thought she was getting arthritis even though she was only 53 years old. She finally told me that she had to meet a friend for lunch, reminding me that she was in a time zone two hours later.

After hanging up with Mom, I worked on my various school assignments and got completely caught up. In fact, I was so absorbed in my work that I almost missed lunch again. I rushed down to the dining hall and hit the serving line at 12:50. As usual, my entrance was noticed by everyone. Instead of cringing in embarrassment, the tingling sensation just intensified, especially when I realized that I had left my binder upstairs. I had nothing to use to block anyone's view of my shaved pubic area. And after my frantic masturbation of a couple of hours before, my labia minora were poking out even further than usual from my already pink outer folds. The embarrassment was a turn on, but being so turned on by it was embarrassing. I felt like I was in some kind of an infinite loop.

I got my tray of food and, remembering that I had wanted to try to sit at my old table, I made my way over. The table was full, but almost everyone was finished eating. In the past, someone would get up and offer me a seat if I came late with a loaded tray. Today, they all just stared at me with dumbfounded looks. I felt unwelcome, outcast.

"Dani!" Liz called to me from three tables over. She motioned to the seat next to her and Bruce, so I made my way over.

"Nice," Liz said as I pulled some extra napkins from the dispenser to use to sit on since I didn't have a little towel with me. "Shave or wax?"

I know I blushed when I said, "Shaved."

"Looks good. Does it make you feel more naked?"

"Yes," I said and realized that I liked that more naked feeling, especially when an air vent or a breeze hit it just right. I knew then that I was going to keep shaving.

The movie theater in the Student Union was playing a matinee of *Citizen Kane*, and during lunch it was suggested that the five of us should see it. All I knew about it was that it had the reputation as the greatest movie ever made, so I agreed to go, especially since I was caught up with all my assignments.

After the movie, we talked about Rosebud and deep camera focus as we played pool in the SU lounge for a couple of hours, with me getting all kinds of looks from people walking in and out. I ignored them as much as I could just so I wouldn't need to go excuse myself to somewhere private. When we finally got back to the dorm, it was time to eat again, so we went straight to the dining hall.

After dinner, I checked my cell phone, which had been set on silent and tucked away in my hand purse, for the first time since my conversation with Mom. It showed three missed calls and one voice mail, all from the same number.

"Hi," a female voice said when I checked the voice mail, "this is Sylvia Smith, and I am a publicist for the university, which makes me, in a way, your publicist. I've been contacted by two local television stations and one national network about your current state of dress, or undress. They all want to interview you in some form, and I wanted to get together and talk with you about it."

She recited her number, but it was already after seven o'clock. I sighed, wondering what to do. I went to Channel Three's website to look at the stories they had aired on their five and six o'clock telecasts. I had declined to talk to the reporter, so surely, they wouldn't have a story on me. But there I was, right at the top of the page. I clicked play on the video and watched in horror as the anchor talked over a pixelated image of me walking back to the dorm this morning.

"The naked girl has been identified as sophomore Danielle Keaton from North Richland Hills, Texas," the anchor said.

"NOOOO!" I screamed.

The anchor went on to quote from Clarissa's newspaper article, about my cousin and my going nude to promote positive body image.

"No, no, no," I repeated throughout the two and a half minute video, which looped the footage of my walk three times as the anchor talked.

As the video ended, I uttered the f-word for one of the few times in my life. What could I do? That story had already aired, and I couldn't get them to take it back. What could they even do, issue a retraction? How would I even get them to do that, march my naked ass into their TV studio? I sat and thought for a long time. My name was now out there, and I was sure that it would become at least as well-known as Andrew Martinez's had. Martinez didn't even have the World Wide Web back in 1992, so I was sure my story would spread faster and farther than his. Outside of blowing the lid off of

Dr. Slater's sociology experiment, which wasn't an option since I knew doing so would cost me my scholarship, there was only one thing to do: I had to take ownership of this. I picked up my phone and returned that publicist's phone call.

"Sylvia Smith," she answered, surprising me since I had figured that she would have gone home by now.

"Uh, hi. This is Danielle Keaton."

"Danielle. Yes! How are you?"

"I don't know. I just saw that channel three aired a story about me."

"Yes, I saw that," Sylivia replied. "They are not supposed to come onto the campus without prior approval from our department."

"Well, I told her that I didn't want to talk to her, but they took footage of me anyway."

"I know. Why didn't you want to talk with Kristen?"

"Well," I said, not knowing how to explain this without saying too much, "I'm not really doing this for publicity."

"You're not? I thought you were trying to make a statement about body acceptance. I figured publicity would be something you would want."

I closed my eyes and imagined my parents, my friends at home, and my pastor seeing the video of me walking naked across campus, first pixelated and then not. It was not inconceivable that HBO or some other cable channel could air a story about me with my naked body shown uncensored. The idea was both frightening and arousing. That tingling sensation was pressing in on me again at the thought that the entire world could be seeing my bare breasts and shaven vulva. What was wrong with me?

"I know," I said as I came up with a decent sounding answer, "but I wanted the focus to be on body image and not on me. I'm not doing this to get famous."

"Well, I think we should talk about this. The local Fox and ABC affiliates want to talk with you. And just this afternoon, I got a call from the Fox Business network. John Stossel is interested in doing a story on you. Do you know who he is?"

"No."

"He used to be on 20/20, that ABC news magazine show, but he now has his own nationally televised talk show. He's a big libertarian, so I'm sure he would be in favor of your right to go naked in public, especially if you have a message behind it."

"National TV," I said and gulped.

"Yes. It's not a done deal of course. They have just expressed an interest. What's your schedule like tomorrow?"

"Um, I have classes from ten until 3:30."

"How about lunch?"

"I have a break from 11:00 until 12:30."

"Perfect," Sylvia said. "I'll buy. Where do you want to go?"

"Um, somewhere on campus?"

"Well, of course. How about we meet in the deli in the Student Union at 11:15?"

"Sure," I said, trying to picture where the deli was.

"Great. Dress casual." She laughed at her own joke and said, "See you tomorrow."

I disconnected and collapsed onto my bed. Could this week get any stranger? As I lay there looking at the ceiling, my eyes moved over to the calendar on the wall. This was the fourth day. I only had 56 to go. Eight weeks. Naked. Constantly naked. How was I going to get through this with any shred of dignity intact?

Chapter Ten – The Visit

Not having any idea what Sylvia Smith looked like, I walked into the deli after my British lit class ended and waited for her to spot me. Of course, every other person in the place also spotted me. I was greeted with that deafening eruption of dead silence that seemed to fall upon every noisy place I had entered since Monday. That tingling sensation in my gut and groin was in high gear, just knowing that every eye in the place was taking in all of my exposed body, when a tall woman in a Coachella Valley University t-shirt and blue jeans scampered over and introduced herself as Sylvia. She led me to her table, and we both sat down.

"I just love casual Fridays," she said, I guess to explain her casual attire.

"Me too," I said with a shrug.

"I'm sorry. I guess every day is casual for you lately."

"I guess." I looked away from her and up at the menu board above the counter.

"Let me know what you want, and I'll get up and go order it," Sylvia said.

I decided on a tuna salad sandwich, and I stayed in my seat while Sylvia got up to order. More than half the people in the place were looking at me. Feeling self-conscious, I clenched my thighs together, thinking that it would hold the tingling at bay. The deli was open to the main entrance hall of the Student Union Building, one of the busiest places on campus. It seemed like everyone walking by took a long look at me. I felt out of breath. Maybe I was hyperventilating. At day five, I should have been getting used to this, but at times like this, I didn't think so. Here I was, the one lone naked person, sitting among more than a dozen people with many others walking past. The foot traffic was something like twenty people per minute. How could people not look at me? The thought gave me a goofy idea for a picture book.

Sylvia brought our drinks from the self-service fountain and sat back down.

"Thank you," I said, taking a sip of Diet Coke from my straw.

"No problem. Thank you for coming."

"I just had an idea," I told her. "We could publish a book with pictures of me in the middle of hundreds of other people, and we could challenge readers to spot me. Instead of 'Where's Waldo?' it could be 'Where's Naked Dani?'"

"That's actually not a bad idea," Sylvia said, smiling. "Although we might run into copyright issues with the 'Where's Waldo?' people."

I shrugged and glanced out into the hall. Two guys bumped into each other while looking at me. I smiled and almost laughed out loud at them.

"That was a great cover story you gave for *The Clarion*," Sylvia said.

"What?"

"Your cousin and the whole body image thing. That was great." She stopped and noticed the questioning look I was giving her. "Yes, I know about Lorraine's 'project,'" she said, using air quotes on the word project.

"You do?"

"Oh yeah. Lorraine knew that the media would be involved, so she brought me on a couple of years ago."

"Two years ago?"

Sylvia shrugged. "Give or take. It took a while to get all the infrastructure in place. The cameras mainly. Those are not standard security cameras. They take very detailed ultra-high definition video." Sylvia shook her head. "I don't know how she does it. She must be a fund raising genius. The people who sponsored this study foot the bill for those cameras. I think that's why the university was so willing to go along with the nudity part of it. They got the best security surveillance system of any school in the country out of the deal."

I gulped at the thought of such ultra-clear high definition video of me naked and in public being watched by members of the university police and the sociology department faculty. I wondered who else would see it. The people who paid for those cameras and who were specifically interested in this project would undoubtedly be getting copies. Who were these people?

"Of course, Lorraine's idea all along is to observe how the world at large, and not just those at this university, reacts to a permanently naked person. She just has to keep you here on campus to keep you safe from arrest and attack. She would have you going naked anywhere and everywhere if she could."

"Great," I said. "So she knew that they would want to put me on TV."

"Oh, she was counting on it. That's why she got me involved. So, let's talk about how to manage that."

She went over the requests she had received, the number of which had apparently gone up since our phone conversation yesterday. Two local Palm Springs stations, one local Los Angeles station, and two network talk shows now wanted to speak with me.

Before Sylvia could talk about the logistics of such requests, our number was called, and she got up to get our food. I sat there reflecting on everything she had told me about the study, and my imagination started running wild.

"Can I ask you something?" I said after she had sat back down and handed me my sandwich and chips.

"Sure."

"This study. It's everything Dr. Slater says it is, isn't it? I mean, she takes my clothes and throws me out to the campus, doesn't give me a cover story, just says not to tell anyone the real reason I'm naked, and has her team follow me around. I'm sure this microphone picks up more of what I say than it does from anyone else. This isn't about me, is it? To see how much exposure a person can take, how being naked all the time can drive a person crazy."

Sylvia chuckled. "No, it's not about that. Lorraine – Dr. Slater – has been working on this study for years. She's on the level."

"Did she have a crush on this Andrew Martinez guy or something?"

"Oh, I wouldn't know about that," Sylvia said with a laugh.

We ate our lunch, and Sylvia talked about my options. She said that she would try to get all the local stations onto campus the same day. They could each do their interviews with me along with any photo or video shoots they wanted. I almost choked on my sandwich when Sylvia mentioned videos, but my image was already in enough places already. More footage shouldn't even matter. Sylvia also promised to talk to the national shows, one of which was on Showtime. I cringed when I heard that, knowing that Showtime would have no qualms or problems showing me uncensored. But part of me, the tingling part, wanted me to do Showtime as well. And this way, I would have control. I would be the person making the statements, not other people.

I thanked Sylvia for the lunch. All I could do now was wait for her to tell me when my interviews would take place. My afternoon classes were as uneventful as I could have hoped for in my naked state, until swimming. I stopped in the locker room to secure my binder and microphone, grab my cap and goggles and headed out to the pool. Without that necklace, I was truly totally naked, at least until I put the cap on. I wore no rings on my fingers, no earrings, nothing. I was as naked as I had been when I was born. That thought alone increased the intensity of the tingling. Why would a little necklace make such a difference?

I grabbed a kickboard and some flippers from the bin and dropped them and the goggles on the concrete on the end of the pool at the lane I always used. After pulling my rubber cap on, I stepped off and dropped into the warm water. When I resurfaced, I turned to grab my goggles and saw Rick walking toward the pool and the lane next to me. He was naked, his penis bouncing with each step, a huge grin on his face. I couldn't help but notice that his penis looked different from the other, albeit few, penises I had seen. The skin completely enveloped the head, and I realized the difference: Rick was uncircumcised.

"Woo hoo!" I heard a girl from outside the fence yell.

Rick blushed and gave a half-hearted wave to the girl.

"What are you doing?" I asked after he had jumped in and resurfaced.

"I am standing in solidarity with my swimming classmate," Rick replied. "And it feels awesome to be so free in the water."

I could agree with him there. Now that I was able to swim naked, I wondered how I would ever be able to wear a swimsuit again. Ms. Martin arrived and got us started on our regular drills. She had to have known that I was swimming nude again since I had become the campus celebrity of the week after that story in the paper, but I don't know if she realized Rick was also nude until we all got out of the pool at the end of class. I saw her eyes widen when she saw Rick's body. She looked over at me and shook her head as if I were to blame. Part of me wanted to tell her to go take it up with Dr. Slater, but I just went back to the locker room, showered, traded my cap and goggles for my necklace and binder, and started back to the dorm. I did see Rick outside the athletic building, fully clothed. I guess he wasn't brave enough to stay naked. But then again, he didn't have a reason to be naked outside the pool area, and I did.

I spent the rest of Friday catching up on my literature reading before eating dinner with Liz, Audrey, Bruce, and Zack. There was a dance that evening at the Student Union, and Liz tried to get me to go with them. Somehow, I didn't feel ready to be naked at such a social function. I spent Friday evening watching TV in my room, feeling like a hermit. Diane had gone to Anaheim with James, so I was going to have the room all to myself for the entire weekend. I wanted to take advantage of the privacy to unwind and reflect. I had made it naked through an entire school week. Five days of constant embarrassment, humiliation, and arousal. I had almost been sexually assaulted, but I had also been guaranteed an A for my four-semester-hour Chemistry course. I could live another eighty years, I thought, and never experience a week as strange as this one.

Saturday morning was usually when I did my laundry, but all I had now were five small black towels and my regular bath towel. It hardly seemed worth the quarters I used to wash them, but I carried on with my routine anyway.

My cell phone had been going crazy since Friday afternoon, with calls from numbers I didn't recognize as well as from friends back home. I had been letting the calls roll to voice mail, but very few people actually left messages. The voice mails from my Texas friends were all pretty generic, saying things like, "Hey, I was just checking up on you. Call me when you get a chance." I thought it was odd that so many people were calling me now, and it made me fearful that the news story about me might have spread. I kept telling myself that it was inevitable that friends back home would hear what I was doing. Sylvia had pretty much said that it was Dr. Slater's intent to expose me to the whole world. Still, I didn't want to have to face anyone back home, either in person or over the phone. I felt somewhat OK here at school, kind of like that Las Vegas commercial, "Whatever happens at CVU stays at CVU." I knew that wasn't true though, with news media outlets swarming Sylvia to get to me.

At noon, I went down to lunch. Liz and Audrey convinced me to join them in the TV lounge over at the guys' dorm next door to watch college basketball. "March Madness" they called it. I had never been a big basketball fan, but sitting with my new friends sounded better than reading a nineteenth century British novel. I felt strange walking naked into a men's dormitory, but I had been walking naked everywhere for going on six days. Everyone who lived in that dorm had already seen me either in the dining hall or out on campus. They would just have to get used to me, which, I supposed, was the whole point of Dr. Slater's study.

Someone had set up a buffet table full of snacks and drinks. Brandon and Kevin were there. I had seen both of them from a distance a few times since Monday's episode, but I hadn't wanted to talk to either of them. I sat between Liz and Audrey as the first game started.

There were about forty people packed into the lounge, most of whom were guys. While the game was on, they were cheering like they were in the arena, but during timeouts and commercials, most of them would sneak peeks back at me. Every time I caught one of them looking, I felt those familiar tingles. I wanted to play with them more, maybe spread my legs apart just a bit and give them more of a show, but I remembered what had happened with the last person I had done that to, Dr. Biden. Still, the longer I sat there, the greater that mix of humiliation, excitement, and arousal. I finally decided that none of the people here had any kind of power over me like Dr.

Biden, as my chemistry professor, had had. I was in a metal folding chair, part of the extra seating added to the TV lounge for the games today, and I wasn't exactly comfortable. I shifted positions often, at one point stretching out with my butt at the front edge of the chair, my legs straight and together, and my arms over my head. I noticed three guys do classic double takes. They kept looking at me until I sat back up. After that, I took more revealing positions, my legs getting further and further apart as the chair became more uncomfortable and as my arousal grew. By halftime of that first game, I needed to get away and give myself some relief.

"I'll be back," I whispered to Liz.

I got up and slipped out of the row. The wetness was so bad that I was tempted to use my little black towel to wipe myself off before I even got out of the lounge. But before I could reach the exit doors, I heard a familiar voice say my name.

"Danielle?"

I thought about continuing, pretending that I didn't hear him, but I stopped. When I turned, Brandon stopped in front of me. He had almost sprinted to try to catch me.

"Yeah?" I said in as cold a voice as I could muster.

"I wanted to say I was sorry about the other day. I was out of line, and… Well. I wanted to say I was sorry."

"OK." I didn't know what else to say. I could have agreed with him and told him that yes, he was out of line and that he had been a total ass. But I didn't.

Brandon looked around uncomfortably. "I guess that's it. What I wanted to say."

"OK."

I turned to leave. "I'll see you around," Brandon said. I waved whatever as I pushed through the door.

My urge for relief wasn't as overwhelming as it had been when I had gotten up. Brandon and his weak apology had put a damper on my libido. I had spent the last four days reprogramming myself to dislike him, so his interference was more of an annoyance than anything else. But the feeling was still there, so I continued on. Since I hadn't put any sunscreen on my already very tan body, I walked through the dining hall to get to the girls' dorm rather than walking outside from one building to the other.

When I walked into the lobby of Holcombe Hall, I stopped

dead in my tracks at the sight of the absolute last thing I wanted to see in my current naked state. My parents were sitting in the very same love seat where Clarissa had interviewed me on Monday. Daddy and Mom both spoke at the same time, looks of shock and dismay on their faces.

"Oh my God!" Mom exclaimed.

"What the hell?" Daddy said.

I couldn't think or breathe. All I wanted to do was hide. I covered my breasts with one arm and my vulva with the black butt towel in my other hand and lurched forward, crouching down behind a sofa at the other end of the room.

"What are you doing here!?" I screamed.

Looking over the sofa, I saw Daddy walking toward me. Mom was still on the love seat, crying.

"I should ask the same of you," Daddy said. "What are you doing here at this school? Get upstairs and put some clothes on right now!"

"Stop!" I yelled when Daddy had crossed almost to the sofa. "Just stop. Please."

Daddy stopped, thankfully. He stood there looking rather dumbfounded. "Why don't you get dressed so we can talk about this?" he said at last.

"I can't."

"You can't? What the hell is going on here?"

"Oh, Dani," Mom moaned, still on the love seat. "What has California done to you?"

"I can't get dressed," I said, tearfully. "I just can't."

"So all that bullshit you said about body image in that article…" Daddy said and then stopped. He rarely cussed in front of me, so hearing certain words come out of his mouth was jarring.

"Yes, it was bullshit," I said, trying to shock him too. They had no business being here, invading my space like this.

"Well, you're coming home with us," Daddy said. "We can get you into another school close to home. One that doesn't tolerate this kind of stuff. Naked! Jesus Christ!"

"No!" I yelled a little more forcefully than I had intended. "I am doing--" I stopped, choking back a sob as the tears rolled down my cheeks. "What I have to do to get my degree. You just—you don't understand."

Daddy looked back at Mom then back at my face over the sofa. "Come on," he said, holding his hand out to me. "Let's go upstairs and get you some clothes."

"I can't!" I yelled again. "I don't have any fucking clothes!"

Springing up from my spot behind the sofa, I rushed toward the front door of the building, ignoring the looks of shock that had registered on their faces over my use of the f-word and of the sight of my tanned naked ass zipping by in front of them.

I needed to get away from my parents, but more than that, I needed help. When I burst outside into the sunshine, I bounded down the front steps, almost tripping because I wasn't watching my footing. The big toe of my left foot turned awkwardly on the concrete, taking some of the skin off and sending a jolt of pain up my leg. I tried to ignore it as I looked all over the grounds, knowing that one of Dr. Slater's research assistants had to be out here somewhere and hoping I would recognize the person when I saw him or her. Two guys jogged alongside the street; two others played Frisbee; and three girls were standing on the corner smoking and talking. All of them stopped what they were doing to watch me limp around the building, my bare breasts bouncing and my toe starting to bleed. I had just been in the men's dorm, so perhaps the RA was outside of it somewhere.

When I rounded the corner of the building, I saw the heavyset girl, Ginger, wearing the green backpack and sitting on one of the park benches under the minimal shade of a line of tall palm trees talking on a cell phone. I bounded over to her, wincing at the pain in my toe.

"She's here," I heard Ginger say when I approached.

"Is that her?" I asked.

Ginger nodded. I held my hand out for the phone, and she gave it to me.

"My parents showed up out of the blue," I said. "I have to tell them everything that's going on. They will pull me out of this school if they think this whole running around naked thing was my idea."

"Calm down," Dr. Slater said. "I'm almost there. Just give me two more minutes, and we'll talk to your parents together."

"We have to tell them the truth," I insisted.

"And we will. Calm down. Everything's going to be all

right."

I turned and looked back toward Holcombe Hall. My parents were walking toward Ginger and me. I sighed and sat down on the bare bench, crossed my legs, and used the black butt towel to wipe the blood off my toe. A flap of skin was torn on the side of it, from the edge of the nail and up over the tip.

"Hurry," I said to Dr. Slater. "They're almost here."

I disconnected and handed the phone to Ginger. She had taken off her backpack and set it on the bench beside me. After zipping it open, she pulled out a little first aid kit in a plastic case and handed it to me. She then turned and moved to intercept my parents.

"Mr. and Mrs. Keaton," I heard her say in a cheerful voice. "I'm Ginger Hall, a graduate assistant in the sociology department here at Coachella Valley University."

I found some alcohol wipes and some gauze and tape in the plastic box and proceeded to clean up my toe with it. I had my leg up in front of me, and I used that to block the view of my breasts from my parents as much as I could. I felt like a child about to get chastised and punished. I winced as I used the alcohol wipe on my ripped toe. A crowd was starting to gather near the bench where I was seated.

One guy stepped forward to take a closer look at either my toe or my vulva, I couldn't tell which, and asked, "Are you all right?"

"I'm fine," I said, as Dr. Slater arrived and joined Ginger in talking to my parents.

I heard Dr. Slater introduce herself as the chair of the sociology department.

"What does any of this have to do with my daughter?" Daddy stammered.

"Why don't we go up to Dani's room and talk about it?" Dr. Slater suggested. She stood between my parents, taking them both by their elbows and trying to guide them toward the dorm entrance. Dr. Slater looked at me and motioned with her head for me to follow. I had just gotten a gauze pad taped around my toe, so I closed the first aid kit and offered it to Ginger.

"Keep it," she said in a quiet voice. "I'll get another one."

My parents seemed to be in a daze as Dr. Slater led them into the dorm and to the elevator with me limping along behind them, out of my parents' line of sight. Getting into the elevator naked with my parents was one of the most difficult things I had ever had to do. They stepped in with Dr. Slater, and when all three of them turned, they saw naked me getting in. Mom visibly shuddered at the sight of me, making me feel even worse. I understood that no one would want their daughter running around naked in public in front of everyone. I turned quickly when I got into the elevator, so all they could see of me was my backside, and rode up to the third floor.

"How can students be allowed to just—?" Daddy started to ask, but Dr. Slater cut him off.

"We'll talk in Danielle's room."

The elevator doors opened with a ding, and I rushed ahead as quickly as my toe would allow, bursting into my room and jumping into my bed, pulling the sheet up to my neck. Dr. Slater ushered my parents into the room like she owned the place.

"Please have a seat," she said, closing the door.

Daddy pulled the chair from my desk out for Mom and then took his own seat on Diane's bed.

"First of all," Dr. Slater began, "I want to tell you that I adore your daughter. She has so far exceeded any expectations I had of her when she volunteered for this project."

My parents looked at each other. "What project?" Mom asked.

Dr. Slater sat at Diane's desk chair and took a deep breath. "Danielle is our subject for a study involving people's reactions to and interactions with a constantly nude person. For the past week, we've been observing her and, more specifically, the people she comes into contact with. It will take a long time to analyze the data we will have collected once the project is done, but the results so far have been interesting. For instance, Danielle has had little association with her frequent acquaintances before she stopped wearing clothes, but she has managed to form new friendships with more accepting people. It will be interesting to see if her former associates ever re-initiate contact with her."

"That's the craziest idea for a study I've ever heard of," Daddy said.

Dr. Slater then went into the same sales pitch she had given me Monday morning, although she had to describe Andrew Martinez's history at UC Berkeley to my parents since they had never heard of him. She talked about the same TV shows and magazines she had mentioned to me and how these things seemed to be signaling a shift in attitudes toward public nudity.

"And you think that's a good thing?" Daddy said.

"I do. Past studies have shown that more frequent exposure to nudity promotes the de-sexualization of the human body. Being nude is to be free and pure, not sexual. The use of pornography, and especially the rate of pornography addiction, plummets when people routinely see each other in the nude. We're not so concerned about sex when we can see others as they, as we, really are. Hiding the body, always covering ourselves, brings about such stress and anxiety. And of course, the biggest obstacle to more commonplace nudity is government. If this study can show that not only is exposure to nudity not harmful but actually beneficial, perhaps it can trigger a reversal of the plethora of anti-nudity laws we have all over this country."

"I disagree with you on so many levels," Daddy said, "but I'm not going to go into that now. My question is, why would my daughter, raised in a Christian home by conservative parents, ever volunteer for such a study."

My parents both turned toward me, expecting me to answer. I looked at Dr. Slater, and she gave a very slight nod of her head.

"I volunteered because…" I trailed off, trying to figure out how to tell them. "You see, I had this paper due the week that Uncle Robert died. I didn't want to miss the funeral, so I kind of stole someone else's paper."

"You cheated," my father said.

"Yeah."

I looked down at my body, covered by the thin sheet.

"What does that have to do with this whole naked study?" Daddy asked.

"I was going to get suspended and lose my scholarship. Dr. Slater said she could get the suspension lifted and the scholarship reinstated if I volunteered for this. So I did."

"So you blackmailed her," my father summarized to Dr. Slater.

"Mr. Keaton, your daughter committed a serious violation of university rules and ethics. By all rights, she should have received her suspension. But, I also needed a volunteer for this project. I had the power to get Danielle's suspension rescinded. So I made her an offer, and she accepted. It's that simple."

My parents looked at each other, and my father slowly shook his head. The room was awkwardly silent for what seemed like several minutes but was probably only a few seconds.

"OK," Daddy said. "You've had her naked for a week. I think that's enough humiliation for her. And it ought to be restitution enough for this paper you say she cheated on."

"The project is to study behavior patterns toward a nude person over a long period of time. To do that, the subject has to be continually nude for at least two months. I had wanted the study to last for an entire semester, but I had to make allowances to get Danielle. I'm hoping that these last two months of this semester will give us enough data, but I do anticipate future studies with other subjects."

"Oh, I don't believe this," Mom said. "You people are all out of your mind. You are really going to make my baby run around naked for two whole months in front of God and everyone just to pay for some paper she cheated on. Unbelievable!"

"It's OK, Mom," I said, finally finding my voice.

"No, it's not OK," Daddy said, still looking at Dr. Slater. "I ought to sue you and the whole school. This could come under cruel and unusual punishment."

"This is not a punishment, Mr. Keaton. What your daughter is doing is contributing to a valuable scientific study."

"Bullshit!"

Dr. Slater looked over at me. I had been frightened and horrified by my parents' sudden appearance, but now I was just angry. I was an adult twenty-year-old woman capable of making my own decisions, but they were trying to take charge of me like I was still a little girl. I think Dr. Slater saw something of that anger in my eyes.

"Why don't you ask Danielle what she wants?" she asked my parents.

My father and mother both looked at me. "Well?" Daddy asked.

My hands were shaking from a tangled mess of fear, anger, embarrassment, and contrition. But I managed to push the sheet off my body and stand up, fully naked, in front of my parents. Daddy took one glance at me and then looked at the floor.

"I signed up to do this," I told them. "I didn't want to at first, but I saw it as a way out. And I was scared to death that first day. But it has gotten easier. And I told Dr. Slater that I would do this for the entire two months, and Daddy, you always told me to follow through on my word. So that's what I'm going to do."

Dr. Slater was smiling like a proud momma while my real mother's frown lifted slightly.

"But you just seem so vulnerable," Mom said.

"I have a team of people who follow and monitor her interactions around the clock. They are ready to step in at a moment's notice for any emergency." Dr. Slater reached over to my bed, grabbed the first aid kit, and held it up. "For instance, this." She set it back down and said, "Your daughter is probably the safest student on campus."

Mom and Daddy looked at each other again. Daddy started to say something, but Mom shook her head.

"I'm doing this," I said in a firm voice. "And I will be all right. I might even become a stronger person because of it. I definitely feel different than I did last week."

Daddy sighed and stood up. "All right then. We don't agree with this at all. And I think you are setting yourself up for future problems. You know that once photos of you wind up on the Internet, there's no getting rid of them."

"I know," I said. "I've thought of that."

"If this study is successful," Dr. Slater said, "seeing photos of nude people engaged in regular every day activity will become a lot more prevalent. Pictures of her will just fade into the rest of the bunch. Hopefully."

"I doubt that," Daddy said.

"I do have to ask that you keep everything I've told you here confidential," Dr. Slater said. "The reasons given for Dani's nudity don't matter to me a bit as long as the people around her don't realize that they are the actual subjects being studied. If they did, they would alter their behavior, and we would not get the honest results we're looking for."

"OK, whatever," Daddy said.

Dr. Slater looked at them and then at me, standing naked in the middle of my room. Daddy still refused to look at me. Mom had looked away too.

"I'll leave you to visit then," Dr. Slater said, rising to her feet. "You all have a good rest of the weekend."

She walked out, closing the door behind her. I sat down on the edge of my bed, but I didn't cover up even though I wanted to.

"You hurt your toe?" Mom said.

"Yeah, I caught it awkwardly on the steps outside. It's OK though. Just a scrape."

"I'm sorry. We didn't mean to frighten you. Your father showed me that news report, and I couldn't believe it. Why didn't you tell me about this when we talked?"

"Ha!" I said. "I wouldn't have begun to know how to even bring that up."

"Well."

We sat there in silence for a minute before Daddy said, "Do you have any other secrets?"

I shook my head, but he wasn't looking at me. "No."

"Ok. Well, we had better get going."

"OK," I replied, not protesting at all.

"We got a room at the Riviera in Palm Springs," Mom said.

"Nice," I said. I would have asked to join them if I could leave campus. And if I wasn't naked.

"And we fly back tomorrow night," Daddy said.

"Well, you have fun," I said. "At least you get a nice weekend getaway out of this little trip."

"Yeah."

"Do you want me to walk you down?"

"No," Daddy and Mom said in unison.

I couldn't help but feel a stab of disappointment that they didn't want to be seen with me. But I think that part of them still couldn't process that I was routinely naked all over campus. It was my life for the moment, as strange as it seemed.

Daddy stood up, and Mom and I rose. It had only been a week since I had seen both of them, although to me, it felt a lot longer. We really had nothing new to talk about except my participation in Dr. Slater's project, and my parents clearly didn't want to talk about that now that they knew the details.

"You keep those grades up, and don't cheat anymore," Daddy said.

"I won't."

He stepped over and gave me an awkward hug. Having his hands on my bare back felt strange and unnatural. The hug lasted just an instant, long enough for him to feel the awkwardness as well, I think. Mom stepped over and gave me a hug too.

"You take care, and we will see you in May," she said as she pulled away.

"We love you," Daddy said.

"I love you too."

They both left, and I let out a big long sigh. I collapsed on my bed and couldn't stop the tears. I was such a disappointment to them, and part of me felt that they were right for thinking of me as a little kid. How had I gotten myself into this, singled out to be the lone naked person surrounded by clothed people? I couldn't stop the tears from coming as I was overwhelmed with sadness, frustration, humiliation, and anger. When they stopped, I sat up in bed and took a deep breath to compose myself.

Walking out of the sociology department office on Monday without any clothes, I remembered thinking that the absolute worst thing that could happen would be running into my parents. The worst had just happened, and in only the first week, but I had survived. I was still naked, and my hopes of a college degree were still intact. I could do this. Once today was over, I would have completed six days. I was one tenth of the way through it. Nothing in any of the subsequent weeks could possibly be as challenging as what I had faced in these first six days. I washed my face in the bathroom and then headed back to the men's dorm to rejoin Liz and Audrey and the guys.

Chapter Eleven – God and Fame

I stayed in my room most of Sunday due to the pain in my toe, going out during the day only to eat breakfast, lunch, and dinner down at the dining hall. I slept in, but as I lay in bed, I thought about my parents and my home. I had gone to church throughout my childhood and teenage years, and I remembered my youth pastor saying at one point that the overwhelming majority of kids who grow up attending church regularly stop going as soon as they move out on their own. Being the dedicated Christian I thought I was, I told myself at the time that I would never do that. But since I'd been away at college, I had only gone to a church service three times, and all three of those were during my freshman year. I had yet to go during my current sophomore year. Sunday mornings just seemed to be a time for sleeping in.

I didn't have a car, so the three services I had attended had all been interdenominational ones right on campus. So technically, I could still go. I didn't know how well they would receive a naked girl though. For all of the arguments that I had read about how simple nudity wasn't a sin, I was sure that the big issue they would throw up at me would be that thing about not causing your brother to stumble. Before going down to breakfast, I Googled "naked in church" and got a lot of weird results. I did see one photo of a fully naked woman standing in church surrounded by people dressed in early twentieth century clothing. It took me a minute to realize that the guy standing next to her was actor Hugh Grant. When I read more about the picture, I learned that it was a still from a 1993 movie called *Sirens.*

I navigated to Netflix and was pleased to see that I could stream and watch the movie there. Before watching it, I went down to eat breakfast, making it to the serving line a mere two minutes before it closed. The dining area was just about empty as I sat down by myself to eat. Of course, the few people there couldn't take their eyes off of me. A couple of guys got up, bused their table, and carried their trays right past me on their way to the dishwasher conveyer belt.

"Wow," one of the guys said, shaking his head, his eyes never leaving my breasts.

I scarfed down the rest of my food before they could come back and try to talk to me. It had been the head shaking more than what he had said that had gotten to me. I questioned myself for the thousandth time: what was I doing? My situation was just absurd, being naked, letting anyone and everyone see all of me, my breasts, my butt, my vulva. The thought, as usual, both embarrassed me and aroused me. Putting myself on constant display was exciting and humiliating, but at least I had that excuse of having to do it to save my scholarships. I really had no choice, and the more I thought about that, the more my suppressed anger at having to remain naked started to come to the surface. Dr. Slater and her backers were making me expose myself. How could they get away with such a thing?

I jumped up, grabbed my butt towel, threw my tray and used dishes onto the belt, and hurried back into the women's dorm. My toe throbbed, but I could at least walk without a visible limp. Taking the elevator up, I rushed into my room, locked the door, and spent the next ten minutes bringing myself to three orgasms. What was wrong with me? In the space of thirty minutes, I had gone from thinking about going to church service to masturbating. What was this project turning me into? This wasn't the me I had grown up with.

Once I had caught my breath, I made a quick trip to the restroom, came back, and removed the gauze from my toe. I put some Neosporin on it, left it uncovered, and propped my foot up on a pillow I borrowed from Diane's bed. I turned on the *Sirens* movie and watched the entire thing. It was a pretty decent light comedy about a minister and his wife visiting an artist's compound. Of course, this artist used nude models quite a bit, something I had just gotten a taste of in the art department here. The scene with the woman naked in church was part of the minister's wife's daydream. She hadn't actually been naked in church in the story.

Why was I so concerned with being naked in church? I hadn't been in a year, so why did I suddenly have the urge to go to a service? Was it because my parents had just been here, and that I had spent my entire life with them going to church every Sunday? I didn't know. Maybe I had the urge to go to church for the same reason I felt I had to masturbate so much more often, to keep myself from going crazy, to stay on the right path and not become something I didn't want to be. Of course, it was too late today to go to service, but if I felt the same calling next week, would I go? And how would I be received if I tried to go naked? Would the pastor or others ask me to leave?

I pushed all these thoughts aside as my cell phone vibrated. It had been ringing so much that I had to keep it on silent and check every incoming call. I didn't answer most of them and just let them roll to voice mail. I still had twelve messages that I hadn't even listened to yet. The number calling now was one I recognized though, so I answered it.

"Hello."

"Hi Danielle," Sylvia said. "How are you on this lovely Sunday?"

"I'm OK. I hurt my toe yesterday, so I'm just hanging out in the dorm."

"Oh, I'm sorry."

"It's OK though. I can walk without a limp."

"That's good because I have some news for you."

My stomach clenched. I wasn't sure I wanted to hear her news. "OK," I said with a bit of waver in my voice.

"Camera crews from three different local stations will be here filming on campus tomorrow. They want to get footage of you walking across campus and going to class. Maybe even a few shots of you in class if your professors are OK with it."

"Oh," I said. "Tomorrow?"

"Yes, tomorrow. Isn't that exciting? You are big news!"

"Great," I said with as little enthusiasm as I could muster. I wasn't news; my naked body was.

"I pulled your schedule. I hope you don't mind. You have swimming for fitness from 3:00 to 3:50, right?"

"Yes."

"Great. Those will be great shots. And when you're done, the stations all want to do separate on-camera interviews with you. I've got them scheduled back to back to back for four o'clock right there outside your dorm."

"Outside?" I said.

"Oh yes. They all wanted to show you in a campus environment, out in the sunshine. So make sure you pack extra sunscreen to put on after your swim class."

"OK."

"I'll be there in the morning with them. You don't have to do anything extra until the interviews at 4:00. Just go to class like you usually do, and the camera crews will do what they do."

I took a deep breath, resigned to my fate. This is what Dr. Slater wanted, probably part of her plan all along, to see how the world reacted to Naked Dani. "All right," I said.

When I hung up, I sat on the edge of my bed, staring at the wall and thinking about how much my life was changing. I would forever be known as Naked Dani. People would be looking at pictures of me naked for years to come. Perhaps when I am old and gray, I will look back and be glad that the world will remember me as a youthful naked girl, but right now, it just seemed like I was going to be judged an exhibitionist slut. At least my parents already knew about the project, had even seen me naked outside on campus. Nothing else could be as bad as that.

I moved to my computer chair and pulled up Facebook. When I had deactivated my account, I had received a message saying that to reactivate it, all I had to do was log back in. When I did log in, everything looked like it had before. I clicked on the Update Status field and started typing.

"Hi everyone! I'm back on Facebook after deactivating my account for a few days. I had to do some soul searching about this unusual and special project I am doing. I want my friends here to know before you see it on TV (if you haven't already) that I am making a statement for humanity, for body image and self-acceptance. I am committed to finishing the current spring semester without ever putting on any clothes. Yes, that means I am naked everywhere I go, to classes, to meals, and anywhere else on campus. People are making a bigger deal out of this than I thought they would, so I felt I had to say something to my friends and family out there. We are all created in God's image, yet we all spend 99 percent of our lives covering up that image, always hiding parts of it. Here's hoping that what I'm doing means that we don't have to hide as often in the future."

I proofread what I had typed twice before hitting the Post button. It was a bit less profound than any of the Andrew Martinez quotes I had read just a week ago, but I didn't think it was too bad. As much as I wanted to sit and watch to see if anyone commented or clicked Like, I was hungry. I put a band aid on my toe and went down to eat lunch. I did have my iPhone with me, so I could log back into Facebook there, but part of me was afraid to see what my friends in Texas would say. The law students were in the dining hall when I got my tray, so I ate with them and didn't look at my phone.

When I got back to the room, I worked on my reading assignments for the two literature classes. When I finally did check my Facebook, I was surprised that even though I had over 500 friends, there were only just twenty-something likes and thirty-four comments. None of the comments were overwhelmingly negative, so I could only figure that the people who disagreed with or didn't like what I was doing had remained silent. The comments that weren't completely positive were from people perplexed as to why I would consider doing such a thing or how going naked on campus could be legal. I looked at every comment but refrained from replying to anything. I didn't want to get into any arguments with anyone, especially when I was afraid of slipping and saying something about Dr. Slater's study. So, I just let it be.

Diane and James got back from their weekend away just as I was getting ready to go down for dinner. I was standing up, making sure I had a black butt towel in my hand purse when they both walked in. James stopped and just laughed. He seemed drunk, and I hoped that Diane had been the one to drive back. And even though James laughed at me, I never felt the urge to cover up. After one week of this, was I really becoming accustomed to being seen nude all the time? As I walked the hall toward the elevator, my hand brushed against my bare hip giving me a little reminder that I wasn't wearing any clothes. I rode down with three girls and a guy. They snickered but didn't say anything. I was a novelty, and somehow, I was becoming OK with this.

After dinner with Liz and Audrey and the guys, I took a short walk outside. My toe still hurt, but I could walk normally. I was tired of being cooped up in my room, and besides that, Diane and James were probably still up there. I looked around to see who from the sociology department was following me and was very happy to see Greg. But when I turned and started walking toward him, he shook his head. I frowned at him, but I turned and walked toward the Student Union building instead. People smiled politely as I passed them, although I noticed many of them, both guys and girls, taking peeks down at my breasts and pubic area. I didn't feel any embarrassment anymore. Just knowing that people were looking at me, at the parts of my body that had always been private, aroused me more than it ever had. This project had to have jarred something loose in my psyche.

I walked into the Student Union building and went up the stairs toward where the church services I had attended last year had been held. I wasn't too surprised to see that they were holding a Sunday evening service; my subconscious knew they would be. It was sparsely attended with only about two dozen people. I stopped at the glass doors, listening to them sing a song I had never heard. It wasn't one of the old hymns I had grown up with. My phone had a Bible app on it, and I could follow along with whatever the sermon or lesson was about. But I was naked. They would never let me in.

I was about to walk away when someone acting as usher pushed the door open in front of me. About half the people turned their heads mid-song to look at me. I felt like running away. Who did I think I was, coming into a place of worship as naked as the day I was born? But I only saw two faces with shocked expressions, one of which belonged to Stacy, the Resident Assistant on my floor at the dorm. The others seemed to be smiling (or were they laughing as James had just laughed at me?). The song leader, a man in his forties whom I recognized as having been the preacher last year, motioned for me to come in. I took a deep breath and hurried in, like jumping in a pool of cold water, and took an aisle seat on the very back row, pausing only briefly to get my little black towel situated on the metal folding chair.

Everyone was standing to sing, and the lyrics were projected onto a screen behind the song leader/preacher. It was a song I had never heard before, so I mouthed the words and pretended to sing. I couldn't believe that I was standing naked in a worship service. I had the row to myself. The guy who had opened the door for me sat across the aisle in the next to last row. He kept glancing over at me as if he too couldn't believe I was stark naked there. Or perhaps he just liked looking at my body. As I stood for the song, I felt that very familiar conundrum of what to do with my arms while standing at church. My natural inclination was to cross them over my chest, under my breasts, but I thought that always made me look either bored or angry. And doing that now would only push my breasts up and draw even more attention to them. I used to force myself to hold my arms behind my back with my hands clasped, unless, of course the song was an upbeat one that we could clap to. The current song was not upbeat, but I couldn't figure out how to hold my hands behind my back without seeming to thrust my naked breasts out. So I held arms in front of me with my hands clasped for a moment until I realized that this made it seem like I was trying to cover my pubic area. And trying to cover it up only drew more attention to it, so I unclasped my hands and just held them at my sides, with everything on display. The air conditioner vent above me blew cold air across my body, and I broke out in goose pimples. What was I doing here? I felt like I was crashing the place.

The song mercifully ended, and the pastor broke into prayer. When he was done, he motioned for all of us to sit. When I did, the back of the chair was cold against my bare skin, so I leaned forward to avoid touching it. I crossed my legs, and pulled my Bible app up on my phone. The pastor started into a lesson on the dangers of temptation, with references to the story of David and Bathsheba in 2nd Samuel 11 and the adulterous woman in Proverbs 7. The pastor looked directly at me throughout most of the sermon. Had this guy planned this particular topic, or had he decided to switch to this when he saw me come in? I struggled with an impulse to just leave, or to at least cover myself, but I also wanted to stand up and tell him that Bathsheba hadn't done anything wrong, that in the days before indoor plumbing everyone bathed outside, that what David did when he saw her was all his sin, not hers. What was a girl, married or not, supposed to do when the King, who had the power of life and death over all of his subjects, initiated sex with her? And as for the adulterous woman in Proverbs 7, I wanted to tell this preacher that it was right there in the text that she was DRESSED like a prostitute and that everything else alluring about her was because of her actions and attitude. Even though I was naked, I was sure that nothing in my current actions or intent was designed to lead anyone astray, especially after the episode with Dr. Biden. It would probably do most of these guys good to see more naked women in regular every day activities, so they didn't drive themselves crazy fantasizing about what we looked like under our clothes. I was sure that if they did see more regular girls naked, they wouldn't turn to porn so often, building up unrealistic expectations. But I kept my mouth shut. The guy talked for over thirty minutes, but I had tuned him out as I thought about the benefits of my nudity project for everyone else. I may have even, for the first time, felt just a bit proud of what I was doing, if such a thing were even possible. When the preacher finally closed, I slipped out during his prayer before anyone could stop me.

The campus is mostly quiet on Sunday evenings with students all inside doing last minute work for the week ahead. The day had been cooler than it had been the previous week, with temperatures in the early evening only in the low seventies. Still, I avoided the concrete walkways and enjoyed the feeling of the cool, freshly watered grass on my bare feet. My hurt toe was numb, and stray blades of grass clung to the band aid around it. A gentle breeze ruffled the leaves of the palm trees far above me. As disappointed as I had been with the preacher, I was glad that I had gone to the service just for the opportunity to process my thoughts and feelings about how to reconcile my constant nudity with my beliefs. It had taken a week, but I was OK with this. I was going to be able to make it through the semester; I no longer had any doubt of that.

Perhaps my good feelings after the service were just a coping mechanism for how my life was. I don't know. But in spite of the looming television coverage, I was feeling good about everyone on campus seeing me naked all the time. And it had only taken a week.

I slept OK Sunday night, waking up once in the two o'clock hour needing to pee and stumbling around in the dark looking for a nightshirt to throw on before remembering that I was now naked all the time. Old habits are difficult to break, especially when one is only one-quarter or so awake. My first class Monday was at eleven o'clock, so I didn't get out of bed until after nine. After pulling a brush through my hair a few times, I grabbed my hand purse with my room key, my iPhone, my meal card, and a black butt towel and took the elevator down to breakfast. The buzz of conversation was louder than usual, so the silence that ensued when I entered the room was even more pronounced than normal. I went through the serving line and got my breakfast. Liz waved me over to her table, much to the consternation of the law students who were also making a place for me. I shrugged to them as I made my way over to Liz.

"Hey, did you see the vans outside?" Liz said as I sat down.

"No."

"Six of them, at least," Audrey said.

"What!" I exclaimed. Sylvia had said there would only be three stations taking footage.

"Are they here for you?" Bruce asked.

I sighed and nodded, pulling my phone out of my hand purse.

"Damn," Liz said. "When is your first class? I may want to walk with you so I can get on TV."

"Eleven o'clock."

"Crap. Mine's at ten."

I suddenly had little appetite for the scrambled eggs and sausage in front of me. I found Sylvia's number in my phone and hit the dial button.

"Good morning Danielle," Sylvia said in a loud voice.

"Hi."

"Are you ready for your big day?"

"Not quite," I said. "I'm eating breakfast now, and then I'm going to shower."

"Wonderful. There have been a few changes since we talked yesterday, and I want to go over them with you. Are you in the cafeteria?"

"Yes."

"All right. I'll see you in just a bit."

She hung up without giving me a chance to ask anything over the phone. I grabbed my fork and took a few bites of egg while watching the door for her and shrugging off everyone's questions about what was going on. When Sylvia did walk through the door, I jumped up, grabbing my tray and all my things, and hurried over to the dishwasher conveyer. Sylvia saw where I was heading and met me there just as I set my tray down with my plate of half eaten eggs and untouched sausage. I thought better of letting that get away and grabbed the sausage patty.

"All right," Sylvia said, "I know you still have to shower and get ready, so I'll make this quick. In addition to the three local stations, we now have two major networks and one private production company. And since we have so many, I've moved your interviews up to twelve o'clock, right after your first class. Two of the crews will be taking footage inside your classroom. I've already cleared this with your professor."

"What's the private production company do?"

"I don't have a list of all of their credits, but I know they have done shows for HBO and Showtime."

Great, I thought, two networks that could and probably would show my naked body completely uncensored.

"Make sure your hair is nice and that you put on some make up," Sylvia continued. "And I want you to use these interviews to promote the school. Make sure you say 'Coachella Valley University' in each of your interviews and talk about how precious it is to have the freedom to express yourself and make a statement about our world."

"Yes ma'am," I said as we walked out of the dining hall. Everything was going too fast for me to argue with her. Having someone from HBO or Showtime here bothered me since so many people I know have one or both of those channels and could be seeing me walking naked across campus without any digital blurring. They could probably find uncensored photos or video of me on the Internet if they looked, but that was the catch: they would have to look. If I were on HBO, they could stumble upon naked me just by accident.

"You go get ready and come out the front door at 10:30, OK?" Sylvia said as we approached the elevator.

I nodded and hit the button to go up. Was this really my life? Walking outside without a stitch of clothing on to multiple cameras that would be airing stories about me all over the country? It didn't seem real. The elevator arrived, and I stepped on.

"Remember to smile when you walk out of the building," Sylvia said as the doors were closing.

Life is just a show, I thought to myself as I hurried into my room, eating the sausage patty as I went. Diane was still in bed, but she was stirring. I ate the last of the sausage, grabbed my shower pack and towel, and hurried off to the bathroom. As I waited for the shower water to heat up, I noted to myself that it had been exactly one week since I took off my yellow dress in that office next to Dr. Slater's, and I hadn't worn any clothing since. I wondered how many other people could say that they had spent an entire week naked. There were a few I was sure, but as a percentage of the population, that number had to be extremely small.

I spent a little longer than usual in the shower shaving my legs and pubic area, and more time still at the sink, putting on just a bit of makeup after brushing my teeth. I even used the blow dryer on my hair, something I rarely did. By the time I got back to the room, I was dismayed to see that it was already 10:25. At least I didn't have to take any time to get dressed. I grabbed my binder, put a fresh band aid on my toe, and sprayed on a coat of sunscreen so thick that my body glistened. Upon leaving my room, I turned and started to take the side stairs before remembering that Sylvia had told me to walk out the front door of the dorm. I took the elevator down with two perplexed freshman girls from the upper floors.

I stopped in the building foyer and peeked out the window next to the door. Six news vans were parked on the street in front of the Holcombe Hall, and several men with cameras on their shoulders were lined up on the grassy area between the curb and the sidewalk. I thought about my future husband, whomever he might be, and our future children. Everything so far had been local or on the web, things that could be buried over time. National network coverage was something else entirely, especially HBO. I had HBO at home before Daddy got tired of paying for it and had had it cancelled a year or two ago. I had caught episodes of a show called *Real Sex*, most of which were produced in the 1990s but were still being aired twenty years later. Walking out that door guaranteed that this time of my life, as the naked girl on campus, was going to follow me forever and affect that future husband and children. Sighing, I tried to remember what I had thought last night during the worship service, that what I was doing could have long-lasting beneficial effects for everyone, leading to a healthier view of our bodies and each other. My future family would just have to be understanding of this nudity project and of my reasons for doing it.

I forced a smile onto my face and pushed through the doors of Holcombe Hall and out into the mid-morning sunshine. All of the cameramen sprang into action, pointing their cameras at me and jockeying with each other for position. I tried not to look at them, to just walk normally, looking forward like I always did. Two of the camera guys stalked off ahead, to get full frontal shots of me walking, while the others were content to stay behind, getting shots of my backside and of the reactions of people I passed. I wondered how the cameras behind me avoided having the other cameramen in front of me in their shots, but I also figured that they were shooting far more footage than they would use in their final reports. Sylvia was standing next to one of the news vans talking to several well-dressed people.

People turned to stare during my walk to class, but this time they weren't only looking at me but also at the media circus all around. The camera guys in front of me had moved off the trail and took footage of my profile as I walked. Once I had moved away from their view, they jogged ahead, set up, and took more video. For some reason, I thought of Princess Diana trying to get away from a mob of photographers before crashing to her death, and I felt a new empathy for her. At least she got to wear clothes when the photographers hounded her. I had thought I was getting used to being nude, but having all these video cameras pointed at me made me feel more naked than ever. I wondered how many millions of people in the years ahead would see the footage being taken of me right now. The thought was enough to almost make my legs buckle. This wasn't fair, to be forced to show myself naked to the entire world. People not even born yet would be watching this walk across campus, with me the only naked person in the midst of all these normally dressed people.

Dr. Trostle was in class early when I arrived, being briefed by a couple of television producers.

"Both cameras will be in this corner, so we're not shooting each--" one of them was saying before he stopped when I walked into the room. "Wow, I knew what we were here to shoot, but I guess I didn't actually believe it until seeing you in person. You must be Danielle."

"Yes," I replied.

"I'm Shane from Stellium Productions," he said.

"And I'm Darren from Fox," the other one said.

"As I was saying," Shane continued to both Dr. Trostle and me, "we'll be shooting from over there in the corner. We'll have Danielle come into the room along with any other students who sign a release to be on camera. And we'll take just a few minutes of you lecturing in front of the class before we clear out."

"OK," Dr. Trostle said. I was surprised that she was going along with this given how serious she was when conducting the class and talking about the works we were reading.

"What is Stellium Productions?" I asked.

"We're independent, so we work for whoever hires us. Today's job is for a possible revival of an old Showtime series, if it gets picked up."

"What series?"

Shane smiled. "Not really supposed to say. But think about a particular Vegas magic act and the letters BS."

Great, I thought. I had seen several episodes of *Penn & Teller's Bullshit*, and they did not shy away from showing nudity whenever possible.

The two cameramen who had been shooting my profile during the walk over lumbered into the room, and Shane pointed them over to the front corner, away from the door. I took my regular seat, and watched the other students file in, all of them talking to each other about the news crews on campus. Before they were all seated, Shane addressed the class.

"Could I have everybody's attention? Thank you. Your professor, Dr. Trostle, has graciously given us the first ten minutes of your class to get video footage for a couple of stories we are doing for different network programs. The main subject of these pieces is, of course, your classmate Miss Keaton. I realize that some of you may not want to appear on television, and if that's the case, you can stay where you are and your faces will be obscured when the show airs. But if you do want to be shown, I have releases here on the desk that I would need each of you to look at and sign. There are blanks for your signature and your printed name. It's a simple release and shouldn't take too long to read. It just gives the network permission to use your face. And since we want to get footage of you entering class, you can come up, sign the release, and wait in the hall."

Almost everyone in the class rose and began crowding around the instructor's desk. I stayed in my seat, not wanting to push my naked body into the crowd. When the last two signed and started out into the corridor, I got up and went out with them. I figured that I didn't have to sign, but Shane called me over and pushed a release toward me. I wondered briefly if they would just all pack up and go if I refused, but I picked the pen up and filled out my name and signature.

Shane and Darren followed me out into the hall and picked four people to walk into class first. "Start shooting," Shane called to the camera guys before releasing the four students, telling them not to look directly at the cameras. Dr. Trostle sat at the instructor's desk, making the scene seem more like high school than a university. I walked in after those first four students, naked and carrying my binder at my hip. My nipples tingled when I stepped over the threshold and realized that I was being recorded for network TV. Of course, I had been recorded for a week by the university's security system, with, from what Sylvia had told me, its ultra-high definition video cameras, so I wasn't sure why this felt different. Maybe it was because two men were being paid to point the cameras specifically at me. I took my regular seat, discreetly plopping one of my little black towels into the chair. The rest of the students filed in, and Shane called "Cut!" from the hall.

"All right," he said to Dr. Trostle as he and Darren walked in, "go ahead and start into your lecture like you usually do. We just need about a minute or two of that."

Dr. Trostle stood up, looking at Shane and Darren. When they nodded, she started speaking. "Good morning class. Today we are starting on *The Mill on the Floss* by George Eliot, who, as most of you know, was actually a woman writing under a male pen name. Now why would she do such a thing? The main reason was to differentiate herself from other female writers of the day. One of her last essays before she started writing novels was called "Silly Novels by Lady Novelists."

Dr. Trostle went on for another minute before Darren stopped her. "Thank you very much, all of you," he said. "I think we got some great footage."

The four men cleared out of the room, and Dr. Trostle went on with her lecture as if she had never been interrupted. I had trouble paying attention to her. My mind was on what I was going to say when the reporters interviewed me on camera. Still, I managed to take a few notes in the Kindle before class was dismissed.

"I know, that was wild," I heard one student say to another.

"You are becoming quite the celebrity," the girl next to me said.

"Yeah. This isn't quite what I had in mind though."

"Well, what did you expect when you just suddenly stopped wearing clothes? That's not something that falls under normal behavior."

For some reason, that hurt. She must have seen it in my face because she shoved her books into her backpack and left in a hurry. I knew it wasn't normal behavior, but I hadn't had a choice in the matter. But I couldn't tell her that. I couldn't tell anyone that. I had to go on pretending that this was all my idea, that running around naked *all the time* was something I had decided to do on my own. I zipped up my binder and walked outside where Sylvia and a hoard of media people awaited me.

They had decided to set me up in the Commons, right in front of the library, rather than going all the way back to my dorm. Sylvia walked me over to the chosen area where the camera men were already set up. Cables were strewn across the walkway as technicians and on-air reporters tested their sound equipment. And everyone, no matter how busy, kept stealing glances at me.

"Do you have more sunscreen?" Sylvia asked me.

I nodded, zipped my binder open, and pulled out a fresh bottle. Sylvia took it and commenced spraying me from head to toe, pausing only to allow me to set my binder down. A large crowd of students had gathered around and behind all the media crews. Campus police were keeping the area between my spot and the library free from onlookers.

"They want the background behind you to show activity," Sylvia explained when she noticed what I was looking at. "They want people moving, walking into and out of the library, not standing around and watching. If they want to watch, they can get behind the cameras like everyone else."

I nodded and didn't say anything. My mouth felt dry, and I had a sudden fear that I wouldn't be able to speak whenever the first reporter asked me a question and stuck a microphone in front of my face.

"Do you have any water?" I whispered to Sylvia.

"Of course, darling. Anything you need."

She turned and grabbed a bottle of water from someone and handed it to me. I screwed off the lid and took a long slow drink. When I finished, Sylvia stood in front of me and took a long look at my face and hair. She brushed at my bangs with her fingers, pushing hair back from my temples.

"How do I look?" I said.

"Gorgeous. Remember, be yourself, but say good things about the university."

I nodded. Sylvia took me by my shoulders and guided me over a couple of steps to just the right spot, then turned me so that I was facing the reporters, the cameramen, and the crowd. My nipples tingled at the sight of so many people looking at me. And I was naked. That word flashed through my consciousness, NAKED, NAKED, NAKED… I was acutely aware of the delicate and sensitive folds of skin and tissue between my legs, devoid of hair, visible now to hundreds of people. I didn't dare look, but I could feel the breeze caress the little bit of inner labia peeking out from the fleshier parts of my vulva. My knees shuddered and almost buckled. That little bit of pink labia tissue probably glistened from my wetness; my only saving grace was that my entire body also glistened from the sunscreen Sylvia had just sprayed on me.

I can't remember much of what I said to the reporters and their cameras. The questions all seemed to be a rehash of the ones Clarissa from the school newspaper had asked me, and my answers were paraphrases of what I had already said. I do remember seeing Clarissa in the crowd, taking notes, probably for another story in the school paper, this one about all the media here to talk to me and how she had gotten to me first.

Each station wanted its camera set up with a different angle than the one before, trying to get a different look exclusive to its own news show. I thought each interview was going to drag on and on, but Sylvia kept tight control over the proceedings. When the final reporter had asked his final question, I was ready to collapse, but I still had three classes left to attend, one of which was the exhausting swimming for fitness.

"What time is it?" I asked Sylvia.

She handed me a tuna salad sandwich from the deli and said, "12:50. Just in time to make your next class."

I tore into the clear plastic container to get at the sandwich, scarfing it down as the media circus dispersed all around me. Two of the camera men stayed put though, I assumed to get more footage of me.

"I won't have to talk to anyone this afternoon at the dorm?" I asked Sylvia between bites.

"Oh no, this was it."

"Good. I have a feeling swimming is going to wear me out."

I finished the sandwich as Sylvia carried my binder and walked with me to class. The two cameramen followed us. I saw Dr. Slater from a distance, standing just outside of Carlisle Hall, which housed the sociology department. She smiled and gave me a thumbs-up sign. I turned away without acknowledging her and took my binder from Sylvia.

"Thank you," she said. "You were magnificent. Beautiful. Wonderful."

I sighed, thinking that the entire world had gone crazy right along with me. Sylvia stopped just outside the door to the History Building. She took the empty plastic sandwich container from me.

"I'll throw this away for you. And I'll see you soon. We may have a network doing a live show here on campus in another week or two. I'll keep you posted."

I nodded to her and stood in front of the entrance of the building watching her bound away, only going inside when I felt the two cameras and the eyes of about thirty other students on me.

Chapter Twelve – Uncensored

My memories of those first ten or so days of nudity are so vivid, every encounter and conversation, each little milestone, the first time being seen naked, the first time going to class naked, my first time naked in the dining hall, etc., that it seems strange how most of my memories of the subsequent days seem to merge together. There are, however, several events that stand out and that I will never forget as long as I live.

The day of those multiple media interviews still seems surreal when I think about it. I did go to all my afternoon classes after the reporters dispersed, with the remaining two cameramen following me from class to class until I got back to my dorm. In swimming, Rick came out in his regular swimsuit. I think the television cameras frightened him out of doing the class naked again. When I got back to the dorm, I didn't look to see what the cameramen did after I went inside; I rode the elevator straight up to my room and took a nap. I got up that evening to see that my Facebook had exploded. The local affiliates had aired their stories, of course, but the *NBC Nightly News* also ended their national broadcast with the local channel's report. Parts of my body were pixelated, of course, but my full name and hometown were both mentioned. When I logged onto Facebook, I had over one hundred new friend requests from people I had never heard of, most of them men. Sunday's status update, the one I had typed right after reactivating my account, had been shared several dozen times and now included over two hundred comments. It was all too much, and I logged out of Facebook and went to dinner. Later, after returning to my room, Diane made several comments both to me and to whomever she was talking to on her phone that her naked roommate was now famous.

After my lit class the following day, I got to model again. I was more comfortable the second time, and I think I held the poses better. Matt booked me for two more classes over the next two weeks. I was feeling great until Mom called that evening. By the sound of her voice, I could tell that she was still feeling down. When I asked her how the weekend with Daddy at the Riviera had gone, she said it had been tense. Daddy was still very upset.

"To make things worse," Mom said, "there was a nudist resort right across the street. Right in the middle of town. And they weren't secretive or anything. 'Desert Sun Resort and Spa: Enjoy Palm Springs Au Naturale' it said right on the sign facing a busy intersection. You father was just appalled. We don't understand what this world is coming to."

"It's just California," I said for lack of anything better. I'd never even heard of the Desert Sun Resort & Spa, but then again, I had spent very little time in Palm Springs during my time in the Valley. But Mom did say that they made it back home OK. I didn't ask if either of them had seen me on the news again.

During that first week and a half, I had been so intent on counting down the days until I could wear clothes again that I had almost forgotten the other countdown on my calendar. Luckily and maybe subconsciously, I included a couple of tampons in my binder Wednesday morning and wound up needing one after Spanish class that afternoon.

Everyone knows that women menstruate, and in theory it is nothing to be ashamed or embarrassed about. But I still didn't want people who saw me to know that I was on my period right then. So I tried tucking the string in those first few times, but it kept slipping out. Walking around campus naked with a tampon in my vagina added a new level of embarrassment to my situation. I was also suffering from cramps periodically, so I was already not feeling great.

I finally took to cutting the tampon strings off before inserting the tampons, but that made getting them out problematic. A couple of times I just had to push them out while on the commode. I know flushing them is one of the worst things one can do to bathroom plumbing, but I wasn't about to stick my fingers into toilet water filled with urine and blood to get them out. Luckily, I never heard anything about any stopped up toilets in the dorm, so I didn't feel too bad about it. I mean, representatives of the university were practically forcing me to go naked everywhere I went, so if the result of that was a backed up toilet, then they could just spring for the plumber. I did wind up skipping my swimming class that Friday because of my period, cramping, etc. We were given two free absences for the semester without affecting our grade, and I hadn't used one yet. By the time the following Monday rolled around, my period had ended along with, thankfully, the cramping.

That Monday, day fifteen of my constant nudity, was also the day that Sylvia called my cell phone while I was at lunch in the dining hall with Liz and Audrey. Even though my Facebook continued to go wild with friend requests and comments until I had gone in and set my profile to private, the number of calls to my cell phone had decreased. The number was known only to my family and friends back home and just a very few people here in Coachella Valley. I had finished eating by the time the phone rang, so I picked it up and answered it as I piled my trash on the tray and picked it up to take it to the conveyor.

"Hello Sylvia," I said.

"Hi Danielle, how are you?"

"I'm OK. Just finishing lunch and about to head to my history class."

"Good. I do have some news for you."

"I figured you did," I said.

I was walking out of the dining hall and back toward the women's dorm. People passing by me smiled and said, "Hi Dani." Since I had gained celebrity status, everyone called me by name whether I knew them or not. I wondered how Dr. Slater accounted for that in her study. As for myself, I was feeling more confident and more comfortable in my own skin. Everywhere I went, I was noticed by practically everyone, and the number of hostile or disdainful looks seemed to be decreasing all the time. Even some of the people I used to hang out with before the nudity study were talking to me again.

"I just heard from the producer of the show *Stossel*," Sylvia said over the phone. "John Stossel wants to do a live show, but they've had issues with the network. They want to show you without pixelating any of you. And of course, doing the show live would make it easier to do that. There is a seven second delay of course, which allows them to bleep out any bad words, but pixelating out any nudity is a little difficult."

"Did anyone there think to ask me? I mean, what if I don't want to do the show?"

"Oh Danielle, you have to do the show," Sylvia said. "Our new student applications are up 32 percent just from last week's news stories."

"Is that what I am? A marketing tool?"

"No, no, of course not. It's just that this is such a rare thing, a very special time in your life. You should take advantage of it."

I walked into the foyer of the dorm. Quite a few people were sitting around studying, but of course, they all looked up when I appeared.

"Take advantage of it?" I said, turning and stepping outside through the front door and out of earshot of anybody. "Ha! I feel like I'm being taken advantage of. Dr. Slater makes me run around naked all the time, and I mean ALL the time, and I have to let people take pictures and video of me for TV. It's all -- I don't know. When I really think about it, I still can't believe it."

"I know it's difficult," Sylvia said. "I can't imagine having to do what you are doing. But you have done so well. You've come so far, and I can't imagine you stopping now. What I was trying to tell you is that the producers ironed out everything with the network. They're shooting here on Thursday evening, in Studio A in the Radio and TV Building."

I had started walking away from the dorm and away from the Commons and was now at the very edge of campus. I stopped and looked across the street at a strip shopping center with a couple of fast food restaurants in front. They were far enough away that I didn't think people could see me clearly, but I jumped when a car honked as it went by. I turned around and walked back toward the dorm, the small group of guys who had followed me at a distance dispersing at my sudden change of direction.

"No," I said to Sylvia. "I'm not going to do it."

I had thought a lot about my media day and about the video

that had been taken by Stellium Productions. Nobody knew how many months it would take *Penn & Teller's Bullshit* to come back on, if it ever did. And if it didn't, what would happen to that footage of me? I imagined the production company selling it to some other less than savory late night cable show. My unease at all of this was so heavy that I wanted to resist anything that would add to it.

"You won't do it?" Sylvia asked.

"No, I won't. I have to draw the line somewhere. This whole thing has been crazy. I've been naked for two weeks and had my name thrown out there with all kinds of pictures and video. Seriously, thousands of people have seen parts of me that only my doctor had ever seen. I still have to live after this, find a job and a husband and raise a family."

"What do I tell the *Stossel* producers?"

"I don't know. You'll figure something out."

"Well," Sylvia said, sounding subdued and defeated, "I'll have to tell Lorraine. She may have something to say about it."

"Whatever," I replied. "I'm sorry."

"If you change your mind, call me."

I ended the call and hurried back into the dorm to get my binder and head to Dr. Finfrock's history class.

Swimming class that afternoon was more interesting than usual, with Rick going back to swimming naked. One of the other guys swam naked too, and seeing them walk out of the men's locker room together, their penises swinging with each step toward the pool, one of them circumcised and one not, was highly entertaining. My nudity was definitely having an effect on the rest of the student body. I had seen a group of streakers out early in the evening on the previous Wednesday night, two days after media day. At the time, I had thought it was a fraternity initiation, but it might have just been a group of fans. About eight naked guys ran past me, clapping and singing at eight in the evening after I had taken a study break and gone for a walk. I'd had to stop and laugh while watching their bright white untanned buttocks zip past me.

The swimming exercises were exhausting, and I dragged as I made my way up the elevator to my room. When I opened the door, I was so shocked to see Dr. Slater sitting on the side of my bed that I dropped my binder.

"Hello Danielle," she said with a smile.

"Uh, hi," I said, bending to pick my binder up off the floor.

"Why don't you close the door?"

"How did you get in my room?" I asked as I stood back up and shut the door, locking it. The lock wouldn't keep Diane out for long if she came back, but we would hear her try to get in before having to find her key.

Dr. Slater waved her hand as if to say that her getting into my room wasn't important. "Let's talk about the project. We're two weeks in. How are you feeling?"

"I feel fine," I said, my voice becoming tentative with the last word as I noticed a copy of the contract I had signed lying on my computer desk.

"Good! I have to say that you have, so far, done very well. The data that we are getting back regarding your interactions here at the university has been beyond expectations."

"I'm glad." I said, as I pulled my desk chair out and sat down.

"However, there is a bigger picture to this, beyond the microcosm of the university, and that is how the world in general reacts to you. You were so brilliant when you did the interviews with those local stations. How did it feel, being the center of attention?"

"I don't know. Surreal, I guess. Uncomfortable. But at least I knew they couldn't show everything. People watching would know I was naked, but they wouldn't be able to actually see it because of the blurring."

"You didn't look uncomfortable. You looked like a natural, answering every question they asked you with confidence, even though you and I both know that most of your answers had to be lies."

"There were parts that were true," I said. "Like when I said that I felt that seeing regular people naked was actually healthy."

"Yes, that was especially brilliant. I'm glad that you've come to that viewpoint. And yet, you told Sylvia that you don't want to do the *Stossel* show. Do you understand what a monumental landmark this episode would be?"

I had known why Dr. Slater was here the instant I saw her, of course, but I sighed when she finally got to it. "I know what it means to me. There's a difference between my friends and family back home knowing that I'm running around naked out here in California and actually seeing it for themselves on their TVs."

"Do you know what the producers had to go through to get the network to OK this broadcast, with the lawyers and the FCC regulations, looking for loopholes, fine amounts, etc.? But in the end, they agreed to it! It's unprecedented. A regular cable news channel is going to show full nudity on a prime time telecast."

"How could they even get away with that?" I said.

"Because it's news. The nudity is the story, and Stossel feels that the people watching should see what everyone here on campus sees. And because of the episode's theme, he thinks it would be hypocritical to censor the nudity. I don't think you understand what a huge step forward this is, and it's all because of you and this project. It's what I dreamed of when I first outlined this proposal years ago."

"I'm sorry, but there has to be some line drawn. I still have to carve out a life for myself after this."

"This could be the foundation of that life. Fame is easy to capitalize on, especially with something as groundbreaking as this."

"I just don't think I can do it." I expected to see a look of disappointment on her face, but instead, I saw her eyes narrow, her jaw set.

"You've come so far and done so well," she said. "I would hate to see you throw it all away, your scholarship, your degree program, over this."

"What do you mean?"

She took the contract off my desk and handed it to me. "When you signed this, you agreed to everything in it. I suggest you take another look at paragraph eight."

I almost didn't need to read it; her pointing it out to me told me everything I needed to know about what it said. But I read it anyway, how I was to fulfill every media request at the instruction of the university's publicist to the best of my ability.

"So you see," she said when I looked up, "refusing to do the *Stossel* show would be a violation and would render the contract null and void."

If I backed out now, two weeks of constant nudity would have been for nothing. I would have humiliated myself and still not gotten my scholarships or my degree. And without the degree, I couldn't go to law school. What was worse was that everyone already knew about my naked activities, and my parents had even seen it firsthand. I had to keep going. After these two weeks, what difference would another six make. I had already in my own mind committed myself to going nude for the rest of the semester. Dr. Slater had me, and I knew it. I had to do the show. I was going to expose my naked body to a national TV audience. Millions of people would see my exposed nipples and shaved vulva. No one else had ever done such a thing on such a wide scale. I would be alone, naked, with an audience of millions. The thought should have made me sick, but instead I felt that tingling that seemed to draw my nipples inward, hardening them, and caused wetness down below. How could something so unthinkable arouse me so?

I was going to agree to do the show, but I also wanted to save face, to not let Dr. Slater feel like she had such complete control over me.

"OK, I'll do the show if –"

"If what?" Dr. Slater said when I hesitated, and I still didn't know what concession to ask for.

"Greg," I finally blurted.

"What about Greg?"

"I want to be able to talk to him," I said. "When I tried to approach him the other night, he waved me off, shook his head. I don't know what you told him, or the rest of them."

"Given the secretive nature of the project, I instructed the RAs not to be seen associating with you. It seemed implausible that a sophomore English major would have so many acquaintances in the graduate sociology program."

"I'm the famous naked girl on campus. Everybody says hi to me, and I have so many people introducing themselves to me that I can't keep track of them all. It's not implausible that I would have acquaintances anywhere in the university. And, I'm just talking about Greg, not the whole team."

Dr. Slater's face softened into a sly grin. "So you like Greg, huh?"

"We talked some after that thing. With Dr. Biden. I'd like to continue talking to him."

"Ok. I'll talk to Greg, tell him that you are not 'off limits' anymore."

She sat looking at me as if to say, "Anything else?" "OK," I said, finally.

"Good. The Stossel shoot is Thursday evening at six o'clock, so be there at five. You know where the Radio and TV Building is?"

I nodded, feeling like I was on a runaway freight train and knowing that jumping off would hurt me worse than staying on would. Dr. Slater stood up and smoothed her skirt.

"All right then. I will be in the studio audience, so I will see you Thursday. Smile."

I looked up at her and forced a smile.

"You know, you are the perfect person for this project, the perfect mix of beauty, naivety, purity, and worldliness. I wouldn't have wanted the type of girl who would have readily volunteered for this. It would have been turned into something sexual, a 'Let's see what I can get away with' type of thing." She sighed as she looked down at me. "I do wish I could be in your place," she mused, seemingly more to herself than to me. "But, I have responsibilities and expectations now. And besides that, I'm 51 years old and don't look nearly as attractive as you do."

I wanted to say something, suggest we switch places, but I didn't. Of course, I did not believe her when she said that she wanted to be in my position. Why would anyone want to be in my place, practically forced to exhibit myself to anyone and everyone?

"Well, all right," Dr. Slater said.

She walked out and closed the door behind her. I moved over to my bed, curled into a ball under the covers, and had a good cry, thinking of everyone back home, my parents, my friends, my old boyfriends, my pastor, all gathered around a TV watching me naked.

The next three days went by in a haze. Both the anticipation and dread of the TV show hung over everything I did. I found myself tuned out during class lectures, staring out the window of my dorm room when I should have been typing up a paper on my computer, and lying awake at night unable to go to sleep. I finally took a melatonin on Wednesday night to help me sleep, hoping that I would be well rested for the day of the TV show broadcast.

Chapter Thirteen – Live!

I arrived at Studio A in the Radio and TV Building at 4:45, full of nervous energy. I had started the day off in a fog because of the after effects of the melatonin I had taken the night before, but by the time my American literature class ended, I was mostly awake. I modeled for an art class that afternoon, one pose for the duration of the three hour class, with periodic breaks to stretch my limbs. The long pose gave me a chance to meditate over what I wanted to say during the telecast. I had been exchanging emails over the previous two days with one of the show's associate producers about the theme of the episode and the kind of questions John Stossel would ask me. This associate producer and I had even spent an hour on the phone the previous night, semi-rehearsing what both Stossel and I would say.

Sylvia, dressed in blue jeans and a western style button down shirt, was in the center of a hurricane of activity near the newly constructed set for *Stossel* when I was admitted into the studio by the campus policeman stationed at the door. He hadn't asked me for any kind of identification, and I wondered if he would have let just any naked girl in. Sylvia and everyone else in the studio immediately stopped what they were doing and looked at me.

I had watched clips of past Stossel episodes on Youtube, recognizing both him and the show as something that my father had watched every once in a while. In the clips I had seen, John Stossel sat at the end of what looked like a large desk. I had hoped that I would be sitting behind the other end of that desk, where I could sink down and hide myself. This set looked much smaller than anything I had seen on Youtube, with three chairs and a small table between the right and middle chairs. I assumed that Stossel would sit in that right hand chair (the chair was on the left if standing on the stage facing the cameras) using the little table for his notes and that I would be in the middle, completely uncovered and exposed. There were two large cameras on wheels and another medium sized shoulder mounted camera, all of which were being worked on and adjusted by crewmembers, or at least they had been before I walked into the room. The studio itself was smaller than I expected it to be, with seating for no more than fifty people in chairs on three tiered levels along one side of the room opposite the stage. The ceiling and everything suspended from it, rails and lights and cables, were all painted black.

"Dani!" Sylvia exclaimed, rushing toward me. "We have so much to do." She grabbed my hand and pulled me into what looked like a dressing room while everyone in the studio resumed what they had been doing.

The dressing room was actually a green room with about a dozen people inside, along with a rack of clothes on hangers, a long table upon which sat three well-lit makeup stations, and an office desk.

"Give me your necklace," Sylvia said. "They've got a microphone of their own for you. We don't want to have any conflicts."

"OK," I said, reaching behind my neck and unsnapping it. She took it and slipped it into her pocket.

We started at the desk where Sylvia and a lawyer-type guy from the production company had me sign a few legal releases. Sylvia then took me to the makeup station, bypassing wardrobe of course, and sat me down. A technician fitted a small device over my ear which had a little microphone tube that extended halfway across my cheek, taking short glances down at my breasts and pubic area as he worked. When he finished, he tested it, listening for the sound of my voice on his headphones. He gave Sylvia the thumbs up and moved on. A girl spent twenty minutes wetting, drying, and styling my hair, using a liberal amount of hair spray on it, while another girl applied theatrical make up to my face. I could hear the buzz and bustle of activity outside the room as the girls worked, and I figured that the studio audience was being admitted. A well-dressed fortyish woman sat at one of the other make-up stations, and another pair of girls put a barber's drape over her, protecting her clothes, and went to work on her hair and make-up. I heard a warm-up comedian begin to work the crowd. I couldn't hear what he was saying, but I could hear the laughter from the audience. My foot started tapping, my leg bouncing. I tried to stop it, to take a deep breath and try to relax as the make-up girl urged me to keep my head still, but the leg kept jumping. Just as the girls were finishing up with me, John Stossel himself, in his regular suit and tie, walked into the room, smiling and greeting everyone. I stood up and moved away from the chair, feeling more naked than usual with so many well-dressed people around.

"And you must be Danielle," Stossel said.

"Yes," I said. We shook hands, and I searched for something to say.

"Or do you go by Dani?" he asked.

"Either. But Dani is fine."

"OK, good. I'll introduce you as Danielle Keaton, but I'll call you Dani for the rest of show."

"Sounds good."

Sylvia introduced herself to Stossel as he continued making his way around the room. The make-up girl took my hand and asked me to stand in the far corner away from everyone else.

"This will give your skin a nice sheen to it for the camera," she said as she pointed an aerosol can of something at me and started spraying it all over me, motioning for me to turn around when she finished with the front of me. When she finished spraying, she set the bottle down and began spreading the stuff on me with her hands. "OK, stand here for about five minutes and let that dry," she said when she finished. Then with a giggle, she said, "We don't get many naked people on the show."

I was left to stand by myself, naked. The good thing was that everyone else seemed too busy to look at me. Or was that a bad thing? I had gotten so used to being looked at all the time that I thought I was beginning to like it, maybe even crave it. The make-up girl's hands on me had given me a little flutter, especially when her fingers had glazed over my nipples. Being naked around normally dressed people seemed to keep me always at the edge of arousal, and the make-up girl had just tipped me over that edge.

John Stossel had left the room, and I heard a loud burst of applause from the audience outside. Sylvia ran over to me and grabbed my hand.

"OK, you're up," she said.

"What, the show is starting?" I asked, not nearly ready to speak on live TV.

"No not yet. They just want to introduce you to the audience and show you where to go on the set."

We stood at the doorway of the green room looking out at the stage. We couldn't see the audience from our view, but I could hear them. It was the well-dressed woman from the make-up station next to me who was alone on the stage. I couldn't see John Stossel anywhere. The comedian, dressed in a white tuxedo and standing on the floor just in front of the audience, read from a card in his hand.

"And here is the star guest of tonight's show, CVU's own Danielle Keaton!"

Sylvia practically pushed me out into the studio, and I stepped forward toward the comedian. Everyone was already clapping, and I saw them all rise when I walked in. With a flourish, the comedian gestured me toward the stage. I stepped up onto the four inch high platform in front of the middle chair, and a voice in the speaker in my ear told me to face the crowd. Turning, I was almost blinded by one of the lights. I heard a couple of catcall whistles in the middle of the applause. Not knowing what else to do, I smiled and waved.

"And the star of our show!" the comedian yelled over the applause, "JOHN STOSSEL!"

The audience kept applauding as Stossel jogged out into the studio and jumped up on the stage next to me. He waited for the noise to die down before speaking.

"Thank you. I want to thank Coachella Valley University for hosting us, and all of you for coming and being part of our studio audience. We should have a great show today. Given the content, it may be, will be, a landmark episode. Thank you all for being a part of it. There are several challenges to doing a live TV show, so if you will just bear with us while we get everything set before that 6:00 PM start time."

He turned to one of the producers who stepped up to us.

"Good," the producer said and turned to me. "Normally, we wire people for sound under their clothes, but since you're not wearing any, we are trying something new. So far, everything is working, but be ready if I have to hand you a microphone to speak into."

"OK," I said, nodding.

He turned to the well-dressed lady and talked to both of us. "We'll start with the two of you backstage. John will be out here and will give an opening monologue, introducing the show. Dani, you will be introduced after a few minutes, and you will walk out, come straight to this middle chair, shake hands with John, and sit down. He'll ask you to give your story, and when you're done, he'll have some follow up questions. John doesn't ad lib too much, so it will mostly be what we discussed over the phone."

I noticed that one of my black towels was already positioned in the seat of the chair. The producer addressed the well-dressed woman as Rhonda and gave her similar instructions about coming out when called and shaking hands with John and me.

"Two minutes!" a guy next to one of the big cameras called.

The producer had someone usher us back to the green room, showing Rhonda to the office chair at the desk but holding me ready at the door. John Stossel sat down in his chair as someone applied some last second touches to his make-up. A monitor at the edge of the stage switched from a color bar to a frozen still of the Stossel show logo. The guy next to the camera, the director I assume, started counting down the seconds out loud from ten down to five and then silently using his fingers. The audience settled into a nervous silence as the "Applause" light was off. When the director's one finger turned down and made a fist, the image on the monitor sprang to life. Stossel himself sat silently as his recorded voice played over the images of the screen, rednecks wearing Confederate flags, gang bangers with the waistbands of their pants around their hips revealing their plaid boxer shorts, Miley Cyrus naked on a wrecking ball.

"These days, people are offended by everything," Stossel's recorded voice proclaimed as the images played. "Some groups of people seem to go out of their way to find something to be offended about. But aren't we supposed to be the 'Land of the Free' as the 'Star Spangled Banner' proclaims. The Bill of Rights declares that we have the freedom of speech, that we should be able to freely express ourselves. Nowhere does it say that we have the right to not be offended by something. And yet, students are being suspended from school for wearing clothes with Confederate battle flags or religious messages perceived to be anti-gay hate propaganda. A city in Tennessee recently passed a law making it illegal to wear one's pants more than three inches below the tops of the hips. Where does it all end? If we don't have the freedom to offend someone, are we really free? That's our show tonight."

The studio erupted in light and sound as the Applause light came on. The animated *Stossel* show opening played on the screen before the picture switched to Stossel, sitting in his chair.

"Good evening," he said. "We are broadcasting live from the campus of Coachella Valley University just outside of Palm Desert, California. The question tonight is, are we really free to express ourselves if society and even our legal system keep prohibiting certain messages because someone somewhere finds our message offensive? The wearing of Confederate flags has recently come under fire by some, with lawmakers in cities all over the country trying to ban them. And sometimes it's not what you wear but how you wear it that some people find offensive. In Pikeville, Tennessee, for example, one can be cited for public indecency for wearing pants below the hips, even though all that's being revealed is a pair of boxer shorts. Now, the ordinance claims to be in the interest of public safety as, and I quote--" he paused while picking up a card from the table, "'"there is evidence that indicates the wearing of sagging pants is injurious to the health of the wearer as it causes improper gait."'"

In spite of my nervousness, I laughed at John Stossel's facial expression as he read that part of the ordinance.

"I don't know what's worse," Stossel continued, "prohibiting sagging pants because city leaders find them offensive or because they claim to be interested in the health of the wearer? In a free society, we would all have the right to freely express ourselves, both through our speech and our appearance, how we present ourselves to others. In the midst of all these incidents, with people being offended by everything, comes a student here at Coachella Valley University named Danielle Keaton who wanted to make a statement about who we are as human beings, how we accept ourselves and our bodies. To make that statement, she did not wear anything with flags or slogans that anyone could find offensive. She, in fact, didn't wear anything. After spring break, she stopped wearing clothes and started going about her daily activities in her body's natural state. Naked. She goes to class, to meals, and to campus functions all wearing nothing but a smile. Of course, some people, quite a lot actually, find that offensive, and in most locales, what she's doing would be illegal, punishable by jail time. But so far, here at Coachella, she is still at it after two and a half weeks. We are going to bring her out now, and since this is a live show, some of you may be offended at the sight of her. If you are, then you certainly have the freedom to turn the channel. But I think her message needs to be seen and heard by those who would listen even if some do find it offensive. Those who would stop her from expressing herself in this manner would be doing the rest of the world a huge disservice. But here she is, Danielle Keaton."

The director motioned me out of the green room, but he didn't have to; I was already stepping out when I heard John Stossel call me by name. The audience applauded more loudly than ever as I stepped up onto the set, shook Stossel's hand, turned to face both them and the cameras, and sat down. As they quieted down, I wondered if the seven second delay had yet passed. As I sat waiting for Stossel to ask me to tell my story, people all over the country, hundreds of thousands of them, maybe millions of them, were right then watching me walk onto the platform. Why did I have to stand and acknowledge the audience, giving the cameras a full frontal shot of me, my breasts and shaved pubic mound visible in high definition on televisions all over the country, the world? The little flutter that the make-up girl had given me was like a raging torrent now. I should be ashamed, embarrassed, covering myself as the camera operators jockeyed for position. Instead, I felt excited, confident, and aroused. I took a quick glance down at my breasts when Stossel started talking, hoping that the cameras would be on him. My nipples were as hard as concrete.

Stossel asked me how I came up with the idea to go nude on campus, and I told him the same story I had told to Clarissa from the school newspaper and to the reporters from the local TV stations. We went into body image and body acceptance, and I told him how I thought my thighs were too thick, although they were mostly muscle, and how my butt was too big and round. I mentioned the fabricated story of seeing the Walk of Shame scene from *Game of Thrones*, how perfect Lena Headey's body double had seemed. We talked about other nudity in media, especially Lena Dunham who was both a producer and a lead actress on an HBO show I had never watched. Stossel put a photo of her, clothed, on the screen, and I thought she looked great without having that Hollywood body and that I would have applauded her nude scenes if I had seen them, especially knowing that she was also a writer and producer on the show. We talked about Miley Cyrus and how she had at one time suggested doing a nude concert, with both herself and the audience all nude. That suggestion had never gotten off the ground, and I tried to act sad that it hadn't (I honestly didn't care one way or the other, although it might have been fun to go naked in a place where I wasn't the only naked person around).

"How have the rest of the students, faculty, and staff here at Coachella Valley University responded to you since you started this?" John Stossel finally asked me after the second commercial break, and I knew that this question was supposed to lead into the introduction of the other guest.

"I got a few rude looks and some rather risqué remarks from a few guys when I started, but things have settled down now. I feel a lot of acceptance from most of the people I interact with."

"But you have to know that not everyone agrees with allowing you to do this?"

"I would be surprised if no one had a problem with it."

"And that brings us to our next guest. Rhonda Zurich is an assistant professor of theology here at Coachella Valley University and has been the most outspoken critic of Dani's public nudity on campus. Please welcome Dr. Zurich."

John Stossel and I both stood and the audience applauded as Dr. Zurich walked onto the set. If she had been such an outspoken critic, I wondered why I had never heard of her before now. She shook Stossel's hand and merely nodded at me before taking the third seat.

"So tell me Dr. Zurich," Stossel said, "why do you object to Dani's freedom to go around campus in the nude?"

"Please, call me Rhonda. I think the thing we need to ask ourselves is how much freedom does an individual have before that freedom infringes on that of everyone else. A person has a reasonable expectation of carrying on with his or her day without being confronted by something provocative."

"Provocative, how?"

"This is a college campus filled with 18 to 22 year old men. Seeing an attractive nude girl such as Danielle here might provoke them into actions that they might not otherwise take. Perhaps they may be more aggressive toward their own girlfriends, or perhaps they might engage in unhealthy fantasies. For the good of society as a whole, the freedom to expose oneself has to be curtailed. That's why we have community standards."

I started to say something, but Stossel had already resumed talking. "But in a free society, each person has to be responsible for his or her own actions. You can't blame any misdeeds on something the perpetrator saw someone else do. He has to be held accountable himself."

"That's why we have to protect these young people from seeing things like Danielle strutting around naked in public. They are already vulnerable enough without someone like her putting thoughts into their heads."

"What do you mean, someone like me?" I said in a loud voice, trying to get a word in this time before Stossel did. "There is nothing about my actions, the things that I do, that is designed to provoke anyone. So what if I'm not wearing clothes. Let me tell you something, dressing in skimpy outfits, showing just a little bit, is far sexier than going nude."

"Going nude in public is, in itself, an action. You could make a strong statement about body acceptance without showing everything you've got to every young man at this university. I frankly think that what you are doing is crazy, a sign of extreme exhibitionism or nymphomania, and that makes me concerned for you and for everyone you've been with."

"For one thing," I said as I felt the blood vessel in my temple pound against my skull, "you don't know anything about me. Everyone I've been with? Let me tell you something, if you are referring to sexual partners, that number is zero. I'm a Christian; I grew up in the church; and I am still a virgin, by choice. Being naked doesn't have anything to do with sex. Is it sensual? Yes. Is it comfortable, especially in this desert heat? You bet. Am I trying to seduce anyone by being naked? Absolutely not. The thought never even entered my mind. In fact, I would have a better chance of finding a guy, the right guy, with my clothes on. But that's not my focus in life right now. So quit making assumptions about me. And by the way, if you're such an outspoken critic of me, why haven't I ever heard of you before today?"

"You must not read the right publications," Rhonda said as Stossel talked over her.

"Why don't we take a break and come back to this topic right after a word from our sponsors."

The *Stossel* theme music played as the logo filled up every monitor visible in the studio.

"And we're out," the director said.

"Really, who are you?" I said, turning to Rhonda.

"Relax," she said. "I'm a friend of Lorraine's. She just wanted to make this interesting."

The show producer rushed up to us and said, "Are you two going to be able to continue together?"

I must have been staring at Rhonda with an open-mouthed dumbfounded look on my face. I caught myself, shook my head a quick time or two, and said, "Yes. Sure."

Two of the crew members had brought us glasses of water, and Rhonda and I both took long drinks.

"That was good stuff, you two," Stossel said. "But let's try to keep it civil. We do only have one more segment left."

I glanced out into the audience and saw Dr. Slater sitting on the second row. Greg sat next to her, without the green backpack I was so used to seeing on him. Dr. Slater wore a smile so big she was beaming. Greg smiled and winked at me when I caught his attention. I smiled back and probably blushed.

I was much calmer when the show resumed. Rhonda took my earlier statement about being a Christian and asked how I could reconcile that with my constant nudity. In answer, I was able to articulate everything I felt in and after that Sunday night church service I had attended. I also brought up God telling Isaiah in Isaiah chapter 20 to spend three years naked in public to spread a warning against Egypt and Cush as proof that public nudity wasn't either sinful or anti-Christian.

"We're all curious," I said at one point, "all of us. If one guy out there satisfies his curiosity about the female anatomy by looking at me instead of turning to pornography with its lies about how people normally look and behave, isn't that a good thing?"

"It would be, if something like that happened," Rhonda conceded. By the end of the show, she was much less argumentative, making me feel like I had won some kind of small victory.

As John Stossel wrapped up the show, I was anxious to get up out of my chair. I wanted to stand up, let the viewing public get another full frontal look at me. Part of it was vanity: sitting like this made my belly compress and look bigger than it was. But the thought of those multitude of people looking at my naked body in a standing position, seeing my bare pubic area, the soft flesh of my vulva visible to all, was such a turn on. What was this thing turning me into? I was the first and only person in television history to be shown completely naked on a regular news channel, and all I wanted was to keep exposing myself.

"I'd like to thank our guests Rhonda Zurich and the beautiful Danielle Keaton for sharing so much of herself with us. It was certainly a first for Fox Business Network and this show. Good night."

The closing credits rolled on the monitors, and I jumped out of my seat. Stossel quickly got up and leaned toward me. "Hold up right here," he said in my ear as the audience applauded.

"OK, we're out," the director called after a few seconds.

"Thank you so much for appearing on the show," Stossel said. "That was certainly something." He turned to the producer and said, "Teddy, what's the word from New York?"

"Switchboards have been flooded with calls. Sixty percent positive so far."

"What about ratings?" I asked, wondering just how many people had seen me naked.

"We'll get preliminary numbers in the morning," Teddy said. "But the response is, for a Fox Business Network show, massive."

My knees felt weak. Now that the show was over and the moment passed, remorse and regret flooded into my psyche. I had to ask myself, what have I done? I stepped off the stage and almost fell down. Greg caught me and held me up, his hands cool and soft against the bare skin of my waist.

"Dani, you were awesome!" he said. "Beautiful, brilliant, and just amazing. You totally owned Dr. Zurich."

"I don't think she was trying that hard," I said.

"Still, you came across as very smart and articulate. I just couldn't believe how good you were."

Sylvia had me by the elbow and was guiding me toward the green room. "Let's get that makeup off of you," she said. "And I agree, you were brilliant."

I turned back to Greg as Sylvia tugged on my arm. "Are you going to be around for a while?" I asked.

"Sure. You want to get a bite to eat?"

"Yes. I'm starving."

"Cool. Oh, there's a movie playing in the Student Union. A classic. Part of that Oscar Mistakes series, films that didn't win the Best Picture award but should have. Or at least, Dr. Barker thinks they should have."

Dr. Barker was the well-known chairman of the university's film department and was very active in promoting his department. This was southern California, film capital of the world, after all.

"Oh yeah," I said. "I saw *Citizen Kane* there a couple of weeks ago. What's playing today?"

"*Double Indemnity*."

"Never heard of it," I said. "But I'd love to go."

Sylvia gave my elbow another impatient tug. I smiled at Greg as he said, "OK. See you in a bit."

I turned and followed Sylvia into the green room; my regret vanished as I felt the lightness of having been asked on a date by Greg. The worst was over, I told myself. I had made it through the media gauntlet, school newspaper, local stations, and a live national broadcast. And I was proud of myself for negotiating a chance to date Greg. Life was good.

Chapter 14 – Festival

A replay of the *Stossel* episode started on the monitor in the green room while one of the girls used some kind of cream to take the make-up off my face. I was anxious to see just how much of me had been shown, especially during my walk to the stage. I listened to Stossel's introduction and opening monologue and had the girl stop wiping my face when I heard him say my name. On the monitor, I walked out fully naked, with side and rear views as I stepped up and shook hands with Stossel, cringing at the sight of my round bubble butt. I gasped when I saw myself turn and face the audience. The camera had captured everything from my head to my feet, my body glistening in the stage lights, my nipples hard, my shaven and bare vulva looking swollen and wet. That image had gone out on the broadcast to millions.

"Oh my God!" I said, wanting to cry.

How could I have allowed myself to be seen so naked like this by a national television audience? It had felt exciting when I was on the set, turning and letting everyone in the audience see me, but now that it was done, now that I was off that adrenaline kick and could think clearly, I was mortified. How could I ever face any of my friends and family again? Maybe I should just run away and become a hermit.

The make-up girl continued cleaning me up as I listened to myself on the TV tell my partly made up story. When the girl proclaimed my face clean, I looked at the screen again, dismayed that my full breasts and nipples were exposed in each shot. Couldn't they have zoomed in just a bit more so that just my head and shoulders were visible?

I couldn't watch the rest of it. All I wanted to do was go back to my room and hide under the covers of my bed, but I had just made a date with Greg. Going to eat in public, even if it was on campus, and then watching an old movie in the SU theater suddenly did not appeal to me. People on campus were used to seeing me out and about naked, but I wondered what their opinion of me would be after seeing me on a regular network TV show exposing myself to millions. Still, I would be with Greg. If I heard anything negative, I could just get him to walk me back to my room. He would understand, I told myself.

He was waiting for me just outside the back door of the Radio and Television Building. Stossel's people were going in and out, carrying equipment and parts of the set to the two trucks that were parked in the side lot. Greg saw me and smiled, but his smile seemed to fade when he saw my expression.

"Did you see any of the show?" I asked him as we walked toward the Student Union.

"It was on the monitor next to the set during the taping. I kept looking over to see how much the camera was showing."

"My God, they showed everything."

"You didn't think they would?" he asked.

"I don't know. I don't know what I thought."

"This was all part of Dr. Slater's idea," Greg said. "She thought whoever volunteered for this – you -- would make a bigger splash in today's media than the naked guy at Berkeley did. You're an attractive female for one thing. And everyone is more connected now than they were back then. News spreads so much faster with the Internet."

"Yeah, tell me about it," I said, thinking of how my parents had found out after less than a week.

Greg took my hand and gave it a squeeze. "What's done is done. Try to relax and have fun, OK?"

"OK."

We had a nice but quick meal at the deli and just made it into the theater in time for the start of the movie. When I read that

Double Indemnity was made way back in 1944, I didn't think I would like it, but it turned out to be one of the most riveting films I had ever seen. The actor who played Keyes, Edward G. Robinson, stole every scene he was in. Greg took a series program, and over the next few weeks we saw three other movies on the list, *Singin' in the Rain* from 1952, *The Searchers* from 1956, and *Network* from 1976.

We never talked about my nudity during that first date or any of the other subsequent ones. I learned that Greg was from the Seattle area originally and was still a big Seahawks and Mariners fan, but that he had also lived in the Dallas, Phoenix, and Denver areas due to his dad's job while he was growing up. As a result of that, he had never developed any close friends and still had trouble relating to people.

"That's kind of why I went into sociology," he said at one point, "to learn how people relate and interact with each other. I never stayed in one place long enough to figure that out for myself."

The physical relationship between us developed very slowly. After watching *Double Indemnity* on that first date, he walked me to the door of the dormitory and ended the evening with a quick kiss on my mouth. We went out once a week after that, usually to the film department's Thursday series since Greg couldn't very well take me to a theater playing any new movies. Those good night kisses gradually got longer and more open mouthed. Greg's hands on my back during these lingering kisses got lower and lower until he was caressing the tops of my buttocks. In the theater during a particularly harrowing scene in *The Searchers*, Greg put his hand on my knee, as if to try to comfort me. I put my hand over his, holding it there before he could take it away. For the rest of the movie, I kept pulling his hand slowly up my thigh toward my crotch. I could sense the change in his breathing with each little move upward and knew that he was feeling something. If I hadn't been so afraid of him removing his hand from my leg, I would have reached over and caressed his.

Though we never talked about it, I do think that he was slow to initiate any physical contact between us because I was so exposed and vulnerable. I think we would have progressed much further and faster if I hadn't been naked all the time, but his gentlemanliness and gallantry in this regard made me like him, and want him, even more. There was also that little thing about my virginity, which I had proclaimed on national television. He never asked me about it, and I took that to mean that he never doubted me.

We saw Liz and Audrey out on campus during a couple of our dates. Greg already knew about them from listening to my audio feed in his capacity as one of Dr. Slater's research assistants, but everyone seemed to get along when I introduced the girls to him. But still, I was surprised when, on our walk back toward the dorm after seeing *Network*, he said, "I talked to Liz this morning."

"Really? What about?"

"The Festival."

By far, the largest event in the area was the Coachella Valley Music and Arts Festival, held each year during consecutive weekends in April. Not many university students went since the tickets were expensive and usually sold out the summer before. The first weekend of the festival had already passed, with the second weekend starting tomorrow.

"She had two extra passes for this Saturday and wanted to know if we were interested," Greg said.

"Ha! I'd love to, but I don't think I could get in."

"I wouldn't be so sure about that," Greg said, smiling sheepishly. "I talked to Dr. Slater about you going."

"Really? She's going to let me put clothes on so I can go?"

"Well, no, not exactly."

I stopped walking and let go of his hand. "What does that mean?"

Greg stopped and turned toward me. "What do you think?"

"I can't go there like this! I'd get arrested!"

"Dr. Slater has some contacts in the Indio Police Department, and she has talked to whoever it is that's in charge of the festival. She thinks that you are now enough of a celebrity that you can get away with certain things that others can't."

I thought of clips I had seen from the festival on news reports, both last week and last year while I was here at Coachella Valley University. The stated attendance for past festivals was somewhere in the neighborhood of 90,000 people. I had, of course, read the reviews and the ratings of my *Stossel* appearance. The average episode of *Stossel* drew 250,000 to 300,000 viewers. My episode had over two million viewers during that live show, and the subsequent airings drew higher than average ratings. Of course, all of those subsequent airings happened after ten PM so that they could air uncensored without drawing more fines from the FCC. That first live broadcast was the most watched hour of television in the history of Fox Business Network.

But all of those millions of people watching me had been spread out all over the country. These 90,000 people would be seeing me in person, in the flesh. The idea was terrifying, and yet, I felt that tingling sensation again.

"You seem to like the idea," Greg said, making it obvious that he was looking at my erect nipples.

"Shut up," I said, putting my hands over my breasts. I snatched them quickly away as my nipples were almost too sensitive to touch and resumed walking toward the dorm.

"It'll be fine," Greg said, taking my hand again as we walked. "Aren't you tired of being cooped up here on campus?"

"Yeah," I admitted, thinking that my taxi ride from the Palm Springs airport after flying back from spring break was the last time I had been off campus. And that was five weeks ago. "But back when I agreed to do this, Dr. Slater said I had to stay on campus."

"She just said that because on campus was the only place where she could guarantee your safety, that you wouldn't be arrested. It's actually not in the contract you signed." He glanced over at me and saw my doubting look. "I've already talked to her about it. She really wants you to go. She thinks it would be good for the project. More data. And you'll have me with you the whole time. Liz and Audrey too. And some of the other RAs will be tailing us with camcorders."

"That figures," I said.

As much as I was afraid of going off campus in my naked state, the prospect of adventure was too exciting. And besides that, everything I had heard about the Coachella Music Festival indicated that it was a truly amazing event with some of the top music acts in the world.

"Okay," I said, stopping at the side entrance to the dorm. "I'll go."

"Awesome!" Greg said, smiling and hugging me. The sensation of my nipples against his t-shirt sent shivers up and down my spine. I turned my face up to him, and we kissed. He had an erection; I could feel it through his blue jeans against my belly. I wanted to take it out of his pants and touch it, see it, to give him both pleasure and release. I was, as I had claimed on the *Stossel* episode, a virgin when it came to intercourse, but I did have some experience with past boyfriends, satisfying them with my hands and, on a couple of occasions, my mouth. I wanted to do that -- at least that -- for Greg. But part of our problem was that he lived off campus where I had always assumed I couldn't go, and my dorm room wasn't private. If Diane wasn't actually in the room, there was always the threat of her coming in.

Greg broke the kiss and pulled back, looking down at me as I tried to catch my breath, his hand still on my hip and curving around to my butt.

"We'll leave right after lunch on Saturday. Sound good?"

I nodded wordlessly, hating that we were having to part.

"I'll see you then." He smiled and gave me another kiss, just a quick peck, before taking off.

I walked into the dorm and climbed the steps to the third floor. The room was empty, and I wanted to pull my phone out, call Greg and tell him to come as I raced back down the stairs to let him into the building, but I didn't. I looked out my dorm room window and saw that he was already out of sight, past the Commons. I locked the room door and took care of myself, relieving my frustrations, at least for a little while.

When I finished, I ran to the restroom to pee and wash my hands. I checked my Facebook when I got back to the room. I had several ongoing message threads with friends back home who had seen me on *Stossel*. Most of them couldn't believe what I was doing, and I felt like I was constantly defending myself in my replies to them. But I couldn't just stop talking to them. I would be going home in a little over three weeks, and I knew I would eventually have to see them in person.

Of course, that meant that I only had to be naked for another 26 days. I had managed to go 33 days without wearing clothes. That had to be some kind of record for a person living and functioning in modern civilized society. I wondered if Guinness might want to talk to me about it for their next *Book of World Records*. Looking at my calendar also reminded me that I was almost due for my period. Maybe that was why I had been feeling hornier than usual around Greg. Just wonderful, I thought. I get to go to the Coachella Festival, but I have to be both naked and on my period when I go.

The next day was Friday, and just like last month, my period started right after Spanish class. This meant skipping my swimming class, which was too bad since I enjoyed watching the naked guys walking to and from the pool. There were now three of them swimming naked, but I was still the only nude girl. It was nice not being the only naked person though. Maybe I should start skipping Spanish class near my period, thinking that there had to be something about Ms. Castillo, the teacher, that made my body want to start expelling excess blood. I did work on my tampon though, tying a knot high up on the string and cutting the excess off. I didn't have to worry about the string showing, and when it was time to pull the tampon out, I could grab that knot with my fingernails.

Sylvia called me that afternoon, just when I would have been arriving back to the dorm if I hadn't skipped swimming. She and I had talked often since the *Stossel* show, and she had been very good at issuing statements on my behalf and keeping the media off my back so that I could concentrate on my school work. That *Stossel* episode had itself made the news, and everyone from Barbara Walters to Britt Hume wanted to talk to me.

"I heard on the grapevine that you are going to the music festival tomorrow," Sylvia said.

"Can you believe it?"

"No. But it gives me a chance to expense a ticket for myself since there will be media there. As your agent, you are going to need me."

"Um, OK," I said, wondering how the five of us were going to get to the festival grounds. Liz drove a Volkswagen Beetle, and Greg had an eight year old Prius.

"Is that OK?" she asked.

"I guess. How much is parking?"

Sylvia laughed. "Don't worry. I'll drive all of you. I have a mini-van."

"Oh cool!" I said.

We talked a bit more about a story on me in *Time* magazine before ending the call. I went to dinner and sat with Liz and Audrey. Bruce and Zack were highly jealous of the rest of us for getting to go to the music festival, but Liz only had the two extra tickets. She wouldn't say where she got them or how much she had paid, and it made me wonder if Dr. Slater or her backers weren't behind the whole thing. I would have thought Liz would have offered those extra tickets to the guys before Greg and me.

Liz, Audrey, and I met Greg in the dormitory foyer at 12:30 the next day, right after eating lunch. I was the only person not wearing shorts and a polo shirt. Greg greeted me with a kiss, prompting Liz and Audrey to both say, "Awe" in unison.

"Sylvia's got her van right outside," he said, "so let's go."

We all walked outside into the bright sunlight. I had put on a thick coat of SPF 90 sunblock and had brought a fresh bottle along as well, giving it to Liz to carry in her purse since it wouldn't fit in my little hand bag. The high temperature was supposed to soar to over 95 degrees, and one weather forecast had us possibly hitting 100. A dark blue Honda Odyssey was sitting at the curb, the motor running and Sylvia behind the wheel. As we all piled in, I couldn't help but feel the strangeness of getting into a van naked. Greg and I took the back seat, with Audrey by herself in the middle and Liz riding shotgun.

Greg made idle conversation as I looked out the window. It had been so long since I had been off campus that the real world seemed strange. Sylvia followed the signs to a place called the Empire Polo Club, stopped at the gate, and then parked the van on a grass and dirt field with thousands of other vehicles.

"We'll have to walk a bit," she said cheerfully.

I had started wearing the sandals within the past couple of weeks since the afternoon temperatures had been getting consistently hotter. Those concrete walkways were too hot for bare feet, and the grass didn't feel much better. Everyone climbed out of the van, but I stopped at the side door, looking around at all the cars in the parking lot, the dozens of people walking toward the gates of the festival.

"Are we sure this is OK?" I asked.

"There's only one way to find out," Greg said, offering his hand.

I took it and stepped out into the sunlight, naked in public, away from the campus yet still forbidden to wear clothing. Audrey slid the side door shut as Sylvia opened the back and asked Greg to lift the cooler out and onto the ground. After closing that back door, I winced at the click when Sylvia locked it with her key fob. I was naked in an unknown place, entrusting myself to four people I had known for less than six weeks. The feeling of vulnerability I had felt when I first left Dr. Slater's office had returned. Greg handed me a bottle of water from the cooler.

"Better stay hydrated," he said.

I opened it and took a long drink. Sylvia passed out the wristbands, and we all helped each other put them on.

"Holy shit, there's a naked girl," I heard a voice say from up the row of parked cars.

That tingling in my core, spreading out to my nipples and vulva, started with that and never stopped the whole day. We walked across the parking lot, stopping at the port-o-potty near the main entrance so that I could change tampons, and allowed our wristbands to be scanned at the gate to get into the festival. The guy scanning us looked at me, smiled, and then giggled.

"You're her, aren't you? Naked Dani?"

"Yes," I said, wishing I had been given a more anonymous nickname. Andrew Martinez had been known as the Naked Guy at Berkeley, but most of the stories coming out about me had started calling me Naked Dani.

There were two police officers at one end of the gate area watching the guy scan me in, and I instinctively hid behind Greg when I got through the gate. They continued to look right at us, but they didn't say anything. Greg looked at the cops then back at me cowering behind him and took my hand.

"See?" he said. "It's all right."

I tried to relax my fears about the police, but we didn't get very far past the gate before a group of high school age kids, both boys and girls, ran up to me.

"Oh my God, I saw you on TV," one of the girls said. "Can we get a picture with you?"

I looked at Greg and said, "OK."

That opened the floodgates. Everyone wanted to pose with me for a photo. People posed standing next to me, an arm around my shoulder or waist, cute guys, pretty girls, older guys, and even a couple of older ladies. I felt like a rock star. Liz was standing back with her phone and getting her own shots of everything. Whenever a cute guy would pose with his arm around my waist, his hand on my hip, that buzz of arousal in me only increased. But people were respectful, and we didn't have any issues with anyone trying to touch me inappropriately. Greg started to fidget, and I could tell he was getting impatient. We'd been inside the gates for a half an hour and hadn't gone more than one hundred yards. I finally started walking, but the requests kept coming. I would stop for just a split second to let the person get his or her photo and then continue on. After one such request, Greg got on one side of me and Audrey the other, and we were able to walk away.

"Holy shit," Liz said from behind us. "They love you."

"They're just not used to seeing a naked person out in public like this," I said.

Sylvia was far up ahead of us, pulling the wheeled cooler behind her. We walked past several art exhibits, sculptures of varying sizes and colors, but we didn't stop at any of them for fear of being held up again by photo seekers.

"Why don't you come up here and walk with us?" Audrey said to Liz.

"I'm enjoying the view from back here," she replied.

"Stop looking at my big butt," I said, trying to cover it with my hands.

"It's not too big," she said with a laugh. "I think it's perfect." But she did skip forward and walk next to Audrey.

We found a spot near the large stage, and Audrey spread out a picnic blanket. Liz sprayed another coat of sunscreen on me, put some on her legs and arms, and passed the bottle around. The crowd started filling in around us as a punk band I had never heard of started their set on the big stage. They sounded pretty good, and we all got comfortable. Sylvia had only brought water, but Greg bought a couple of beers from a vendor and gave me one. People would turn their heads and look at me as they passed by us, and a few of them stopped to pose for photos with me. More bands played, and as the sun got lower, the smell of marijuana enveloped us. I had only ever tried smoking it once, way back in high school, and the burning sensation in my lungs had felt so bad that I had felt no effects of the drug itself. So I was never interested in smoking it again. But the people around us were very friendly, maybe because of the naked girl among us, and someone wound up passing a lit joint to Greg. He took a toke and offered it to me. I shook my head, and Liz eagerly snatched it up.

Not long after that, both Greg and Liz wandered off in search of food. Audrey was next to me on the blanket watching and listening to the band on the stage.

"Where's Sylvia?" I asked her.

Audrey shrugged. I tried to remember the last time I had seen Sylvia and realized that she had been gone for quite a while, at least through two bands' sets. I stood up to look around for her and heard some catcalls behind me. There was no sign of Sylvia though.

Greg and Liz returned with five burgers and fries, and we made short work of them, leaving Sylvia's in the bag for her return. It was after eight o'clock, the sun long down, when Miley Cyrus was announced. Everyone around us stood up, and she put on an energetic, theatrical show. Sylvia returned well into her set and took me by the hand.

"Come on, there's someone I want you to meet," she yelled into my ear to be heard above the music and the crowd.

I looked at Greg and shrugged as Sylvia led me to a roped off area that served as an aisle at the edge of the crowd. She dipped under the rope and held it up for me. When I bent down to pass under, I heard a guy say, "Holy shit!" right behind me. I had to blush thinking of the view I had given him. On the stage, Miley finished a song, waved to the crowd, and disappeared from the stage amidst thunderous applause.

"Hurry up," Sylvia said, almost running toward the stage.

The crowd noise increased as Miley Cyrus reappeared. She wore what looked like a white bathing suit covered in sequins with long sleeves sewn on, her legs bare except for the fur edged boots on her feet.

"Now, I know we are right by Coachella Valley University, home of a hero of mine, Naked Dani," Miley Cyrus said. I was surprised at the loud roar of the audience at the mention of my name. "And I heard through the grapevine that she is actually here tonight."

The area around me seemed to explode as a spotlight hit me. I looked up at the stage and saw myself, naked, on the huge video board behind the band. The crowd erupted in its loudest applause yet.

"Come on up here," Miley said.

Sylvia had abandoned me to the spotlight; I looked all around but couldn't see her. I climbed the steps to the stage with the spotlight following me. Miley rushed to the top of the stairs, took my hand, and pulled me to the center of the stage. I looked out at the crowd packed onto the lawn as far as I could see. 90,000 people were looking at me, naked.

"Thank you," Miley said. "I appreciated what you said about me a couple of weeks ago on *Stossel*."

I remembered the clip of her in the show introduction and talking about her with John Stossel just in passing, but I had no recollection of what I said. So I simply shrugged and said, "You're welcome?"

Miley laughed and asked me, with her microphone on, if I sang. "No, not really," I replied.

"I want you to help me with next song. I think you've heard it before."

The crowd noise increased again as the opening notes of "Wrecking Ball" started up. Miley's microphone was one of those things that attaches behind her ear, kind of like what I had worn on *Stossel*. She stood right beside me, leaning her head into me, our foreheads almost touching, so that audio of my voice could be captured. I tried to sing but stumbled over the words. Miley finally pulled away, and when the first chorus started, the lights exploded, and I was startled to see a large white wrecking ball swinging between us and the band. Miley turned her back to me and pointed to the zipper at the nape of her neck. I grabbed it and pulled it down a few inches. She then turned away, still singing, and pointed at me and then at the ball, nodding her head. I walked over to it, felt it go by, realizing that it didn't weigh much at all. A stage hand pointed me to a small scaffold. I went up the stairs with him, and he caught the ball for me, helping me on, showing me where the hidden straps for my feet were. I grabbed the chain, and he pushed the ball out, swinging me across the stage.

Miley had shed her outfit and was naked except for the furry boots. The crowd noise was deafening, and I could barely hear the song. Back and forth I swung, as the band played and the lights flashed. I was getting a headache, and I knew my tampon needed changing. I only hoped I wasn't making a mess on the giant white papier Mache ball. The song finally ended, but the crowd was still screaming and yelling. The stage hand caught the ball and helped me off. I looked at it and felt relieved to see no mess on it. Miley stood in front of the stage, her arms in the air, legs spread apart and knees bent, showing herself off to her applauding fans. Seeing her made me think of Dr. Slater in my dorm room before the *Stossel* taping saying that she wouldn't have wanted one of the girls who would have readily volunteered for her nudity project.

Rather than rejoin Miley in the middle of the stage, I disappeared down the stairs where Sylvia met me.

"That was incredible!" she said. "I had no idea you were going to get to ride on the ball."

"Me either," I said.

I took Sylvia's hand and led the way this time, back to where I thought our row was. We slipped under the rope and walked between other groups, everyone standing and cheering me, patting me on the back or the buttocks. Miley Cyrus had left the stage, and the announcer was introducing the next band, Nine Inch Nails. We finally found the right blanket, and Greg took me in his arms and kissed me tightly. I kissed him back with passion. He tried to touch my pubic area as we kissed, but I remembered the state of my tampon and pulled away from him. The nearest bathroom was hundreds of yards away through throngs of people. I grabbed my hand purse and leaned back toward Greg.

"Can you take me to the bathroom?"

He nodded, and we made our way through the crowd. I heard several remarks, but Greg's presence kept anyone from touching me again. We finally made it to one of the portable toilets that had a green vacant sign, and I excused myself.

Greg was still there when I came out.

"Sorry," I said.

"No, I'm sorry. I got carried away."

I smiled, wishing I hadn't been on my period, knowing that I would have let him fondle me all he wanted here. We made our way back to the others and enjoyed the music until well after midnight. Sylvia stayed on her phone most of the time, shouting to try to be heard, and I imagined that several news stories about my naked wrecking ball ride and how I had inspired Miley to strip down during her performance would be hitting the airwaves in the next few days.

By the time we had made the walk back to Sylvia's van and emerged from the line of cars leaving the parking lot, it was after two AM. Sylvia made yet another call on her phone, but being so far in the back of the van, I couldn't hear her. Greg had his hand on my thigh, and I leaned over and rested my head on his shoulder.

I must have drifted off because I was startled awake by the side door sliding open on its track. I sat up and looked around. We were not back at the school but in a small parking lot, a busy street behind us. I could see a yellow Denny's sign reflected in the window of a car next to us. Sylvia was standing by the door helping a sleepy Audrey step out of the van.

"Let's get an early breakfast. My treat," Sylvia said.

"What about Dani?" Greg said, his voice sounding dopey with sleep.

"What about her? She can order whatever she wants."

"I can't go in there naked. No shoes, no shirt, no service."

"You have shoes on," Sylvia said. "I've already called ahead, and the manager on duty is thrilled to have the famous Naked Dani eat in his restaurant this morning."

I started to say, "You mean infamous," but I held my tongue.

I got out, feeling the cooler night breeze tickle my body. Sylvia led the way, and I followed. I think Greg, Liz, and Audrey were waiting for me to make the move and fell in behind me. The young kid serving as host took one look at me as we walked inside, and his eyes widened comically.

"Uh, um, just a moment," he said and disappeared toward the back.

A little over half of the tables were occupied, and all conversation had stopped after I walked in. I ignored them all, looking at the stack of menus on the counter. The kid came back with an older guy in a white shirt and tie.

"Good morning," he said, his eyes glued to my body. "I'm Brian, the manager. Which one of you is Sylvia?"

Sylvia raised her hand.

"So nice to meet you," Brian continued, grabbing five menus from the stack. "I have a table ready for you. Right this way."

We followed him back, and I heard several people whispering among themselves. I should have felt a self-conscious embarrassment at being naked in a public restaurant, but after five weeks of constant nudity, I was numb to it. This was how I was, and they could either accept me or not. I caught a young teenage boy staring at me, and I smiled back at him. He blushed and turned away, hiding his face from me. My heart seemed to melt even though my nipples tingled.

Brian seated us in the back area where only one other table was occupied. I draped one of my black butt towels over the seat, and the five of us ordered breakfast. The people at the other table had also been at the festival and asked for photos with me, calling me the Wrecking Ball girl. Once our food arrived, I almost forgot about being the only naked person in the place until we got up to leave. Walking out, I heard snippets of more whispered conversations, but I refused to let any of it bother me. We piled into the van, and Sylvia drove us back to the campus. Greg walked me to the front entrance of the dorm and gave me a quick kiss good night. He looked as tired as I felt. When I got up to the room, I collapsed onto my bed and slept until Sunday afternoon.

Chapter Fifteen – Semester's End

As the end of the semester approached, I started having dreams of being somewhere on campus wearing clothes and, fearful of being disqualified from the project and losing my scholarships, trying to rip those clothes off in a panic but not being able to get out of them, all the while asking myself where I had even gotten the clothes. Most people have nightmares about going to school or work either naked or in their underwear, so even my dreams were becoming backwards.

Sylvia had continued to keep me updated on media requests and the stories being written and posted about me. There was quite a bit of fallout over the Coachella Music Festival, but most of the criticism fell on Miley Cyrus. There had been a clause in the standard Festival contract prohibiting nudity on the part of any performers. I hadn't fallen under that clause, of course, being a non-performer, but the festival organizers had withheld payment to Miley Cyrus for her little naked act. I think that, in whatever state she gets herself into to be able to perform, the exhibitionist in her just couldn't stand to have a naked girl on stage without getting naked herself. And maybe my presence made her feel that it would be OK. But I'm just speculating, of course. She and the festival organizers agreed to some kind of settlement when the festival came under fire itself from a few groups for allowing such explicit R and X-rated lyrics on their stage but not nudity.

I kept my head down and concentrated on my studies. Greg and I did go out to dinner a couple of times, and we also saw the last movie in that Oscar Mistakes series, the original 1996 *Fargo*. I had seen an episode or two of the TV series but had never seen the movie. Greg and I both loved it, although being naked while watching a movie set in a Minnesota winter gave me just a few chills. That wasn't too bad since it prompted Greg to put his arm around me and rub my arms and shoulders to make me feel warmer. Greg also convinced me to go to one of the campus dances which turned out to be really fun. Several people there were inspired by me and took their own clothes off. In all, I would say that about ten of us danced naked out of a crowd of about three hundred. Greg told me that several other naked people had been seen in various places around campus, most of them guys of course. I hadn't seen any myself except for that group of streakers on one of my evening walks and the three guys in my swimming class. And apparently, according to Sylvia, five or six college students had been cited for trying to walk across campus nude in other states where the laws against public nudity were a bit more vigorous.

Sylvia had also told me about all the offers and honors I had received. Penthouse and Hustler magazines wanted me to do both photo and video sessions. I turned both of those down even though the money offered from each was in the six figures. If I did something like that, I would lose the argument with my father (and everyone else) that being nude was not necessarily sexual. The American Association for Nude Recreation had made me an honorary lifetime member, an honor which I accepted, writing them what I hoped was a nice letter in thanks.

I breezed through finals week, feeling very confident that I had aced all of my exams. My last test was in Spanish class, and completing that exam was like a weight lifted off my shoulders. I walked out of the room and didn't know what to do with myself. There were no more papers to write, no more passages to read, no more verbs to conjugate. According to Dr. Slater's contract, I had to remain naked until the last final exam period had ended, so I still had another day to just hang out. Greg was busy helping Dr. Slater with her data organization and working on his own thesis, so I hadn't seen much of him in the last week.

When I got back to the room after finishing that Spanish final, Diane was packing to go home. Her parents and younger brother were in the room waiting for her. I think she was probably delaying so she would get a chance to show off her naked roommate.

"Wow," her brother said when I walked in. "Hello."

After two months, I had gotten used to all kinds of reactions to me. "Hi," I said.

"Well, my goodness," Diane's mother said.

Diane introduced me to her family. Her brother's name was Steven and looked to be about sixteen, fresh red acne scars on both cheeks.

"I saw you on TV," Steven said, smiling and gazing at my breasts. "When Diane said her roommate was the naked girl, I didn't believe her at first."

I shrugged, feeling awkward, like a fifth wheel. Diane's mother knocked Steven in the shoulder, prompting him to look away from me. Whenever Diane's father got a glimpse, he snapped his head toward his wife, trying not to look at me. It was kind of funny, and I wanted to tell them that it was OK to look, that I was used to it now.

"I think I'm all done," Diane announced. She tried to close her large suitcase, but her father gently pushed her aside and did it for her.

"I'll just take this down to the car. Nice to meet you Danielle," he mumbled without looking at me. "Come on Steven."

Diane stood still for a moment after her father and brother left, looking at me. "Well, it was an interesting semester," she said, "especially after spring break."

Her mom and I both laughed.

"Yeah, I guess it was." Although Diane and I had never gotten along much during the year, I didn't have any ill feelings toward her. She was nice, and I had learned that the party girl image that she tried to convey was just a façade, that she was really quiet and reserved and even conservative. "Have a good summer."

"You too," she said, picking up a box of things from her bed and following her mom out.

I sighed with relief, both that she had not wanted to hug and that I had the room all to myself for the next two nights. The last exam period was on Saturday, for those few Saturday sections on the class schedule. The period ended at 11:50, and at that time the spring semester would officially be over. My flight home wasn't until Sunday morning. I dialed Greg's cell phone and was disappointed when it rolled to his voice mail.

"Hey," I said, "I just took my last test, so I am DONE. And my roommate just left to go home, so I'm all alone. I was wondering if you wanted to do something tonight. So call me later."

With nothing to do, I turned on the TV and browsed the list of things I had recorded on my DVR. I settled on *Laura* which I had recorded off of Turner Classic Movies the month before. Since Greg and I had started going to that film series, I had been recording and watching a lot of classic movies. I used all my pillows and made a comfortable seat for myself on the bed, briefly wondering what people would think if they knew that the world famous Naked Dani was all alone in her dorm room watching an old black and white movie, stuck on campus with no car and no clothes and it too hot to do anything outside. My life just didn't seem very glamourous.

Greg called about halfway through the movie. I hurriedly paused it and grabbed the vibrating phone.

"Hey there," I said.

"Hi Dani." He sounded down, without the usual spark in his voice.

"What's wrong?"

"Nothing. It's just that I've so much to do today and tonight. I don't know if I can get away."

"Well, that's OK," I lied, feeling the sting of disappointment. I finally get the room to myself, and he can't make time for me?

"I have to have everything done tonight, so I'll be free tomorrow," Greg said. "OK?"

"Yeah, that's fine. Good luck with all your stuff."

"I'm sorry. I know you're disappointed. I can hear it in your voice."

"I'm just tired. Finals week is always tiring."

We chatted just a bit more before Greg had to get back to whatever he was working on. I resumed the movie and spent a quiet evening in the dorm, going downstairs only to eat dinner. The dorm was emptying out, with everyone heading home for the summer. I stayed up late watching TV, too excited about the end of the nudity project the next day to be able to sleep well.

I walked into the sociology department office at 11:30 AM on Saturday, the last day of the semester. Since it was a weekend, the receptionist's desk was empty, but I could see that the door to Dr.

Slater's office was open. I padded through the front office, my sandals silent on the carpet, and then I wondered why I was bothering to sneak. She probably knew I was here; she'd been tracking my movements, listening to the audio from the microphone around my neck, for two months. She appeared in the doorway to her office before I could make it there.

"Dani!" she squealed with the sound of delight in her voice.

She stepped forward and pulled me into a big hug just as I was saying "Hi."

"We made it," she said, releasing me from her hug.

I felt like correcting her, saying that *I* had made it, not we. But I didn't.

"Come on in," she said, retreating back into her office and waving me in.

I followed her inside. Her office looked exactly as it had when I had last visited two months before except that my big suitcase was sitting upright on the floor next to the door. On her desk, neatly folded, were a bra and panties and the flats I had worn and taken off the last time I was here.

"Go ahead and shut the door," Dr. Slater said. When I did, I saw my yellow dress on a hanger on the back of the door, the last outfit I had worn, two months ago. I must have gasped when I saw it because Dr. Slater laughed. "Come on and sit down. We'll get to that in a little bit."

I pulled one of my black butt towels out of my hand purse, plopped it onto the chair across from Dr. Slater's desk, and sat down. Dr. Slater sat in her chair and leaned forward toward me, her hands on her desk.

"So tell me Dani, how do you feel?"

"I feel fine," I replied.

"I mean, how do you feel about putting on clothes after the last two months?"

Dr. Slater's expression was one of determined curiosity, with an intensity that I had never seen. After the last two months of forced nudity, all the embarrassment and humiliation I had felt over having my friends and family see me naked either in person or on their televisions, I should hate this woman, especially since she seemed to be savoring these last moments of my nakedness. But all I felt was relief that the project had ended, that I had made it through something that two months before I could never have even imagined. And even with all of the shame, there was a part of me that had enjoyed it, being seen and admired by so many strangers.

"I'm ready," I said, my voice sounding shaky. "I mean, it's been such a strange experience."

"I know, it has been. And I know we put you through a lot, with the television appearances and everything. That was part of the goal of this. Yes, I wanted to study people's reactions to you here on campus, but I also wanted to change, at least just a little bit, the public's perception of the nude body. That uncensored *Stossel* episode proves that we did change that perception and for the better. It was something I had only imagined happening, but seeing your full body on that TV, on a Fox network no less, was such a triumph. It was amazing. And you were amazing. So, thank you. From the bottom of my heart, thank you."

She looked like she was about to cry as she talked, and I was convinced that her emotions were genuine.

"Why was this so important to you?" I ventured.

A tear did fall then, and she grabbed a tissue from the box on her desk and dabbed it at her eyes to catch any remaining tears.

"Andrew," she said.

"Martinez?" I asked when she seemed unable to say anything else.

Dr. Slater nodded, and her silence told me everything I needed to know. She had been in love with him, whether he ever knew it or not. She took a deep breath, and thumbed through some papers on her desk, pulling out two sheets and passing them to me.

"As we agreed, you will be credited with six semester hours of Sociology 4999, Special Topics, with a grade of A. Your disciplinary record has been expunged. The suspension has been rescinded, your scholarships restored, and the file on you, containing that plagiarized paper, shredded." She looked at the digital display on her desk phone. "And at 11:38 AM, I am proclaiming the project done. You are free to get dressed and – well, to wear whatever you want."

I took a quick glance at the papers she had handed me. One was just a form stating that I had completed the requirements for the six sociology hours, and the other was a personal letter from Dr. Slater and the sociology department thanking me for volunteering to be the test subject of her study. I set the papers on her desk, stood up, and grabbed my underwear. Stepping out of my sandals, I slid the panties up over my waist, the sensation of the fabric so tight against my skin feeling both strange and familiar at the same time. I slid my arms under the bra straps, pulling the cups over my breasts, covering them, and reached behind me to fasten the clasps behind my back. My arms almost couldn't turn backwards enough to allow me to pull the ends of the bra together; it had been so long since I had put on a bra I had trouble remembering the motions.

Dr. Slater had turned her chair sideways, and she gazed intently out the window overlooking the Commons. Once my bra was secure, I stepped over to the door and slid my yellow dress off the hanger. I put it on over my head, arms extended, letting it fall over me. It felt heavy, like it was weighted down, as I pulled up the zipper on the side. For the first time in two months, I was clothed! I picked my flats up off of Dr. Slater's desk and, after swiping the black butt towel off the chair and onto the floor, sat down to put them on. Dr. Slater turned her chair back toward me and looked at me in my dress, a wry smile on her face.

"Oh," I said, suddenly remembering and reaching over my shoulders to unclasp the necklace microphone, "here you go."

I held it out to her, and she took it. "Thank you."

Dr. Slater dropped the necklace into a desk drawer.

"The charger's still in my room," I said. "I can bring it by—"

"Don't worry about it," Dr. Slater said, waving her hand as if to push my words away. "You can give it to Greg. He's standing by to help get your suitcase back to your room."

I tried not to smile and failed. "Okay."

Dr. Slater stood up and walked around me to open her office door. "Greg," she called before turning around and standing beside her desk.

I stood up as Greg strolled into the room, looking bleary eyed. I wanted to be mad at him for not being available last night, but I was also happy that he was finally going to see me with clothes on. His eyes seemed to light up when he saw me standing there in my yellow dress.

"Hi," he said, smiling.

"Hey," I answered, acting shy by looking down at myself in the dress.

"I guess this is it," Dr. Slater said. "Dani, have a wonderful summer and I hope to see you again soon."

I nodded, not knowing what to say. There was no way I could thank her for anything since the whole project had been more or less forced on me. But I did have my scholarships intact, and I could continue on with my college plans. Greg grabbed the handle of my suitcase and tilted it forward so that it would roll on its wheels. I gathered the sandals and my purse, putting the little black towel inside it, and together, Greg and I walked out of Dr. Slater's office.

We took the elevator down to the first floor and walked across the Commons under the oppressively hot sun. Greg kept looking over at me and shaking his head.

"What!?" I finally asked.

"I'm not used to seeing you like this," he said, shaking his head.

"What, like a normal person?"

"Yeah, I guess."

There were still a few people on campus, walking this way and that, even though the semester had just ended. None of them looked at or appeared to take any special notice of me. I had rejoined the masses. It's funny how we take for granted such simple things. Now that I finally had clothes back on, I couldn't help but be acutely aware of every little touch of fabric as we walked back to my dorm, how my thighs brushed against the folds of the dress with each step or how my bra constricted my chest, squeezing the flesh of my sides up toward my armpits, compressing my breasts into pancake shapes and pushing my cleavage up.

"Did you get everything done last night?" I asked Greg.

"Yeah," he said, with a heavy sigh.

We took the elevator up to the third floor, and Greg wheeled the suitcase into my room, setting it on the floor at the foot of my bed.

"Thank you," I said.

"No problem. I wouldn't have missed it for the world."

We stepped into each other, embracing, kissing with a passion. His hands wandered more freely now that he was touching the fabric of my dress rather than bare skin, reaching down and cupping my buttocks, pulling me up to him. I pulled his shirt tail out of the waistband of his shorts, put my hands on the skin of his lower back, and moved upwards, pushing his shirt up further. He pulled back from me, breaking our kiss, long enough to pull the shirt over his head and off. I stepped into him again after he had flung the shirt away, kissing his chest, his nipples.

I hadn't had my clothes on for fifteen minutes, and I already wanted to take them off. But, just once, I wanted to be clothed while Greg was naked, so I unsnapped his shorts and pushed the zipper down. Greg helped by lowering the shorts along with whatever else he was wearing underneath. His erection sprang forward, and I grabbed it with my hand, relishing the gasp he made at my touch. I looked down at him as he stepped out of his shoes and shorts.

"Well, this is a change," he said, smiling.

"It is. I kind of like it."

"I'll bet you do."

I pushed him onto my bed and kicked off the shoes I was wearing. Greg's penis was above his belly, hard and pointed straight up toward his head, almost defying gravity. We kissed again, and I felt him push the zipper of my dress down. I was ready to get out of it by then, and I was especially ready to get rid of the bra I was wearing.

We spent what seemed like a long time enjoying each other's touch, putting our mouths on each other. Greg went down between my legs and licked and sucked and used his fingers like an artist, giving me an explosive orgasm that made my past self-induced orgasms seem like minor tremors. I returned the favor, intending to get Greg off with just my hands and mouth, but when he didn't come right away like my two past boyfriends, we went a little farther. He had a condom with him. When he reached down onto the floor, pulled it out of his shorts pocket, and showed it to me, I nodded. He rolled it on as I lay on my back, and he entered me slowly from above. I was very wet from everything else we had done, but I still felt a quick stab of pain that turned to pleasure. Even though the rest of it was very enjoyable, I wasn't able to orgasm from the penetration. I certainly never felt anything close to what Greg had given me before, and Greg came quickly into the condom.

"Oh wow!" he said, pulling out and rolling onto his back next to me.

He yanked the condom off, noticed the little bit of blood on it, and tossed it into the trash can under my computer desk.

"Did you come?" he asked.

"Oh yeah," I lied. "It was amazing." But I couldn't help but feel disappointed, like maybe I wasn't good at sex or something.

We lay together catching our breath until I couldn't stand it anymore; I had to pee so badly. I jumped up out of bed and hurried out into the hall and to the bathroom. It was only after I had gotten back to the room that I realized I had gone naked.

"When you gotta go, you gotta go," Greg said, laughing. He already had his shorts back on and was turning his shirt right side out.

"Shut up. It's a habit now."

"I'll bet," he said. "You hungry?"

"Starving," I said.

I looked in my suitcase for a t-shirt and pair of shorts, and when I got dressed, I went braless. Getting used to wearing a bra again was going to take some time. We ate downstairs in the dining hall. Greg, not having a meal card, paid cash for his lunch. It was so late in the lunch hour and in the semester that we had the place to ourselves. We didn't talk much, and I began to wonder if that was how sex was, a replacement for regular conversation.

Greg did try spending the night in my bed with me, but neither of us could sleep well on such a tiny single bed. He finally moved over to Diane's bed at some point in the middle of the night. When we got up, we had another round of sex. Knowing a little more what to expect, I was able to relax and had a couple of fantastic orgasms when Greg was going down on me. He went more slowly during intercourse, and I finally hit that plateau, although it only came when I was thinking of myself naked on that stage in front of 90,000 people, all of them staring at my naked breasts and vulva blown up on the giant video board above me.

My clothes were already packed, so all I had to do was put my other things in the big suitcase. Since I was coming back to take summer classes, I had planned on boxing up my computer and paying to have it stored in the Student Union building, but Greg offered to keep it at his house during the two and a half weeks I would be home in Texas. I wished I could have kept the room, but only one dorm was open for the summer sessions, and Holcombe Hall wasn't it.

"You should get a laptop," Greg said as we were carrying the computer down to his car. He was carrying the tower, and I had the monitor.

"My birthday is coming up, so maybe I can talk Daddy into getting me one," I said.

We had already loaded my suitcase and carry-on bag into Greg's car. Greg sat by the curb with the motor running while I ran back in to turn in my key and meal card. He then drove me to the Palm Springs Airport. I checked my bag at the curbside check in, got my boarding pass, and had Greg walk me to the security checkpoint.

"I'm going to miss you," he said.

"I'll be back before you know it."

"It won't quite be the same," he countered with a fake frown.

I punched him in the shoulder playfully with my open palm. "You," I said, and he kissed me, long and lingering.

"I'd better get," he said. "We don't want your computer sitting in a hot car for too long."

"Bye," I said.

I watched him walk out the doors before I got into the line for security. I looked around at all the people waiting, but no one seemed to take any note of me. After two months of almost constant attention everywhere I went, it almost felt like something was wrong. I began to daydream about taking off my clothes and standing naked in line and then watching the heads turn. Going through security would sure be a lot easier if I just put everything in the x-ray tray and walked through naked, I thought with a laugh. When I got up to the checkpoint, I took off my shoes and emptied my pockets and walked through the scanning machine barefooted, feeling first the carpet and then the cool metal on the soles of my feet. My senses were so much more alive when my skin was uncovered. The sun and wind had made me feel more alive. I shook my head as I waited for the tray with my things to roll out of the machine, telling myself that I had to quit thinking about being naked, that that part of my life was now in the past. I had to look toward the future, and the next thing up in my future was going home and facing my parents and friends.

Chapter Sixteen – Home

The average looking middle-aged man next to me, whose wife was on the other side of him in the aisle seat, kept looking at my profile as if he recognized me but couldn't quite place from where. When I wasn't napping, I kept my gaze out the window at the landscape and clouds below for most of the flight. The guy never tried to say anything to me though, maybe because of that wife sitting next to him or maybe because he would have had to raise his voice to be heard over the constant noise of the jet engines. I kept my focus on the earth below, trying to decide if the world looked any different now that I was no longer a virgin before deciding that it only looked strange because I was 35,000 feet above it and that my sexual status didn't mean much in the grand scheme of things. The plane landed at DFW International Airport on time, and I was happy to see Mom waiting for me in the baggage claim area. She gave me a hug, holding on to me for what seemed like a long time.

"Where's Daddy?" I asked, looking around for him.

"He's on call this week," she said, "so he stayed home."

"Oh," I said. Daddy had always had to be in an on call rotation in the various IT jobs he had held throughout my childhood, but in his current job, which he had had for over five years now, the on call weeks were never busy enough that he had to stay home by his computer all weekend. So I immediately took his absence to mean that he was still upset with me.

"That's a cute outfit," Mom said as we waited for my suitcase to appear on the carousel, and I wondered for a second if she could tell that I wasn't wearing a bra.

For some reason, this gave me a case of giggles that wouldn't stop. I don't know if it was just the irony of hearing her remark about my clothes or as a cover for feeling like such a disappointment to my father.

"What are you laughing at?" Mom said, but she started laughing herself.

My suitcase appeared on the carousel, and I grabbed it before it could start around again. The drive home was quick with the light Sunday evening traffic, and we arrived at the house just before dark. Daddy was sitting in front of his computer typing furiously on his keyboard. Whatever he was typing he didn't want me to see as he took pains to save and close it before getting up to greet me with a hug.

"I'm glad you're home and away from that school," he said.

"You know I'm going back though, right? I'm taking classes both summer sessions. If I do that this summer and next, I should be able to graduate almost a year early."

"You could always transfer to UTA and live here at home."

I shook my head. "I don't know how many of my hours would even transfer," I said, thinking especially of those six advanced sociology hours. "And would my scholarships go with me if I did? No, I have a pretty set degree plan there. I'll be all right."

He didn't seem too happy with this, so I lugged my suitcase up the stairs myself to my old room. It was how I had left it, and being there made the previous two months seem like a dream, almost as if they hadn't really happened.

I spent the next two days at home, sleeping more than twelve hours a night, as if my body were trying to catch up from the busy semester. I tried to sleep in my regular pajamas the first night, but after an hour of tossing and turning and staring at my ceiling, I took them off and slept naked. Those crazy dreams of being clothed on campus and being unable to get undressed still persisted.

On Wednesday morning, my cousin Sally called to invite me to go shopping with her at the Northeast Mall. Sally had long brown hair that hung down almost to her waist unless she tied it up. She was a couple of inches shorter than I was, and she weighed about sixty pounds more. When Sally came to pick me up, she waited until we were out of the house and away from Mom before asking me about the nudity project.

"So who was it that inspired that whole thing?" she asked. "I talked to Gabby, but she says it wasn't her." Gabby was another cousin of ours.

"I never did say which cousin, did I?" I said. "To tell you the truth, I was thinking of you."

"What? You made that whole story up? Why?"

So I told Sally the story of Dr. Slater's study and how I had volunteered for it and that because of the nature of the study, I had to keep the real reason I was naked a secret. I left out the part about my plagiarized paper.

"Why would you volunteer for something like that?" she asked.

"I don't know. Those six extra hours sounded good to me. And being naked was exciting."

"Weren't you scared?"

"The first day, yeah. And the second. But it got easier. Now, I kind of wish I could be naked more often."

We were walking the mall by then, and I tried to imagine myself naked in the middle of all those people. I looked at them, trying to see if any of them took any special note of me, perhaps recognizing me from the *Stossel* show, but no one did.

"That's just weird," she said. "I could never do that."

"I know. I said the same thing to Dr. Slater when she asked me to volunteer." I started to say that the idea grew on me, but I left that part out. I felt a bit disingenuous for telling Sally that I had been a completely willing volunteer, but I didn't want to admit that I had cheated on a paper. She probably would have understood though, since I had only done it so that I was able to come to her father's funeral.

We had fun that day though. After shopping we wound up going to a movie at the Rave Motion Pictures Theater attached to the mall and then to dinner at the Genghis Grill right outside the theater. Dad was home from work by the time I got back, but he barely acknowledged me when I came in. He was busy typing on his computer again, and whenever I would walk up behind him, he would minimize his window. The only thing that I could see was that he was in his email app, and I wondered to whom he would be typing such a long message.

Samantha and Katie, two of my best friends from high school, invited me to a party Saturday night, and I agreed to go even though I didn't really feel like it. Being home after the Project, as I had come to think of Dr. Slater's nudity study now that I was out of it, was different than past visits home. My clothes never felt right, and I wondered if it was the ten pounds I had lost since spring break or if I had really been conditioned to feeling uncomfortable in anything. And Daddy's attitude toward me and his secretiveness on the computer added to the general strangeness of everything.

Samantha picked me up at eight o'clock Saturday evening. I promised Mom that I would try to be home before midnight but that not having a car made me dependent on other people.

"If you need to be picked up, call us," Daddy said.

"I will," I promised before heading out the door.

Samantha had said that the party was at Katie's house, but Katie had apparently moved since high school. Instead of going up to the front door of her new house, Samantha led me around to the gate on the side. I could hear people laughing and splashing in a swimming pool as we walked into the big back yard.

"There she is!" I heard Katie proclaim when Samantha and I approached the patio. "Do you want a beer?"

"You didn't say this was a pool party," I said to Katie and Samantha as Katie, wearing nothing but a black one-piece bathing suit, filled a plastic cup from a keg.

"Oh, well," Samantha said. "Now you know."

"But I didn't bring a bathing suit."

My two friends looked at each other, eyes wide in surprise. "We didn't figure you would want to wear a suit," Samantha said. "After your – well, you know."

"Come on in the pool," one of the guys in the water said. I recognized him as James. He and I had gone out on a couple of dates in the tenth grade, but there had been nothing serious between us.

I looked around at everyone else, visible from the floodlights pointed toward the pool area from the eaves of the house, and saw that almost all of the guests were from my high school class. A couple of them also went to my church. The guys were all wearing baggy swim trunks. Two of the girls were in bikinis, but the rest of them wore one piece suits.

"Come on," another guy said. "It's not like we don't already know what you look like naked."

"EVERYONE knows what Dani looks like naked," someone else said which drew a round of laughter from everybody.

Samantha and Katie stared at me, and I glared back at them, knowing that this had been some kind of set up. My cheeks felt flush with embarrassment. Getting naked in front of my old high school friends was unthinkable, I told myself. But that conflicted with the tingling I started feeling in my core at the thought of getting another chance to be naked in front of people, and as that tingling feeling spread to my nipples and pubic area, I knew that I would succumb to it.

"I didn't bring a towel either," I said weakly.

"We have extras," Katie said with a wicked grin on her face.

Samantha pulled a bikini out of the large purse she had been carrying. "I'm going to go change," she said and started into the house. I followed her until she got to a half bath near the kitchen and closed the door.

There was a small bedroom next to that bathroom, and when I looked inside with the light off, I saw several piles of clothes lying on the bed and floor. I stepped in and to the side as Samantha unlocked the bathroom door. She walked into the dark bedroom and set her pile of clothes in the corner near the door. I shrank into the wall near the closet in the shadow of an upright dresser, and Samantha didn't appear to see me as she turned and headed back out toward the pool. I stood against the wall in the dark room for a full minute, thinking about my high school days and the people outside, the girls who had been my friends, the guys I'd had crushes on and the ones I had even dated a time or two. They had all seen me naked on TV or on their computers. That *Stossel* episode was on Youtube and had over 1.5 million views, so of course they had all seen me. They had all known me and would have been curious, especially with my new celebrity status. I stepped out of my shoes and pulled my shirt over my head and off. I still hadn't adjusted to clothes enough to wear a bra again. I asked myself if I would have come to this party if Samantha and Katie had told me it was a pool party but that they wanted me to swim naked. My answer to them would have been no, but I would have regretted it eventually. As I slipped my shorts and panties down, my irritation with them for this apparent set up dissipated. Naked now, I folded my clothes up and set them on the floor in that shadow of the dresser where I had hidden from Samantha.

When I walked out of the dark bedroom and passed the half

bath, that tingling sensation was so strong that I was tempted to duck inside, lock the door, and get myself off. But I didn't. That anticipation of everyone seeing me, my bare breasts and exposed vulva, was so great that I wanted to get on with it. I reached the sliding glass door and looked outside. Samantha and Katie were still on the patio looking inside through the glass. They both smiled and Katie even clapped her hands twice when they saw me. I slid the door open and stepped out onto the patio.

"Woo hoo!" James yelled from the pool, and everyone stopped what they were doing to look at me. My God, I wanted to rush back inside and put my fingers on my clitoris until I came, which wouldn't have taken very long. Instead I stepped forward and took the plastic cup full of beer that Samantha held out to me.

"Awesome!" she said.

"You really just don't care, do you?" Katie said. "You'll just get naked in front of anyone."

"That's what I did for two months," I said.

"Unbelievable," Katie said, looking me over from head to toe. "How can they let you do that and not arrest you?"

I shrugged and said, "It's California."

I stood around drinking my beer enjoying being the subject of everyone's gaze. As soon as I finished, I set the cup down and stepped into the pool. It was only May, and the water was still cold. The pools in Texas were never temperature controlled like the ones at CVU. They had to keep them controlled out there because the pool water would reach the temperature of a hot tub during the brutal summers.

Once I was in the water up to my shoulders, everyone talked to me normally. I enjoyed visiting with all of my old friends. Every once in a while, under the water, my hand would brush over my bare vulva, my finger caressing my clitoral hood, making my whole body shudder. A fantasy of getting out of the pool and masturbating to orgasm in front of everyone, all of my old friends, entered my mind. But I could never really do that. How could I even contemplate such a thing? What was wrong with me?

I stayed in the pool for a couple of hours, until Samantha offered me another beer. I got out and took one from her, enjoying the feeling of being wet and naked in the warm breeze. Everybody, especially the guys, turned their attention to me once I was out of the pool. I had to pee, but I was still wet with no towel. I sipped my beer and waited until I had air dried enough to go inside to relieve myself. And I relieved myself in more ways than one, giving myself a quick and sudden orgasm after I finished peeing. When I was done, I washed my hands and looked at myself in the mirror. After my orgasm, my pink labia were poking out from between the folds of my vulva, making me look more sexual. There was nothing I could do about it, so I dried my hands and walked back outside.

I spent the rest of the night out of the water, talking with the other guests, mostly guys since they were the ones trying to crowd around me the most. At some point, Katie got Samantha to take a picture of her and me together, and that opened the floodgates for everyone else. I posed with each person attending the party individually and then in small groups. I couldn't count how many photos were taken of me. But after the Project and all the photos and videos of me floating around in cyberspace, how could I say no? I would say that I didn't care, but I found the whole thing stimulating, posing naked for the camera. By eleven-thirty, no one had left the party. I caught up to Samantha and told her that I needed her to take me home.

"OK, hold on," she said.

Samantha disappeared into the house while Katie and James asked me when I was going back to California. When Samantha came back outside, she had changed out of her bikini and back into her regular clothes.

"Hey, I've got to go," I said to Katie and James and everyone else standing around trying to either talk to me or just get another good look at me.

"Awww," some of them said in disappointment.

I headed into the house to get dressed, but when I got into the dark bedroom, I couldn't find my clothes where I thought I had left them. After turning the light on, I saw everyone else's clothes, but mine were gone. I stormed back outside, right up to Samantha.

"Where are my clothes?"

"Relax," she said, "they're in my car."

Most of the people standing around snickered.

"Why?" I asked.

"Come on, I thought you might enjoy a little naked in public adventure."

"Umm, this is Texas, not California," I reminded her. "I can't get away with that sort of thing here."

"Relax, we'll be careful. Someone would love to see you, but he was working tonight and couldn't come. I just texted him and told him that I would bring you by."

"Who?"

"Chris Strong," Samantha replied.

"What!" Chris had been my boyfriend throughout most of my senior year. We had promised to stay together after high school while I went off to Coachella Valley University and he started out at Tarrant County College, but as usual with such relationships, we had drifted apart during that first year. "No," I said.

"What? You don't want to see Chris?" Samantha asked with a tone of amusement in her voice.

"Well, yeah, but not like this."

"Chris sure wants to see you."

Everyone at the party was standing by listening to all of this. I grabbed Samantha's arm and pulled her to the side, near the gate and out of earshot of the rest of the party guests.

"What are you trying to do?" I whispered to Samantha.

"I thought it would be funny. A little joke on Chris."

"A little joke?"

"Come on, you know you want to. When you were on that show, Chris was pissed because he never got to see you naked when you were dating, and now, there you were naked in front of the whole world."

Samantha was right; I did want to go see Chris like this, in my Naked Dani persona. At least, that part of me did. But I was still afraid of getting caught by the local police. How would I ever explain to Daddy why I was arrested for indecent exposure after what he had seen at the college? Would he even believe me if I told him that I was at the mercy of Samantha, my old best friend whom I now barely knew?

"OK," I said, deciding that the best way to avoid getting into trouble was to get my clothes back as quickly as possible, and the only way I saw to do that was to cooperate with Samantha.

"Awesome!" Samantha cried. She turned back to everyone else and said, "All right, we're going. Bye everyone!"

There was a chorus of farewells as I waved at everyone still gathered around the pool in wet swimsuits. I walked out the gate and crept beside the house until I got to the corner. Samantha had parked in the driveway and was getting in her car.

"Is the coast clear?" I asked.

Samantha looked up and down the street and said, "Yes, silly."

I darted out to her car as she sat down behind the wheel. Just as I got to the passenger door, I heard the lock click. I pulled on the door handle anyway, but the door wouldn't budge. Samantha sat in the driver's seat laughing in an exaggeratedly loud voice.

"Shut up," I said, crouching down beside the car.

Samantha unlocked the car, and I yanked the door open, climbed inside, and pulled it shut. Two months of using those little black butt towels had conditioned me into not putting my bare ass on any surface, but I didn't have one of those towels with me. So I sat on my hip, leaning over toward Samantha.

"What are you so shy for?" she asked. "So many people have seen you naked lately, why should you care about a few more?"

"Because I don't want anyone to call the police," I said.

"People only call the police on naked old men, not naked college girls."

I wasn't so sure of that, but I didn't say anything as Samantha backed the car out of the driveway and took off toward the airport. I looked around inside the car but didn't see my clothes.

"Where's my stuff?" I asked.

"In the trunk."

"The trunk! Why are they in the trunk?"

"I didn't want you to chicken out," Samantha said. "Look, we'll stop and see Chris really quick, five minutes tops, and then I'll get your clothes out of the trunk and take you home. I promise."

"Where does Chris work?" I asked.

"The Comfort Inn near DFW. He's on the front desk during the graveyard shift."

"Great," I said, hoping that Chris would be the only person there.

"I'm only doing this because I know you want to."

"What makes you think that?" I asked.

"Because you're an exhibitionist. You have to be to have done all that shit you did in California. How was Miley Cyrus by the way?"

"I don't know. I didn't talk to her except for that little bit on stage."

The clock on the dash of Samantha's car read 11:55. I wanted to call home and at least tell Daddy or Mom that I would be a little late, but my phone was in the pocket of my shorts, in the trunk.

"Remember when we went skinny dipping late at night at my apartment pool," Samantha said.

"Yes," I said, remembering how that memory had resurfaced during my first talk with Dr. Slater.

"I knew then that you were an exhibitionist."

"Bull! I'm not an exhibitionist. At least not back then."

"Ah, so you admit you are now. You were then too. You were just scared of getting caught, like now. That whole skinny-dipping thing was your idea. And then when that drunk guy came by, I had to hold you into the pool and shush you to be quiet. You had wanted to flash him. 'He's not going to call the cops; he's drunk,' you said."

"I did not."

"Did too."

"That's not the way I remember it."

"Then your memory is faulty," Samantha said.

We rode in silence until Samantha stopped the car right in front of the entrance of the Comfort Inn.

"OK, go on in," Samantha said.

"Uh, no. You're coming in with me." I wasn't about to take the chance of Samantha driving off and leaving me there naked.

She sighed and killed the motor. I waited until she was out of the car and standing close enough to the hotel entrance for the automatic doors to slide open before opening the passenger door. After taking a quick look around, I darted from the car into the building. Samantha giggled as she skipped into the building behind me.

"Hey Chris," she said to what appeared to be an empty lobby, "I brought someone to see you."

Chris emerged from the office behind the front desk, and his eyes widened when he saw me.

"Holy shit!" he exclaimed. "Dani, what are you doing here? Where are your clothes? What the hell is wrong with you?"

"It's good to see you too," I said sarcastically. I turned around to go, but Chris disappeared into the side area and walked out into the lobby between me and the door.

"This was Samantha's idea," I said.

He looked at her, saw the expression on her face, and relaxed just a bit. "Yeah, I bet it was," he conceded. He looked me over from head to toe, and I felt that familiar tingling under his scrutiny. It wasn't too long ago that I had thought I would wind up marrying him.

"It really is good to see you," I said.

"Yeah. You too." He hesitated. "But you should probably go. I could get in trouble. And they have security cameras."

"Shit," I said.

Samantha shrugged and said, "OK." She took my arm and walked me back outside. "I'll see you later Chris."

"Bye," he said, turning and watching my bare ass walk away.

Samantha popped the trunk with her key fob, and I grabbed my clothes and started putting them on right there in the Comfort Inn carport.

"Sorry," Samantha said when she dropped me off at home.

"No, it was fun."

"I know. I just feel bad about it now."

"I know the feeling. There were times at the university when I would get carried away, and then, later, I would feel nothing but regret. Like when I stood up facing the camera on *Stossel.* I couldn't believe that I had done that afterwards. It's weird."

"Did it ever get any better?"

"Yeah," I said. "The more stuff I did, the more time I spent naked, the less intensity I felt, both the euphoria during and regret afterward."

"Is that what it was like to be naked out in public like you were? Euphoric?"

I thought about that for a second before saying, "Yeah, that's it. That's how I felt, especially when it started."

"Hmm."

I sat there in her car for a moment, thinking.

"Listen," I finally said, "would you help me with something next Saturday?"

"Sure. What?"

"Go with me somewhere."

"Where?"

"A nudist resort just outside of Decatur." I glanced over and saw the frightened look on Samantha's face. "You wouldn't have to get naked," I explained. "I found the place on the AANR site, and I wanted to go and see how it felt to be naked around a bunch of other naked people."

"What am I supposed to do there if I stay dressed?"

I shrugged. "Sit around and drink beer, I guess. The only place where you have to be naked, at least according to their website, is the pool and hot tub."

"OK," Samantha said. "I guess I owe you after tonight."

"Yes, you do," I said before wishing her a good night and getting out of the car.

The next week seemed to crawl by. My period started Monday, so I spent a lot of the week either in a bad mood or just not feeling well. Daddy worked a lot, but when he was home, he still seemed withdrawn and standoffish. Mom worked too, so I had the house to myself for most of the time. I wished I still had the car I had used during my last two years of high school. Daddy hadn't wanted me to drive all the way to and from Palm Desert, and he didn't want the car just sitting here taking up space in the driveway. So we had sold it, and I had used the funds as spending money during my first semester at Coachella, before I got the job in the Copy Center.

The good thing about having the house to myself was that I got to spend a lot more time naked. I made and ate my lunch in the kitchen, watched TV in the living room, and even did my laundry all while naked, something that would have been unthinkable before I went away to Coachella. I thought a lot about that last conversation I'd had with Samantha on Saturday night about how my emotions had been on a yoyo at the beginning of the Project and how that yoyo seemed to slow down the further along I got in it. I started writing about that first day, trying to remember and describe every little thing that happened and how I felt about it. (If you're reading this now, you will realize that my writing went far beyond that first day.)

Samantha and I talked several times on the phone, and she faithfully showed up at the house at ten o'clock Saturday morning which happened to be the start of Memorial Day weekend. I told Mom that we would be gone all day, and when she asked where, I just told her we were going to the lake with some friends. The drive to the nudist resort took about an hour, although we extended that by stopping at a Panda Express in Decatur to eat lunch. I had made a reservation via email earlier in the week, so our check-in at the resort was quick and painless. A friendly Filipino lady wearing nothing but a pair of gym shorts confirmed our information and took the money for the camp's day fees and then offered to give us a tour of the grounds on her golf cart. I quickly got undressed, leaving my clothes in Samantha's car, grabbed my beach towel and got in the cart. If the fully dressed Samantha was uncomfortable squeezed in between naked me and the topless resort manager, she never let it show. We saw the two pools already populated by several nude people on lounge chairs, the clubhouse, the volleyball and tennis courts, and the hot tub and sauna.

That day, at least the time spent at the nudist resort, was one of the most blissful, relaxing times I had ever had. After the golf cart tour, we were taken back to the office, and we drove Samantha's car back down to the pool area. We had brought a cooler full of snacks and drinks and found a nice shady table on the deck. Most of the other nudists were over forty, but a group of younger people, calling themselves Young Nudists of Texas, were holding a special "Nude Olympics" there, with all kinds of events: tennis, horse shoes, tug of war, and what seemed to be the resort's favorite pastime, water volleyball. Samantha eventually tired of being the only person wearing clothes and stripped down to nothing.

The water volleyball was a blast. I played in four games, with whichever team I was on winning three of them. Samantha and I also spent a lot of time just sitting around the table by the pool, drinking and talking with the other nudists. They were all amazingly friendly, and with all of us naked, there didn't seem to be any class distinction. The people we talked to could have been CEOs or garbage collectors or anything else. We were all just people enjoying ourselves in the great outdoors. The members there invited us to their big potluck dinner that evening even though we hadn't brought anything, so we stayed and ate way too much food.

As I sat in the clubhouse eating a dessert of banana cream pie and listening to two different conversations, I realized that I hadn't once felt that tingling that had stayed with me almost all the time during my two naked months at CVU. Among the nudists, I was part of the norm, a naked person among naked people. That feeling that I craved, and it was only then that I realized I did crave it, was nowhere to be found at the nudist resort. I had felt it the week before, when I had been the only naked person at the pool party, and I realized that what Samantha had said was true: I was an exhibitionist. I thought about Dr. Slater's nudity study and realized what a gift it had been, being able to go naked in the general world and, once I got past the humiliation of being forced to be naked, to enjoy those feelings of freedom, exhilaration, and euphoria.

Still, the day at the nudist resort had been so wonderfully relaxing that I knew that I could be both a nudist and an exhibitionist and that I would be visiting nudist resorts regularly for the rest of my life. After dinner, Samantha and I were invited to stay for the regular Saturday night dance. I, of course, didn't want to leave, and Samantha was also having a great time. I went to the car and dug out my phone to call Mom and tell her that we would be out late. I was surprised to see twelve missed calls on my screen, eight of them from Greg.

Instead of listening to the six voice mails, I dialed Greg directly.

"Danielle," he answered. "What the hell is going on?"

"What do you mean?" I asked.

He gave a little laugh of disbelief. "Are you fucking kidding me? I mean, how could you do this?"

"Do what?" I said, still reeling from Greg's language. I hadn't ever heard him utter a cuss word before.

"Where have you been all day?"

"Out," I replied. "Away from my phone. What is going on?"

"Did you not listen to my voice mails?"

"No," I replied, getting irritated now. "I saw your missed calls and just decided to call you right back."

"Well, you should check Drudge Report. You are all over the news again."

I closed my eyes and imagined the security video at the Comfort Inn. Somehow word had gotten out that I was running around naked back home here in Texas.

"I mean, how could you?" Greg continued which made me

think that this was more serious than showing up on a hotel security video.

"Maybe if you told me exactly what you're talking about, I could answer that."

"You really don't know? OK. *The Dallas Morning News* printed a story about how you cheated on a paper and that Dr. Slater blackmailed you into doing the nudity study and then forced you to lie about why you were naked. All the major networks picked it up. Dr. Slater may lose her position here because of this."

"Oh my God," I muttered in disbelief.

"Sylvia Smith has already been fired. She wasn't a tenured professor, so it was easy to get rid of her. Dr. Hallum, the University president, resigned. Dr. Slater's been hung out to dry, and if she goes, I don't know what's going to happen to the rest of the sociology department."

I sat down in the passenger seat of Samantha's car, feeling suddenly sick to my stomach.

"The university's Board of Regents is holding a special emergency hearing this next Friday to decide whether to initiate a forced dismissal of Dr. Slater or not. Luckily, getting rid of someone with tenure isn't a simple thing."

"Shit," I said.

We were both quiet for a moment, listening to each other's breathing.

"Is it true, about the paper you cheated on?"

"Yes," I said.

"Who did you tell about it?"

"No one."

"Then who told this newspaper person about it?"

"It had to have been my father," I replied.

"Well, fuck a duck."

I sat in the car looking at the approaching darkness and tried to remember when my flight back to Palm Springs was supposed to leave. Summer classes started a week from Monday, so the dorm would be open the Friday before, the day of the hearing. I was supposed to fly back some time on Saturday, but now I knew I had to go back Friday morning. What would Daddy say when I told him to change my flight?

"What time is the hearing?" I asked.

"Three o'clock."

That would give me time to get there if I could get a morning flight. "OK, I'll be there."

"I'm sure you will," Greg said. "You're their star witness against Dr. Slater."

Before I could counter that, Greg hung up.

Chapter Seventeen – The Hearing

Samantha and I left the nudist resort right after my phone conversation with Greg. I listened to the six voice mails while she drove us back to North Richland Hills. Four were from Greg. He was fairly calm in the first one, but the agitation in his voice at being unable to reach me seemed to grow with each subsequent message. The other two were from a representative of the Coachella Valley University's Board of Regents requesting my presence at a closed door hearing on Friday. When I called the number back to tell the guy that I was planning on attending, he asked me to not speak to the media regarding any of this until after the hearing.

We were at the point where Highway 287 merged with Interstate 35W in north Fort Worth when Greg called me back. I was tempted to not answer when I saw his name on my phone display. How dare he be angry with me just because I wasn't surgically attached to my cell phone! But I answered after four rings.

"Hello," I said.

"Hey. I'm sorry. I shouldn't have gotten so bent out of shape."

"Yeah."

"Where were you today?"

"I was out in the country where the cell signal is questionable at best," I said, deciding that I didn't want to reveal that I had left my phone in the car for several hours.

"Well, I'm sorry. And I'm sorry that Dr. Slater did that to you. None of us on the research team knew about the suspension. We just thought you had volunteered on your own to get the six semester hours."

"But you knew about the six hours," I said.

"Yeah. And if she did blackmail you, then I suppose she deserves to be fired. I just – I don't know what's going to happen to all my work. She's my main faculty advisor, and I'm so close to that doctorate now. Do you know how much work I've put into it so far?"

"I can't imagine," I said. We were both quiet for a moment before I asked him, "Were you surprised that she would use that plagiarized paper to get me to do the Project?"

Greg sighed. "Surprised? Yes. Shocked? No, not really. She's very demanding and usually gets her way, one way or another."

"Well, OK."

"Are you flying in Friday?" he asked.

"Yes, I'd better be now."

"Let me know what time and I'll go to the airport and pick you up."

"OK. Thanks. I need to let you go. We're almost home, and I need to go have a talk with my father."

"Good luck with that," Greg said.

"Thanks. The good thing is, at least he waited until after my grade report was issued."

After I ended the call, Samantha looked over at me with a questioning look. "What is all this about?"

So I told her the whole story, since it was, according to Greg, all over the news now.

"That explains a lot," she said when I had finished. "A lot of people around here just thought you had lost your mind, been drinking too much California water or something."

"Nope," I said. "I'm still sane. At least I was at the beginning of the Project."

We had reached my house, and Daddy's car was in the driveway next to Mom's. I steeled myself for what I knew would be a confrontation.

"Good luck," Samantha said.

"Thanks." I got out and walked into the house through the front door. Daddy and Mom were sitting quietly in the living room, with Mom in the love seat and Daddy in his recliner on the other side of the room. Both of them had serious, almost sour, expressions on their faces.

"Hey," I said. "What's going on?"

"Your mother seems to think I overstepped my bounds," Daddy said.

"Well, if what I heard on my way home is true, then yeah, you did," I said. "What were you thinking?"

"I was thinking that that bitch at the college was using and abusing, exploiting my baby girl, and I wasn't about to let her get away with that."

"So your solution was to tell everyone I was a cheat and a liar? Great! Thanks Dad."

"I don't know why you're mad at me. It's my job to look out for you and keep you safe from predators."

"Only up to a certain point," I said. "I'm almost twenty-one years old. You have to let me live my own life, solve my own problems. Sure, I made a mistake, and I paid for that mistake in a way that would have been unimaginable to me a few months ago. But I did it. I had everything under control. Until you butted in and went to the media. Whatever possessed you?"

Daddy stood up and tried to walk toward me, to take me in his arms like he had done so many times over the years.

"Don't," I said, ready to bolt and run up the stairs.

Daddy stopped and stood alone in the middle of the living room, looking lost and miserable.

"I need to change my flight," I said.

"I already did."

"Why am I not surprised?"

"I've got you on the 11:50 flight Friday."

"11:50?"

"That was the earliest one I could get. Don't worry; it lands in Palm Springs at 1:00 local time. You won't have any problem making it to that hearing so you can nail the lid on that woman's coffin."

"Is this a revenge thing?" I asked.

"No, it's justice. Just go to that hearing and tell the truth. If they're human, I'm sure that Board of Regents will do the right thing."

I turned and stormed upstairs to my room. I still had five days in this house before I could get out and fly back to Coachella. I still had to share a roof with Daddy. I paced my room, asking myself over and over how he could have been so presumptuous. I wanted to scream, to throw something, to run away. But I continued pacing until I was calm enough to sit down and surf the Web on my phone, reading story after story about me and the nudity project until my anger at Daddy was redirected at Dr. Slater. The media had really crucified her, made her sound like the devil for taking advantage of a young church-going girl and corrupting her in such a public way. The truth, I realized, was that Dr. Slater did deserve to be removed from her position if only to prevent her from doing to anyone else what she had done to me.

I turned the TV on in my room and found CNN. It didn't take them long to broadcast a report about this latest development in my now very public life. I was surprised no reporters had knocked on my door, but the focus of the story now was Dr. Slater. I watched video of one of the CNN correspondents trying to ask her a question as she walked from Carlisle Hall to her car, but she held up a file folder in front of her face, and ran to get away from the camera. I almost felt sorry for her until I thought about her visit to my dorm room when she had basically ordered me to do the *Stossel* show. It was almost ten o'clock by the time I ventured back downstairs. Daddy was in his recliner, watching an Arnold Schwarzenegger movie on TV. Mom had apparently gone to bed.

"Hey," I said.

"Hey," he replied, his eyes still on the TV. Arnold was hanging on to the landing gear of an airplane as it started taking off. When he let go, he landed in what looked like a very conveniently placed marsh at the end of the runway.

"I'm sorry," I finally said. "I know you were looking out for me. And she does deserve everything she gets."

Daddy looked at me and smiled. "I'm sorry too. I should have checked with you first, seen what you wanted me to do." He stood up from the chair and walked over to me, giving me a hug. "Don't worry about that hearing. You just tell the truth exactly as it happened to you. Whatever happens happens. OK?"

I nodded. Daddy returned to his recliner and to the Arnold movie. When I looked at the screen, I remembered watching the movie with Daddy several years ago. The bad guys had kidnapped Arnold's daughter and were holding her hostage, threatening to kill her if he didn't fly down to South America or somewhere and assassinate someone. Everything Arnold does after escaping from that plane, including the climax when he kills dozens of bad guys, is with a single purpose, to rescue and protect his daughter. I couldn't remember the name of the movie, but it was one of his older ones. As I went upstairs, I had to shake my head at the thought that Daddy had purposely chosen to watch that particular movie on this particular night.

I went to church with my parents the following morning. Daddy and I didn't say much to each other during the ride over, and even Mom was unusually quiet. I hoped that after Friday's hearing we would all be able to put this thing behind us. My reception from the churchgoers was subdued. Most of the people there had just seen me on the news the night before and didn't quite know how to speak to me. I had wanted to ask my old youth pastor about the Project, but I learned that he had moved on to another church, taking a senior pastor position in a small town in east Texas the previous fall. A lot had changed in just two years, new faces and new wrinkles on the old faces, new staff, and even a new wing of the building. It almost didn't feel like the church I had grown up in, and I couldn't decide which had changed more, me or the church. I sat in service like I had sat in so many university classes lately, and I couldn't help but imagine myself naked right there in the pew in the middle of everyone. They would have all freaked out, called the police, prayed over me, and had me carried away in a strait jacket. As soon as the service ended, I didn't feel like talking to anyone and rushed outside to wait for my parents by the car.

Later, when we turned onto our street, I saw two local news vans parked in front of our house. The people outside these vans mobilized when they saw our car, with well-dressed reporters grabbing microphones and shabbily dressed cameramen lifting their heavy video cameras onto their shoulders.

"Crap," Daddy said. "They were supposed to leave you alone."

"Did you really think one reporter could speak for all of

them?" I said from the back, wishing I had Sylvia here to act as a shield.

Daddy opened the garage door with the remote clipped to his sun visor, but we had so much stuff in the garage that we could never fit a car inside it. He parked on the driveway next to Mom's car, and when I got out, the media people converged, stopping at the line in the concrete of our driveway, the two reporters talking at me at the same time.

"Danielle, would you like to speak to us about Dr. Slater's hearing?" the louder of the two asked.

I shook my head and said something I'd heard often on television, "No comment."

I followed my parents into the garage, and Daddy hit the button to lower the door just as I cleared the threshold. Thankfully, the TV crews stayed on the driveway behind our cars. Once we got inside, we ate the casserole that Mom had put into the oven before we left for church and talked about trivial things, avoiding any topics having anything to do with Coachella Valley University or anyone there.

The vans left before we finished eating, and I didn't see them back at all the rest of the week. I did try to watch the news on both of those channels, but I never did see any video of myself saying "No comment." Perhaps I had too many clothes on to be put on TV, I thought with some amusement. Daddy and Mom both worked all week, so I spent the first three days inside, watching movies and playing video games on the PlayStation 3. I was naked most of the time, getting dressed each day at about four o'clock, knowing that my mother usually arrived home at 4:30 and Daddy around 6:00. On Thursday I did laundry and packed my big suitcase as full as it would go. Daddy and Mom took me out to eat at Olive Garden that night, my last in Texas until the Thanksgiving holiday. Conversation topics ranged from the classes I was taking in the summer to my possible graduation at the end of the following summer and which universities had good law schools.

I got up early Friday morning to let both parents say good bye to me.

"Remember, just tell the truth," Daddy said, referring to the hearing, "that's all you have to do."

My mom's advice was a bit more abstract. "Remember who

you are," she told me before giving me a hug and walking out the door.

Once they left, I stood in my living room thinking how strange it was that I would be seeing Dr. Slater that day, attending a hearing over a thousand miles away just that very afternoon. I figured that I would go straight from the airport to the hearing, so I wore my yellow dress, the same dress I had worn to that first fateful meeting with Dr. Slater in March. Wearing it, I thought, would convey my respect for the proceedings without being too dressy. I had my big suitcase and my smaller carry-on bag by the door when Samantha picked me up at 9:30.

"Wow, you look great," she said when I opened the door.

"Thanks."

I hefted the big suitcase into the trunk and put the carry-on bag in her back seat. Samantha switched on the radio as she turned out of our neighborhood and toward the access road for Airport Freeway. We weren't on the freeway long when we came to a sudden stop.

"Shit," Samantha said.

She turned the radio to 1080, an AM 24 hour news station, and caught a traffic report. A fatality accident had occurred on the freeway at Central, and all lanes were closed.

"I'll try to get you there on time," Samantha said, moving over to try to exit the freeway.

The side streets were backed up as well. After waiting through at least six cycles of the stop light, she managed to turn left and get under the freeway, finally making it over to Harwood Street. We turned right there, and made our slow way over to Highway 121, which would take us up and around the airport, letting us take the North Entry. Samantha kept talking, trying to keep me calm, but I kept thinking about my flight, what I would have to do if it missed it. Would another flight get me there in time for the hearing? Once Samantha got onto 121, she floored it, driving at least 80 miles an hour most of the way. My legs wouldn't stop moving just from nervousness, and I had to pee. We pulled up to the terminal at 11:15, but I still had to check in and get through security.

"All right, hurry, and good luck," she said.

"Thank you so much for the ride," I said as I jumped out of the car, grabbed my bag from the back, and sprinted into the terminal. I was able to check in at the machine without waiting in line, grabbing my boarding pass and going straight to security. Thankfully, there wasn't a long line there either, but as I got close to the table with the trays for my shoes and things, my need to pee started to become overwhelming. I started bouncing from one foot to the other, a classic pee-pee dance. I got my bag onto the belt, loaded the tray with my purse and my shoes, and hurried through the checkpoint as rapidly as I could while still following the TSA agents' instructions. I grabbed my stuff from the other side of the X-ray machine and didn't even stop to put on my shoes before running to the nearest rest room.

Once that crisis was averted, I hurried to the gate where I expected to be the last person on the plane only to see a big crowd waiting. The sign behind the counter said that the flight status was delayed and was now departing at 1:15. I did some quick calculations in my head. The flight took three hours and ten minutes, minus the two hour difference in time zones, and that put me in Palm Springs at 2:25. I would only have 35 minutes to get from the airport to the hearing, and that was only if there were no more delays.

I pulled my phone out of my purse and called Greg.

"Hey there," he said. "Shouldn't you be on a plane?"

"My flight has been delayed by almost an hour and a half."

"Why?"

"I don't know. I just wanted to tell you that I would be late. That's not going to give us much time to get to the hearing."

"It'll be all right," he said. "We don't have to be there right at the beginning. Once you get off the plane, I guess we'll have to wait on your baggage."

I froze. "Shit!"

"What?"

"I left my suitcase in the trunk of Samantha's car."

I had to shake my head. It had been less than two weeks ago that my clothes had been locked in Samantha's trunk, and now they were there again, this time almost everything I owned. I laughed at the thought, and Greg probably thought I was hysterical.

"What?" he said.

"Nothing," I said when I finally stopped laughing.

"Just take it easy," Greg said. "Maybe you can get her to ship it to you."

"I'm not even worried about that now," I said. "Just be ready to go when I get off the plane."

"I will," he said.

I hung up the phone and hung out at the airport, visiting the newsstands and the gift shops in the terminal. When my boarding group was finally called, I felt drained after rushing at a hundred miles an hour only to come to a dead stop and sit around waiting. I spent the duration of the flight with my head against the window fading in and out of sleep.

I was sitting near the back of the plane, and I tried to maintain my composure while waiting for everyone ahead of me to get their stuff from the overhead bins and disembark. I called Greg while I waited and just told him to wait in his car by the curb where he had dropped me off two and a half weeks ago. Once I was finally off the plane, I hurried through the terminal, almost running into a lady taking a photo of her family members with the bust of Sonny Bono. Cars lined the curb outside the terminal, and I found Greg's car several hundred yards back from where I had hoped he would be.

"Sorry," he said when, out of breath from running, I slipped into the passenger seat after dropping my carry-on bag into his back seat.

"Just go," I said.

Greg went, somehow avoiding any traffic citations, and dropped me off on campus as close to the Administration Building as he could get with all of the news vans around. I grabbed my carry-on bag and hurried inside, ignoring any questions aimed at me from the people near the vans. The hearing room was easy to find with all of the reporters outside waiting. I pushed my way through them and was stopped at the door by two students in suits and ties.

"This is a closed hearing," one of them said.

"I'm Danielle Keaton. I'm supposed to be here. I'm late."

"Ah," the other guy, looking too young to be college age with his skinny frame and smooth face, said. "I talked to you on the phone last weekend. Come this way. I'll take you to a room where you can wait to be called."

I followed the kid around the corner and down the hall. "I'm Wilson, by the way," he said. "And I'm a big fan. Every time I saw you last semester, you were just – well, if I can say it -- beautiful."

"Thank you," I said to him when he opened the door into a

small conference room with a round table and plush chairs and a door on the far wall.

"Just make yourself comfortable. I'll let them know you're here, and they will call you when they're ready."

"Thank you," I said again.

Wilson closed the door behind him, and I set my bag on the floor in the corner next to the far door. I picked a chair, sat down, and tried to calm myself by taking long slow breaths. I closed my eyes and tried to clear my mind. At some point, the hum of the building's air conditioner shut off. Without that noise, I could hear faint voices from the overhead vent. I slipped my shoes off and climbed onto the table, trying to hear the voices better.

"Why, for a first offense, was probation not an option?" a man asked. I didn't recognize his voice.

"Because we were trying to get tough on academic dishonesty," someone else said, and I recognized that voice as belonging to Dr. Hallam, the now former president of the university. "We had implemented a new zero tolerance policy at the beginning of the academic year."

"And was Miss Keaton the first student to have received such a suspension for a first offense?"

"No, she was not."

"How many were there before her?"

"I can recall two young ladies receiving suspensions."

"Two young ladies? Did these young ladies receive the same proposal from Dr. Slater that Miss Keaton did?"

"I don't know. I don't recall. You would have to ask Dr. Slater that question."

"No male students received suspensions during this time frame?"

"Not that I can remember," Dr. Hallam's voice said.

"I have in front of me a list of the disciplinary actions taken during the current academic year. Dana Mitchell, one semester *SUSPENSION*. Michael Cooley, one year *PROBATION*. Jennifer Adcock, one semester *SUSPENSION*. Joseph Mitchell, one year *PROBATION*. Benjamin Sharp, one year *PROBATION*. Can you explain this disparity?"

Before I could hear Dr. Hallam speak, the building's air conditioner kicked back on, blocking out the sound of any more voices. I climbed down from the table, remembering something Ginger, the research assistant had said that first day when she had come to my room to pick up my clothes. Two previous girls had volunteered but had failed to even make it out of the building, she had said.

I knew then that, at a minimum, Dr. Slater was going to lose her position at the university. And with that certainty came the realization that I didn't want her to lose it, no matter what rotten things she had done. I was sure that the university owned the video from all the security cameras, and it probably owned everything else related to the Project. If she was dismissed, everything I had done, exposing my body to thousands of people, over those sixty days would have been for nothing. No one else would have her passion for this project, and therefore, no one would follow up on all the data collected.

But what could I do to stop her dismissal? I couldn't perjure myself to the Board; I would have to answer all their questions and tell them exactly what Dr. Slater had done to persuade me to take part in her project. But I could also say that I was glad she had done it, that I had experienced so much, learned so much about myself, and even become famous. But I knew that, in light of all this evidence, just my saying these things would have little or no impact on the members of the Board. I had to do more than just tell them what participating in Dr. Slater's nudity project had meant to me. It was a longshot, but I knew what I had to do.

I was ready when the door to the hearing room opened. Dr. Hallam and a woman I had never met before entered the conference room and froze in their tracks when they saw me.

"Um, you're Danielle Keaton," the woman finally said.

"Yes."

Dr. Hallam nodded to me as he passed by and exited through the door to the hallway.

"I'm Dr. Cynthia Jones. I'm a member of the Board of Regents. Please come in, I guess."

I followed her into the hearing room. The other seven members of the board, five men and two women, sat in a semi-circle on a raised platform on one side of the room, each of them behind large stained wood desks, arranged so closely together that their corners were touching the corners of the desks next to them. Dr.

Slater and another man were seated at one end of this semicircle, facing it. At the other end sat a stenographer, busily typing on her stenotype machine until she saw me and paused for just a few seconds, her eyes wide in shock. Dr. Jones gestured me toward the leather upholstered wooden chair in the center of the room, also facing the platform. I padded in my bare feet to that chair, ignoring the looks of shock on the faces of everyone in the room except Dr. Slater. I placed the little black towel I had taken from my carry-on bag onto the seat of the chair and stood in front of it, waiting for direction from someone about whether to sit or stand when I took whatever oath I expected I would have to take.

"What is the meaning of this?" one of the men asked. "Should this even be allowed?"

"Miss Keaton," one of the other women said, "why are you not dressed?"

"Because after the study I helped Dr. Slater with, this is how I prefer to be."

The members of the board all looked at each other. Some of them leaned over and whispered to each other. Dr. Jones took her seat at the end of the semi-circle, and the man in the middle, whose nameplate read, "Melvin Miller, Chairman" beat on his desk with the gavel.

"Let's have order, please." When the room quieted, he looked at me and said, "Please sit down Miss Keaton."

I sat, and the questions started. Each member of the Board seemed to take turns asking the questions, and through my answers I told them everything about how I had gotten a copy of Amanda's history paper and edited it to make it look like mine, how I had been caught by Dr. Finfrock and been sent to a disciplinary hearing, and how Dr. Hallam had called me the Sunday before classes resumed and told me to go see Dr. Slater. I went through the entire story of that first meeting and how, if I accepted the deal, I had to strip right then and leave Dr. Slater's office naked.

"How did that feel, walking out of that office with no clothes on?" Dr. Jones asked. It was the first question about me rather than about something factual that had happened.

"Scary," I said after a pause. "Humiliating. Embarrassing. Exciting."

"Exciting, how?" she asked. "Sexually?"

I probably blushed at her blunt question. "It was more the sense of adventure that made it exciting. I was doing something I had been taught that I wasn't supposed to do."

"But being naked in public didn't arouse you sexually?"

The man sitting next to Dr. Slater spoke up then. "Objection. Dr. Slater's study had nothing to do with sex, and this line of questioning to Miss Keaton seems inappropriate at best."

"Your objection is noted," Chairman Miller said.

The room got quiet for a moment until I realized that they were all waiting for me to answer.

"At times, yes," I admitted.

"I take it by your appearance here that you grew to like being nude on campus," one of the men said.

"Yes," I said.

"Why is that?"

I paused to think of the right words. "Because of the freedom. We're all living, breathing human beings with bodies, but we always cover those bodies, put up barriers between ourselves and nature and each other. The more comfortable I got in my own skin, the more I realized what a rare and special gift Dr. Slater had given me. Me, of all people."

The questions continued, and I told them how I hadn't wanted to do the Stossel show, especially since I knew that my body would be seen uncensored by my friends and family back home.

"But Dr. Slater forced you to do it, using the contract you signed?"

"Yes."

"And after the show aired, how did you feel?"

"I was mortified. Regretful. At least at first. Now, I'm glad I did it. It did make television history."

I don't know how long the questions lasted, but I must have sat in that chair for at least an hour. I knew the questioning was coming to an end when they asked me what I thought should happen to Dr. Slater.

"If this Board determines that the evidence suggests Dr. Slater committed the crime of extortion against you to secure your participation in her study, we would therefore turn over the minutes of this hearing to the District Attorney. If that happens, would you want to press charges against Dr. Slater?" The question came from

Chairman Miller.

"No," I said promptly and with force. "Absolutely not."

"Would you like Dr. Slater's employment with the university to be terminated?"

"No, I would not."

"Why not? After all she's done to you, forced you to do?"

"Because if she goes, what happens to all the data from those sixty days I spent nude on campus? I don't want it to have all been for nothing. And there's another reason. I was brought up Christian, taught to love our enemies, to be both giving and forgiving."

"That all sounds fine and dandy," one of the other Board members, the one who seemed the crankiest, said. "I sense a bit of Stockholm syndrome here. You think you can come in here naked and help Dr. Slater stay out of jail, maybe even keep her job. Then you get dressed and go on your way. There doesn't seem to be much resolve or commitment there."

"You know, that sixty day experiment is not something I would have ever signed up for or done voluntarily. But when I'm older and looking back on it, I know that it will be one of the few truly special times in my life, when I discovered who I am, that I can put shame and embarrassment aside and stand tall and brave and beautiful. What Dr. Slater has given me is something that I can never repay. Just an amazing experience. And you want commitment, evidence that this isn't some kind of show? All right. I will commit right now to staying naked on campus at this university, twenty-four hours a day, seven days a week, from now until I graduate. And if I go to law school here, I'll stay nude throughout that too. I just ask you to please allow Dr. Slater to continue her research, to go through the data, write her articles and her books, and make what I've done so far something worthwhile, that benefits all of humanity, that helps us all become more open, more honest, and more free."

The Board of Regents fell silent, and while I tried not to look directly at Dr. Slater, I saw her wipe the tears from her eyes.

"Thank you," Chairman Miller said. "You're excused."

Dr. Jones got up from her spot on the end of the semi-circle and walked me back to the conference room. I had folded my dress and put it and my shoes into my carry-on bag. I picked that bag up and walked out into the hall, naked, and instead of taking the back stairwell, I walked out into the throng of media outside the main door of the hearing room. When they saw me, they all converged, cameras pointed at me, microphones shoved into my face, questions from so many people that I couldn't discern any one in particular.

"I'd like to say," I said and waited for everyone to fall silent before continuing, "that over the two months of that nudity study, I came to respect Dr. Slater and what she was trying to accomplish with this project. I hope the Board sees fit to allow her to continue the work. Thank you."

I put my head down and started walking forward, ignoring the countless undiscernible follow-up questions and the incidental contact with my breasts and buttocks as I made my way through and out of the throng. I felt good, empowered, and exhilarated. When I stepped outside, the hot late afternoon sun felt bright and loving on my bare skin. Greg, who had been sitting on one of the benches near the entrance of the Administration Building, stood up, smiling and shaking his head when he saw me.

"Oh my God," he said when I got close to him. "What happened in there?"

I told him all about it as we walked to my summer dorm to get myself checked in, from what I heard over the air conditioner vents to what I had told the Board.

"So you're going to do it?" Greg asked. "Stay naked for the rest of your time here at the college?"

"I might as well," I said. "I enjoy the feeling of being naked; everyone on campus is used to seeing me this way; and, all my clothes are still locked in Samantha's trunk."

"Except for your yellow dress," Greg added.

"Well, I need something to wear for my trips home."

Epilogue

The Board of Regents censured Dr. Slater, placing her on probation for a year, but she got to keep her job. The University offered to reinstate the two female students who had been suspended, with free tuition for the rest of their degree plans to avoid any lawsuits. I went to Human Resources during the first week of the summer session and asked that Sylvia be rehired. I was still getting a lot of requests from the media, and I knew Sylvia could handle those. Dr. Slater put in a request as well, and Sylvia came back the following week.

The summers here are so brutally hot that not many students take summer classes at the university. As I'm writing this in early July in the extended weekend break between the first and second summer sessions, yesterday's high temperature at the Palm Springs Airport was 116 degrees. The high number of tourists that seem to wander onto campus makes up for the lack of students and faculty, and most of the tourists seem to always be on the lookout for the naked girl. I suppose it's like how every visitor to Loch Ness always looks for the monster, Nessie, except in the case of Coachella Valley University, the naked girl actually exists. If tourists approach me nicely, I'll even pose with them for photographs. Greg, of course, worries about my safety since I don't have a team of research assistants following me around day and night anymore, so he bought me a can of pepper spray to carry in my little hand purse. I doubt that I will ever need it, but it's nice to have, just in case.

The good thing about living in the dorm in the summer is that I was assigned to a single room, without a roommate, and the absence of that second bed makes the room seem so much bigger. I have applied to keep this room for the fall semester, but I haven't heard anything yet. The air conditioning has trouble keeping the building cool enough at night, so I've taken to sleeping on the top sheet completely uncovered. So I really am naked all of the time. I looked at my calendar and counted 176 days between that hearing and my flight back home for the Thanksgiving holiday. That will blow my 60 day naked record out of the water if I can make it. Of course, I don't have Dr. Slater and her contract forcing me to stay nude, only a non-binding commitment I made in front of the Board of Regents. But I am holding to that commitment, especially since I find staying nude to be easier now than ever. It's just a part of who I am, no matter how much my father complains about it.

Two days after Sylvia called me to tell me that she was back on the job, I stopped in the deli in the Student Union to buy an iced tea after my morning class. Dr. Slater stepped up behind me as I was in line.

"You are looking more tan than ever," she said.

"Yes. This desert sun will do it to you."

After I ordered and got my drink, she touched my arm before I could leave.

"I want to thank you," she said. "You didn't have to do what you did. And you really didn't have to do this," she added, looking down at my naked body.

"But I wanted to do this. I love it. I love the feeling, and I love being the center of attention everywhere I go. I don't know what I'm going to do when I leave this college and don't have this freedom anymore."

"Perhaps you doing this now will bring about that freedom in other places."

"I hope so," I said.

"You know, we have thousands of hours of footage of you from the project. A major Hollywood director has approached me about using some of that for a documentary. I don't want to say who it is, but you would recognize the name if I told you. I want you to know that I will make sure that you are included in the deal, that you get well compensated."

"Thank you," I said. The thought of movie goers seeing me naked on screen caused that little tingling sensation to kick into a higher gear.

Dr. Slater and I stood looking at each other for a moment before I decided that it felt just a bit awkward.

"Well—" I began, meaning to tell her good bye.

"But thank you for what you said and did in that hearing," she said before I could finish. "I thought I was a goner for sure."

"It was nothing."

"Why? Why did you do it? I used you, manipulated you, and you could have taken all that out on me."

"What good would that have done? It would have made me a vengeful, spiteful person. And I don't want to be that person. Before I left the house, my mom told me to remember who I was. And waiting to go into that hearing, I did." I shrugged and said, "I'm Naked Dani."

CPSIA information can be obtained
at www.ICGtesting.com
Printed in the USA
FSHW021944060619
58830FS

9 781534 635241